GRACE TURNER

SOMETHING to SOMEONE

CONTENTS

To anyone who likes a little bit of trouble.

CONTENT NOTE

This book is intended for adults and contains sexual situations. *Something to Someone* is a super spicy book that contains light BDSM (bondage, blindfolds, spanking, etc.), spitting, and pegging. The book also contains mentions loss of a partner (boyfriend) earlier in life (off-page) as well as cheating. Again, earlier in life (off-page and *not* a main character).

If you have any questions about the content of this book, or feel anything should be added to this list, please feel free to reach out to me on social media (@graceturnerauthor) or email me at graceturnerauthor@gmail.com.

PROLOGUE
DANGER!

Caroline

RYDER CALAWAY WOULD BE THE DEATH OF ME.

He held a thin strand of my hair between his fingers, a blonde lock that had fallen loose from the bun on top of my head. Toying with it like it was the most beautiful thing he'd ever seen, the back of his finger brushed my cheek.

He didn't miss my sharp intake of breath.

And before I could stop, I found myself admitting, "You, Ryder Calaway, are *very* dangerous." The words spilled from my lips before I could choke them down.

Wild blue eyes flashed to mine, and I was frozen in place. The simple sentence was enough of an admission, I knew he wouldn't let it slide. I'd known, or at least guessed at, Ryder's crush for years, but I'd been careful not to hint at my newfound attraction.

Until today.

He was my best friend's son. I wasn't supposed to find him attractive or enigmatic or so freaking annoying. But I did, and for whatever reason, it all contributed to that pull. Of course, those feelings hadn't started until much later. With eleven years between us, we'd met when he was only fifteen.

Until recently, he was just my friend's son. I didn't think too much about him, but over the past year, something had changed. I couldn't pinpoint it, and I couldn't explain it either, but enough had changed that when he bowed his head and brushed his nose along my cheek, I didn't pull away.

His lips hovered next to my ear, and I could feel his warm breath flutter over my skin. Like he was breathing me in, he inhaled deeply and hummed low in his throat. Likely an involuntary sound he couldn't control.

"You say that like it's a bad thing, Caroline," he said, and I ground my teeth, trying not to react to the way he said my name. It was all deep and growly. A sound I never expected to hear from his lips. "But isn't it the dangerous rides that leave you breathless? They leave you panting, your heart racing, and your thighs weak. Danger is so much fun."

The last words were punctuated with a brush of his lips against my skin which finally snapped me from my trance. I raised my hands and braced them against his chest. His *firm, toned* chest, which were not things I should have noticed, and I willed myself to push the thoughts to the back of my mind.

"This isn't happening, Ryder," I warned, and he blessedly took a step back. I needed space and air that wasn't clouded with...*him*. "Let's just grab the food and go back to your mom's."

His mom, and my best friend, Natalie, was waiting on us. As was her new-ish boyfriend, Theo, who also happened to be Ryder's best friend. It was kind of a mess, but we were making the best of it.

Ryder found Theo in bed with his mom almost a week ago, and while he was doing fairly well given the circumstances, he was still coming to terms with the fact that his mom and his best friend were in love.

After he'd found them together, Ryder came to my house just

down the street. He'd busted through the door like his ass was on fire, anger so intense vibrating through him that he couldn't speak. He sat on my couch for an hour before he finally confessed to what had happened. Not long after that Natalie had begun texting me, too.

Then she'd shown up at my door, and Ryder hid in my bedroom like a dirty little secret. The last thing he wanted to do was speak to or see his mom, and I didn't think either of them were prepared for that confrontation just yet.

Only Natalie had sensed something was off and implied that the man hiding in my bedroom was there for something more. Which was a good guess, but it hadn't been true. No matter how much Ryder wanted it to be.

And whether he was trying to put on a brave face or not, I knew the man in front of me was still reeling from his mom and best friend's secret affair. He wasn't in the right mind to insinuate that we should cross a line we couldn't come back from.

"Why?" he asked simply, and I groaned as I grabbed one of the dessert dishes we'd come back for. I shoved it in his hands, and he huffed out a breath at the impact.

A triumphant smile slipped over my lips.

"There are so many reasons why we shouldn't. It's a long, *long* list."

"Name a few."

I leveled him another look, one that often made people think twice about their actions, but it didn't seem to affect him at all, which was a little unsettling. But still, I pushed on.

"You're too young. You just turned twenty-one, and you're my best friend's son. That's a line I shouldn't, and *won't*, cross."

"Those are really just excuses, Caroline, not—" Thankfully, I had my back to him as I added a new layer of tinfoil over the dump cake, I'd baked so he didn't see my reaction to my name yet again slipping from his lips.

"You just found out about your mom and Theo," I reasoned, turning back around with the newly covered dish in my hands.

"I think this is a direct reaction to that. Maybe some part of you wants to get back at her, and what better way to do that then to sleep with *her* best friend."

He was shaking his head before I finished speaking. "That's not true."

"Whether it is or isn't, this isn't happening, Ryder."

"You say that now," he said with a smirk that made my insides melt. "But your reactions say something different. And I know one day you'll change your mind, so I'll wait. I'm very patient."

I brushed past him and ignored the way his eyes lingered on my face. "You seem very sure of that," I challenged. I could hear his steps as he followed me toward the door, and I found myself walking faster.

With my hands full, I was struggling with the door when he stopped behind me.

His lips once again brushed my ear, and I felt the heat of his body at my back.

"I'm very confident, Caroline. *Very* confident."

ONE
WINE ABOUT IT

Caroline

One and a half years later

"THAT TIMELINE WON'T BE AN ISSUE," I CONFIRMED WITH THE prospective clients on the video call. The two men lived overseas and wanted a quick turnaround for their wedding ceremony and reception.

It was barely April, and they wanted to travel back to the US in July for the wedding.

I'd planned weddings and parties with shorter timeframes before, so I wasn't concerned. And with the new assistants I'd recently hired, I knew we could make it work.

"Perfect!" Stephen said, smiling at his future husband, Miles, with so much love I could feel it through the camera.

"Do you have any other questions you want to discuss?"

They looked at each other quickly and both shook their heads. "Nope," Miles said. "Send over the contract, and we'll get it back to you tomorrow. We're going to have one of our friends step in with a few in-person things like touring venues and food tastings."

Excited about the possibility of planning their big day, I jotted down a few notes on my notepad and nodded. "Sure, no problem. I understand it can be helpful to have someone around who knows you both personally."

We said our goodbyes, and I logged off the call. Blowing out a long breath, I slid lower in my chair and leaned back. It had been a long day full of meetings and client calls, but I wouldn't have it any other way. I loved the work I did and the business I'd built.

I'd started Grant Events not long after I graduated college, and now it was known as one of the foremost event-planning businesses in the state. Ten years of hard work and dedication meant I had a business I could be proud of.

There was a knock on my door a second before it opened. Although most of my office was glass looking out into the hallway to my left and to the parking lot below at my back, my door was wood, so I didn't see Addie's face until she appeared in the small space between the doorframe and the door itself.

"How did it go?" she cautiously asked.

I waved her in and sat up straight although my back was yelling at me not to. "It went really well. Can you ask Julia to send the contract and questionnaire to them when you leave?"

"Yeah, definitely. You're leaving, right? Julia said you were already at your desk when she got here at seven this morning, and you've barely come out of your office."

I twirled my hair around my fingers and fished a clip out of my desk drawer, eager to get it off my neck and out of my face.

"Yes, I'm leaving," I said, closing my laptop and shoving it into my bag along with any other items I'd spread out on my desk during the day.

I wasn't necessarily a workaholic, but I did occasionally have longer days. That was part of owning my own business.

"You should probably leave, too."

She rolled her eyes but agreed to head out, too. I'd hired Addie a few months earlier after she applied via one of the many job listings we'd posted. She already had a full-time job as an events coordinator at a luxury senior living community, but for whatever reason, she needed the extra money that came with a part-time job.

She didn't offer up any details, and it wasn't my business to ask. She was one of the best employees I'd ever hired—upbeat and always on time. She genuinely enjoyed helping people which extended to me apparently.

The blonde ushered me out of the office and to the elevator before I could even think to argue. She waved at me as the elevator doors closed, and I sagged against the wall.

The doors opened a few seconds later, and I stepped out into the lobby, pulling out my phone and sending a quick text to Natalie letting her know I was on my way to the wine bar.

The entire drive I fantasized about the wine and cheese I was about to consume, and how much I needed some serious girl time.

Natalie had been my best friend for...I'd lost track of how long we'd been friends. It had to be eight or nine years at least. We'd been friends immediately, hitting it off at a Fourth of July barbecue on our block. We started gossiping about our neighbors, and the rest was history.

When I stepped into the dimly lit bar, I spotted Natalie already seated at a table toward the back, next to a stone wall and a wine rack that stored well over a hundred bottles. She was already perusing the menu and didn't notice me until I slipped into the seat across from her.

"Red, white, or rosé?" she asked by way of greeting, and I couldn't help the smile.

Simultaneously, we both said, "Red," and she snapped the menu shut.

Her smile dropped slightly as her eyes raked over my face. Natalie was too nice for her own good sometimes, and as blunt as I was, she took a little bit more of a careful approach to her words.

"Are you...doing okay?" she asked, and I narrowed my eyes as I hung my bag onto the back of my chair.

Our waiter interrupted before I could respond, and we ordered a charcuterie board and a bottle of wine.

The second he left, I asked, "I'm fine. Why?"

She sighed and tucked her long, dark hair behind her ear. "You look tired."

"Ahh," I said, taking a sip of my water. "I am, but I'm good. Work is just busy, and business is booming. So, I can't complain."

"Didn't you just hire a bunch of people not too long ago who were supposed to take the stress off of you?"

The waiter set our bottle of wine on the table and poured us each a glass. We tapped our glasses together and took our first sips. "I did, but I still like to do the new client meetings, especially for the larger weddings and events."

Always worried about my health and well-being, Natalie gave me an incredulous look over her wineglass. "You need to slow down. Otherwise, you're going to give yourself a heart attack by the time you're forty."

I shook my head and took another long sip of wine. The blackberry and chocolate notes hit my tongue, and I savored the taste. Although Natalie was giving me shit, the longer I sipped and sat across from her, the more I could feel any stress or lingering anxiety leave my body.

"And you would know, wouldn't you? You have, what? One more year until you're forty?"

"Wow, thank you for that beautiful reminder," she said sarcastically. "Honestly, I'm not scared of turning forty. I know the best years of my life are still ahead of me."

Her smile was genuine, and I was happy for my friend. Thankfully, her divorce several years earlier was amicable, but that didn't keep the scars of a years-long loveless marriage from rearing their ugly heads. It wasn't until Theo came into her life that she realized what she'd been missing all those years.

"Is that because you have a really hot twenty-five-year-old boyfriend with a perfect...?" I asked, pointing to my lap and obviously indicating what appendage I was alluding to. This all happened at the same time the waiter appeared with our charcuterie board. He blushed quicker than I'd ever seen and stammered out something about letting him know if we needed anything else.

I was surprised there wasn't smoke billowing behind him the way he rushed off.

Natalie leaned over and smacked my arm. "Now, he's never coming back. And yes, Theo is a contributing factor, but everything else feels right, too. Work is going well, and I just feel more comfortable and confident with myself now than I did when I was in my twenties."

"That's really great, babe. You have seemed like you've come into your own even more in the past year."

"Thanks," she said with a smile. "But anyway, I want to get back to you. I know work is a lot, but busy is good, right?" I nodded, unable to speak with a mouthful of cheese and crackers. "What about on the relationship front?"

I swallowed before I started coughing and managed to clear my throat before a cracker went down the wrong pipe.

Natalie was supportive of all my life decisions, but she was also a hopeless romantic who was in a relationship so healthy it made me sick. So, of course, she thought that was a possibility for everyone. But I had all but given up on relationships a long time ago. Love was stupid and only led to heartbreak. I was cynical—sue me.

But the past was funny like that. It had this great ability to remind you of all the shit you would much rather forget.

No matter the past, a relationship wasn't my priority. Or at that moment, anywhere close to being on my radar.

Natalie also, up until a little over two years ago, had been with the same penis all her life, and that couldn't be me. Especially since the first boy I'd slept with was in ninth grade, and we'd had to have an anatomy lesson about my genitalia prior to insertion. I hadn't really wanted to have sex anymore after our impromptu science class, but back then, I was tired of carrying around my "V" card like it made of lead in my pocket. It was a preposterous thought now, but I was barely fifteen and hormones were a bitch. As was peer pressure.

"Sorry, I know they're not relationships," Natalie corrected without judgment. "You just haven't told me about any of your recent hookups. Usually, I get to hear all the details."

I laughed and scooted the pickles in her direction as she pushed the olives in mine.

"I think you had more fun with it when you were living vicariously through me. Now, you have your own stories."

"You're deflecting," she stated.

I sighed and popped an olive in my mouth. "Yes, but I thought I was doing it quite well." The band at the front of the bar was doing a soundcheck, and in the short time we'd been sitting there, the crowd around us had doubled.

"I know you better than that, and I love you enough not to let you deflect," she said above the noise of the bar and with her eyebrows expectantly raised.

Pursing my lips, I decided to tell her the truth, knowing that she'd get it out of me one way or another. "I've had a bit of a dry spell."

"*You've* had a dry spell?" she repeated back to me. There was surprise laced in her tone, and I shrugged. I was a woman who enjoyed sex, and I was unapologetic about it.

Which was harder for people to understand coming from a woman than from a man. Because what was worse than a successful woman who didn't want her entire life to be settling down and procreating? If I was going to do that, it needed to be with an exceptional man who made my life better. And nothing less. And the likelihood of finding someone so exceptional was growing less and less by the second.

"A self-inflicted dry spell?"

I pursed my lips and tried to hide my expression behind my wineglass.

"Somewhat, I guess. No one has really interested me recently. I just want to focus on myself."

She nodded, and I could see she wanted to pry further, but she refrained. "That's never a bad thing."

"Nope," I said, popping the "p." "So, tell me about work. You said you had someone quit recently? Without telling you? Did they just stop showing up?"

She dove into the story, and I was more than happy to change subjects. Not only because I wanted to hear about my friend's life, but because I wasn't sure how I was supposed to tell her that the reason I was going through a dry spell was because I couldn't stop thinking about her son.

After our encounter in my kitchen almost a year and a half ago, I hadn't been able to shake the feelings he'd stirred awake within me.

I'd known about his crush—I would have had to be completely oblivious to *not* notice his occasional flirting and long looks—but he was that way with a lot of people. He was outgoing and charismatic toward everyone. But his confirmation that it was more than that, it sparked something inside me.

And I hated him for it.

If he hadn't brought it up, I would have continued living my normal life, and I wouldn't be plagued with questions of "what if"? Or the idea that, God forbid, he was actually right, and I would change my mind no matter the very real, horrible consequences that would come with it.

After that afternoon in my kitchen, he'd toned it down. Only flirting casually and keeping most of his feelings locked down. There was nothing too out of the ordinary—just the random text or wink when we saw one another. Maybe a reason to touch my hair or be close to me. But he hadn't tried anything so forward again. He was so casual for so long that I thought maybe he'd changed *his* mind. Until recently, when, for whatever reason, something had changed again.

He was no longer shy or quiet about how much he still wanted me. And every day it was getting harder to ignore.

"...since it's Ryder's birthday."

Realizing I was a crappy friend, and I'd stopped listening for a second, I peered up from my bowl of olives in surprise when I heard her say his name. But I knew it was Ryder's twenty-third birthday.

"Right, yeah," I said, trying to recover, but Natalie didn't buy it for a second.

"When did you stop listening?"

"Sorry, just say the last sentence again. I was lost in thought."

She took a deep breath and repeated, "Theo is out of the house since it's Ryder's birthday, so if you want to come over later, we can watch that movie you were talking about the other day. The one with the blond guy?"

I didn't have to respond, apparently my expression told Natalie how I felt about the offer without me having to open my mouth.

"Or not, that's okay," she said.

She sounded a little dejected, and I immediately felt awful. "Not because I don't want to spend more time with you," I reasoned. "It's just been a long week, and I kind of want to go home and take a bath. Can we do it on Sunday instead?"

"I totally understand. And Sunday should work for me. Also, do you want real food?"

"Yes, do they have real food?" We both glanced at the tables around us and saw a variety of dishes. The pasta the man was eating at the table next to us looked creamy and thick, and that's exactly what I wanted.

Natalie pushed her stool back and hopped down to the ground. "I have to run to the restroom. I'll find our waiter that you've scarred for life on my way."

"Good luck!" I called after her. While she was in the bathroom, I refilled our wineglasses and riffled through my bag until I found my phone.

There were the expected texts and emails from clients waiting in my inbox, but what I hadn't been prepared for was two messages from Ryder. My thumb hovered over the screen for several seconds, trying to decide if I should risk opening them while Natalie was in the bathroom.

He'd already responded to my early text wishing him happy birthday with some dumb GIF. He shouldn't have been texting me again.

But my curiosity won, and I opened the message.

Ryder: Heyyy beautiful

Ryder: What are yuo doing.?

The two messages were sent within a minute of each other and had the classic drunken typos. I rolled my lips to suppress my smile. It wasn't funny. Not at all.

Me: Are you having fun?

Texting back wasn't the best idea, it never was, but I didn't have a chance to think about it before his response lit up my screen.

Ryder: I'd be having more fun if you were here

"Who are you texting?" Natalie appeared beside me, and my phone leaped from my hands. That was the only apt explanation for how it went almost completely across the table, somehow managing to dodge the wineglasses and plates.

I saw her wide-eyed, shocked expression out of the corner of my eye as I scrambled for the phone.

"Umm…okay. That was a little dramatic," she said slowly, sliding back into her seat and offering me a menu. I tucked my phone back in my bag and took the menu without looking at her. Hoping she didn't see my blush, I held the menu a little higher than normal. She would know something was even more off if she saw the color of my cheeks.

I didn't blush.

I chastised myself for my stupidity as she continued, "You usually don't care if I look at your phone, so it must have been really dirty. You sure about that dry spell?"

Oh, if only you knew.

TWO

SPLISH, SPLASH

Caroline

I SLIPPED DOWN INTO THE WARM WATER AND LET IT WASH everything away. Thanks to Ryder, my relaxing girl's night had turned into me sitting across from my best friend feeling guilty and horrible for what I was keeping from her.

Not that there was much to tell anyway, and it wasn't like she needed to know every thought I ever had. Or every one of Ryder's flirty remarks. But those were convenient excuses I told myself to feel better.

I was self-aware enough to know I was delusional.

Soft music filtered through the bathroom, and I swiped my fingers through the bubbles gathered on top of the water. The warm scent of sandalwood and lavender wafted around me, and I closed my eyes.

I felt myself begin to drift off. I wasn't going to fall asleep in the bathtub, but lingering in that place just before the drowsiness took over was calming. It was a state where, although those thoughts were still plaguing me, they were duller and less critical.

It was nice until my phone started buzzing on the edge of the tub. I squeezed my eyes shut and willed it to stop. When it continued, and I realized someone was calling me past midnight, I begrudgingly leaned forward and grabbed it.

Glancing at the screen, I rolled my eyes and set it back down. The vibration continued for another second then stopped.

Of course it was Ryder, but I already had enough to feel guilty about. Answering the phone was bound to add more to that list.

I hadn't even closed my eyes again when the vibration started. Letting out a loud groan that echoed off the tile, I quickly answered. It was a split-second decision to answer, make sure there wasn't something urgent, then hang up.

"Why are you calling me?" I bit out, wiping one hand on the towel next to me then switching hands.

He took a deep breath and said, "I can't stop thinking about you."

Suppressing my initial emotional reaction, I scoffed. "Is that all?"

"It's my birthday," he said, his words slightly slurred but not enough to keep me from understanding him.

"I know."

"And you haven't wished me happy birthday yet."

"Yes," I said slowly. "I texted you this morning. You responded to it as well. Have you started to lose your memory in your old age?"

He laughed, and it was loud and unencumbered. "I'm not sure twenty-three is considered old, but you do have a point. I meant you haven't *told* me happy birthday. A text isn't very personal—"

"Happy birthday, Ryder," I said.

"Fuck," he groaned, and the low, muttered curse shot through me and settled between my thighs. Not all my reactions were so easy to suppress, especially the physical ones I couldn't seem to control.

Startled by my body's response, I took a breath and started to pull the phone away from my ear. "Bye, Ryder."

"Wait, no," he said quickly. "Don't hang up yet. Just—"

I hadn't noticed it before, but there was music in the background. It was loud, the beat heavy, and raised voices carried down the line.

"Are you at a bar?"

I could hear his steps against the ground and assumed he was outside and walking away from the bar as the noise grew softer.

"Ehh, it's more like a club," he explained.

"Either way, you're at a club, and you decided to call me?" I trailed my fingers through the water and leaned back against the cooler white porcelain.

"Yes, because listening to your voice is better than anything that's currently happening in there." He said it so matter-of-factly and without the usual playfulness tinging his voice that I was stunned into silence. He was so serious, and I wasn't used to it.

I opened my mouth to say something, but nothing came out. I couldn't find the words, and I was uncomfortable with how off balance it made me. Readjusting my position, I wasn't paying attention and hit a shampoo bottle poised on the edge of the tub. I gasped and tried to catch it, but it slipped through my fingers and splashed into the water.

Water splattered everywhere, and in the process of trying and failing to catch the shampoo, my phone slid from my ear. I fumbled for it and managed to grab it before it hit the bubbles.

My heart was pounding like I'd just run a freaking marathon, and I'd almost forgotten about Ryder until I heard his voice coming from the speaker.

"What was—are you taking a bath?"

Annoyed by everything that had just taken place, I said, "I'm hanging up now."

"Do you really want to hang up, Caroline?" he asked.

"Because just imagining you in the bathtub right now...the mental image is fucking amazing."

He waited, and when I didn't say anything, he continued. "I bet your hair is pulled back, isn't it? All your blonde hair in one of those big clips to keep it out of the water. And showing off your neck. Until I met you, I didn't know a neck could be beautiful. But—are there bubbles? Fuck, because in my mind, there are bubbles. But only enough to slightly...umm, what's the word... obscure your body under the water."

As he imagined me, I imagined him, standing outside of a club on his birthday with his eyes closed and the phone to his ear, describing in awe-filled wonder the scene in his head. One that almost perfectly matched what was happening in my bathroom.

My breath came out in short, quick pants, and I slipped deeper into the water, further from the judgment of the world. It couldn't reach me there. And the longer the phone call went on the, the more I needed to hide.

"I feel like you would add Epsom salts, too. And the entire bathroom would smell slightly sweet, like flowers in sunshine because that's what you usually smell like. But I don't really care about what it smells like because the bubbles are slowly dissolving, and the water is lapping across your chest. Just the tops of your tits are peeking out, and you're—"

"Ryder—" I said quietly, effectively cutting him off. Thankfully, because I didn't know if I could have lasted another second. There was a definitive tightening in my core that I couldn't ignore, and my skin was heating even as the water cooled.

Another groan and I almost threw my phone. "Just say my name one more time, then you can hang up on me."

Swallowing, I took a breath and said, "Goodbye, Ryder," before I hung up the phone.

THREE
THE MORNING AFTER

Ryder

WITH HOW MUCH I DRANK THE NIGHT BEFORE, I WASN'T SURPRISED to wake up face down on my bed with a raging headache. At least I'd made it back to my bed.

Last night withstanding, I wasn't a huge partier. I had the occasional night out during my four years in college, and I enjoyed a beer or two with friends, but clubs were not my scene. Unless it's my birthday, and then I guess I was more likely to give into peer pressure.

I groaned, lifting my head and blinking the sleep from my eyes so I could reach for my phone which was miraculously plugged into the charger on my bedside table. It was almost noon, but it felt like I'd only been asleep for a few hours. If I remembered correctly, we'd stumbled into my apartment just past two in the morning.

I managed to roll onto my back and dug the heels of my palms into my eyes. I needed water and meds and something greasy and—

There was a knock on my door, and I opened my eyes

enough to see Theo step into my room. With the glorious items he held in his hands.

"Oh my gosh, I could fucking kiss you." I pushed myself up until I was sitting upright against the headboard and swallowed down some mild nausea.

He shook his head and set the plate, water, and medicine bottle on the table beside me. "No, you wouldn't, I'm not your type. I'm not blond."

I looked back fondly on the people I'd dated before. And although I didn't have a preference when it came to someone's gender, they did usually have blond hair. Weird.

"You're right," I agreed and grabbed the water and meds first, swallowing those down before I grabbed the plate and gazed down at the hearty breakfast sandwich. I took a bite and groaned in satisfaction. "Thank you so much," I said around a mouthful of food.

Theo cringed but nodded all the same. "I knew you'd feel like shit."

"Why did you let me drink so much?"

"Me?" He pointed to his chest like he was offended by the insinuation. "I had nothing to do with that. That was all Connor. And when I did try to stop it, you told me to *'let loose'* and *'stop acting like a grandpa.'*"

"Hmm," I hummed. "Not sure I remember that, but it does sound like something I'd say."

He gave me an unimpressed look, and I smiled.

"What else happened that I might not remember?"

He sighed and leaned back in the chair that I thought I remembered him sleeping in the night before. I stowed that question away to ask later.

"Well, after you bought everyone in our vicinity shots, you told us you had to make a very important call and that you'd be right back. Only you were gone for twenty minutes and left me with Connor."

My hands stopped the sandwich midway to my mouth. *That*

I remembered. Shaking off the memories that rushed back and deciding they would also be dealt with later, I quickly took a bite and put the sandwich back on the plate.

"So, what happened?" Theo asked, and I pointed to my mouth, slowly chewing my food so I could consider how to answer.

Theo knew exactly what I was doing, but I wasn't going to tell him that I walked out of the club to call Caroline just so I could hear her voice for a few minutes.

"I don't remember," I lied. Theo braced his elbows on the arms of the chair and pressed his fingers to his lips, probably trying to decide if he wanted to pry for more information. But Theo wasn't a big talker, so he let it slide.

"Right, well, now that I know you're alive, I'm going home."

"Oh yes, I'm sure my mom misses you," I muttered as he stood.

He ran a hand through his hair and stopped halfway to the door. "I thought we'd moved past that. Are you still—"

I shook my head and rolled off the bed. My entire body was sore, and I swore my kidneys ached, but I crossed to him at the foot of my bed. "No, we're good. Just tired still, and you know I like to give you shit."

For a while I couldn't comprehend their relationship—my best friend and my mom were the last people I expected to fall in love, but they had. It had been almost two years, and I still had my moments where it was a little odd. Like when I saw them showing each other affection or remembered that they were living together.

But they were the happiest I'd ever seen them, and being two of my favorite people in the world, it was easier to accept.

I opened my arms, and he knew what was coming. He half-heartedly sighed and let me hug him. It didn't last long, though. A second later, he was shimmying out of it and pointing toward the bathroom.

"Go shower, you reek of liquor," he instructed. He didn't wait for me to respond before he walked out of my room.

"Love you, too!" I called after him. The front door closed a second later, and I walked into the living room to lock it behind him. I was expecting a bigger mess, but there were only a few cups left on the kitchen counter and the couch was a wreck.

I reached to start cleaning, but then I smelled myself and realized exactly what Theo had been talking about. A shower had to happen before anything else.

I stripped as I walked to the bathroom and deposited my dirty clothes in the laundry hamper in my closet. When I turned on the shower and impatiently waited for it to warm up, more memories flooded back from the night before, particularly of my short yet very memorable conversation with Caroline.

Just the thought of her had my blood heating. I stepped under the still-cool water to try to douse the reaction before it could take over, but it wasn't so simple.

My crush had started so long ago, I couldn't remember what it was like *not* to want Caroline Grant.

My mom dragged me to a Fourth of July party in our neighborhood. I was only fifteen at the time, so everything felt like a chore, and that party was the last thing I wanted to do. But I went, and that was the first time I'd laid eyes on her.

She was nothing less than perfect. With precise recollection, I remembered every single thing about that moment. She was wearing a red, white, and blue bikini which was peeking out from beneath her open white button-down shirt. Her cutoff shorts were light blue and fraying at the hem.

But it was her smile, the joy radiating off her that made me stop in my tracks.

And my crush hadn't waned in the past eight years, it had morphed into something more than a schoolboy crush on the hot older woman. There was more to it than that.

Which was how I wound up confessing those feelings to her in the middle of her kitchen a year and a half ago. I'd found out about my mom and Theo a week before, so my emotions were raw. Caroline had also been paramount in keeping me from going off the rails.

It was the perfect storm, and I couldn't keep my feelings locked up any longer. An eleven-year age difference didn't feel like it was insurmountable, and with my mom and best friend shacking up, why couldn't I pursue who I wanted, too? Even if she was my mom's best friend.

So, I took a leap and stopped holding my tongue. I'd always been a little flirty—it was hard not to be with Caroline especially when the banter was so good—but I crossed that line I'd been careful to tiptoe next to for so long.

And her response had been nothing like I expected. The second she told me I was dangerous, I was done for. She couldn't admit it then, but I knew she would eventually—everything I felt, she felt it, too.

I wasn't the type of guy to keep pushing when it wasn't reciprocated or wanted, though. That was gross. So, I took a step back. Went back to casually flirting when the opportunity arose, but I was still intent on keeping myself at the front of her mind.

I was careful until recently, and especially until this weekend. I was a case study on how easily alcohol could lower your inhibitions.

And yet again, her response was nothing like I expected. She pretended to be annoyed, but it was just that, an act. She could have hung up the phone at any moment, but she didn't. I gave her an out, but she stayed on the line.

And she was taking a fucking bath? How cruel was the universe?

I braced my hands on the shower tiles and let my head hang as the spray streamed down my back. Straightening, I started my normal shower routine, grabbing the shampoo and lathering it in my hair. Rinse and repeat.

But the monotony of the motions did little to help the direction of my thoughts. I could control them as well as I could control my raging hard-on. I ran my soaped-up hands over my arms and chest, continuing down my stomach until they were hovering above my cock. I gritted my teeth and finally gave in to the need.

A quick jerk just to take the edge off. That was all I needed.

I wrapped my fingers around my shaft and let the soap guide my hand up and down. But when I closed my eyes and braced my free hand against the wall, it was Caroline's slender fingers encircling me. I bet she would grip me hard and enjoy the twinge of pain that it would elicit before the sensation transformed into pleasure.

So, I tightened my own hold, my hand shaking with the excitement of impending release. Blood pounding, my cock swelled and leaked, thinking about the possibility of her touching me that way. My eyes dropped, and I watched the fat head push through my fingers. I was leaking everywhere and fantasizing that it was her fingers, her pussy that was squeezing around me.

"Fuck, fuck, *fuck*," I moaned as I shot against the wall and all over my hand.

Trying to catch my breath, I straightened and washed away the proof. It felt good, of course it did, but it didn't curb the craving like I wanted it to.

I had a feeling little would have that desired effect. Nothing except *her*.

FOUR

BEST MAN

Caroline

MY HEELS CLICKED AGAINST THE REFURBISHED HARDWOOD FLOORS, and I spun as I stared at the newly restored, intricate ceilings.

The venue was relatively new, and it was my first time seeing the space. I hadn't been able to make the opening party they'd invited me to several months prior, and now, I regretted not fostering a relationship with the owners sooner.

They were going to be booked solid for the next several years, and I knew a lot of the couples I worked with would love it.

It was a mansion built so long ago that it took them years to restore all the original features and fixtures that they could. The ballroom—yes, it had a ballroom—had stunning mahogany floors that I was sure ran throughout the rest of the house and ornate crown molding around the perimeter of the ceiling.

It checked off all the boxes Stephen and Miles had given me —it was *not* modern, it was romantic and elegant and absolutely stunning. And it had on-site rooms where the wedding party and family could stay that weekend.

"You look speechless, Ms. Grant," Chuck, one of the owners,

said as he stepped into the ballroom. He was older and rugged with dirt under his nails and wrinkles from time in the sun.

I smiled at him and tossed my arms out to my sides, motioning to the beautiful place they'd created around us. "Honestly, I am. This place is…stunning."

He peered around the room with a content smile as he walked toward me. "A lot of time and hard work went into making this place what it is now. It was in shambles when we bought it, but we knew we could make it something beautiful again."

"How long did it take exactly?"

He thought for a moment. "Almost three years, but I don't want to bore you with those details just yet. Are we waiting on anyone, or should we get the tour started?"

I glanced toward the front entryway and then down at my phone in my hand. The "best man" had already missed our first venue tour that morning, and now, he was late to the second.

Miles told me he'd forwarded the venue tour schedule to the guy, so I wasn't sure what the issue was. I'd texted them asking for the best man's contact information, but with the time difference, it was the middle of the night in Tokyo.

"I'm really not—" I began to say but was interrupted by the sound of steps coming from the front of the house.

"I'm so sorry I'm late," a familiar voice called. I looked up from my phone, and my jaw dropped.

I didn't think there was much that could surprise me, but there I was, proving myself wrong.

Ryder strode into the room and stopped to introduce himself to Chuck as I attempted to wrap my head around what was happening. But it felt like my brain was short-circuiting at the sight before me. Not just that Ryder was *there*, but that he was there, *and* he was wearing a suit?

I don't think I'd ever seen Ryder in a suit before, and I hated how I had to force myself to swallow and look away.

SOMETHING TO SOMEONE   35

Chuck stepped aside, and Ryder smiled at me. That stupid, cocky smirk, I cleared my throat and raised an eyebrow at him.

"Hey, Caroline."

"Ryder, what are you doing here?"

He laughed quietly, and Chuck looked between us. "I'll be up front, Ms. Grant. Come find me when you're ready to start the tour."

I nodded apologetically. "Sure, thanks. We'll just be a second." I waited until he was out of the room and hopefully out of earshot to turn back to Ryder. "What the hell are you doing here?"

Ryder stuffed his hands in his black slacks, and I caught myself watching the way his pants tightened across his hips with the motion. Or how the jacket shaped his broad shoulders perfectly and the blue of his shirt was a few shades lighter than his eyes.

"I'm the best man," he said.

"Of course you are," I muttered, and he quirked an eyebrow at me in silent question. He'd introduced me to Stephen and Miles, I just hadn't realized they were that close. "The universe is just..." I shook my head and waved him off. "Why were you late then? I'm guessing the suit has something to do with it?"

He shrugged. "I had a job interview. I'm sure you're aware that I'm graduating soon, and I need to be able to make money after. That's why I'm late, but I also told Miles this. I'm guessing he didn't pass on the message?"

"Nope."

He dragged a hand through his black hair and glanced around the ballroom. "Well, I'm here now, and this place is...insane."

"How'd the interview go?" I asked instead.

Ryder answered without looking at me. "It went well. It was with an engineering firm downtown. Is this place in their budget?"

I looked down at the paperwork in my hands and found the

cost. It was hefty but within their budget. "Yeah, their budget is large enough, they could afford almost anything in or around the city. That's not going to be an issue."

He nodded slowly and ran his fingers over one of the oak tables toward the edge of the dance floor. With his back turned, I took a second to take a deep breath and shake off the lingering thoughts that were trying to press in on the edge of my mind. Thoughts of a dirty phone conversation days before.

You're working, I chastised myself. *Control your thoughts. Do not think about how much you liked him explaining what you looked like—*

"Caroline?" I blinked and glanced up at Ryder.

"Hmm?"

He smiled like he knew exactly where my thoughts had been, but he didn't call me out for it. "Do you want to go get Chuck and start the tour? I know we're on a tight schedule."

"Yes," I said, but it came out a little rough, so I cleared my throat and tried again. "Yes, let's go."

FIVE

DANCE WITH ME

Caroline

THE GROUNDS AND EVERY OTHER ROOM IN THE MANSION WERE AS beautiful as I expected it to be. Each of the guest rooms were decorated in the same elegant style but with their own unique twists.

And the exterior was breathtaking. The front had an expansive manicured lawn, and the back had a garden with pristine hedges and extensive gravel paths. There was even a fountain in the courtyard just off the ballroom. I loved the dark ivy climbing the walls and told Chuck as much as we walked back inside.

"It's one of my wife's favorite features as well. Something she was sure we had to replicate when we bought the place," he said, opening the door for me and waving me inside. The air conditioning felt nice against my warm, flushed skin. It wasn't too hot yet, but the weather was changing quickly. Spring was disappearing, and summer was fast approaching.

"And you said you have fans and misters for the courtyard if they decide that's a space they want to utilize?"

Chuck nodded emphatically. "Yes, and an air-conditioned

tent we can put up if necessary. We want to make everyone as comfortable as possible."

"I think Stephen and Miles are really going to like this place," Ryder said. He stood in front of the doors we'd entered through and snapped a picture of the ballroom from that angle.

Chuck cleared his throat and glanced between us. "Excuse me, but…is it two men who will be getting married?"

Ryder and I looked at each other, and my heart dropped. "Yes," I said matter-of-factly. No point in hiding it, they would have figured it out eventually. I just hated bigots.

"Oh, no, no," Chuck said quickly, waving his hands in surrender. "Not like that. I'm sorry, I didn't mean to imply I had an issue with it. They will just be our first gay couple. We've only been open a few months, but I think that's exciting. I… umm…I also have a grandson, he's only sixteen, but he helps with weddings occasionally, and he just came out to me. I think it would be nice for him to see and experience."

I smiled in relief, and I noticed Ryder relax from a few feet away. "That's amazing. Stephen and Miles are great, and I do agree with Ryder—they would love this place. I'm going to snap a few more photos, then we'll get out of your hair."

"Take your time," Chuck said. He waved and headed back up front.

I tossed my papers onto the closest table and considered the size of the room. They had almost three hundred guests, which was larger than the average wedding I planned but not uncommon.

With the size of their guest list in mind, I observed the tables available and the arrangement possibilities. "I'm worried that the dance floor may be too small," I muttered, thinking out loud. "That was on their list of things they absolutely want. There's only tables enough for two hundred people right now, so if we double the amount, then we'll—"

I squeaked in surprise as a strong hand landed on my hip and spun me around. Then Ryder was there, in front of me, reaching for my right hand and guiding my left hand to rest on his shoulder.

"What are you doing?"

Instead of answering, he started moving us around the open space between the tables. With one hand pressed against my lower back, he kept us close as he guided me toward the middle of the dance floor. I heard the music faintly from a nearby table and realized he must have started playing it from his phone.

"What are you doing?" I repeated through clenched teeth.

"Dancing," he said like it wasn't odd at all that he'd randomly decided to sweep me up.

With a soft growl, I tried to plant my feet and push away, but Ryder was having none of it. He just held on tighter and pressed us together. My breasts flattened against his taut chest, and all the air was swept from my lungs.

"Why?" I tried again, breathlessly.

"I don't think the dance floor is too small."

"This may be one of the weirdest things you've ever done, and I can't even hear the damn music."

He chuckled and looked down at me. My eyes traced the line of his sharp jaw and up over his smooth cheek until I met his blue eyes. It was an unsettling sort of blue, one that someone with less willpower than me might easily get lost in. Especially when said person's heart was thudding against their chest, and they couldn't help but inhale and be overwhelmed by his deep, clean scent.

"You're right," he said. "The music is a little soft." Then he started singing the lyrics loudly, drowning out the soft background noise. When the room wasn't filled with linens and flowers and people, sound carried, and Ryder's voice bounced off the walls around us.

"Ryder, you've got to be kidding me!" I angrily whispered, tugging my hand free and slapping it over his mouth.

We stopped moving, but he didn't let me go. His hand I'd dropped appeared on my other hip, and his hold on me tightened. My eyes bounced between his, and I swore I saw excitement sparking behind his irises.

"What is your problem?" A shrug was his response. Not that he could speak with my palm covering his mouth, but that was beside the point. "Are you going to stop singing if I remove my hand?"

Another shrug, then a slow smile tilted his lips. I felt his grin against my palm, and the excitement I thought I saw before was truly blazing in his blue eyes.

Ryder made everything exciting and fun, and, fucking hell, it was contagious. I had no control over the twin smile that tugged at my mouth. With his eyes glued to my face, Ryder didn't miss a second of it. He saw me struggle with my grin by rolling my lips.

It only made his smile widen, and the brush of his hips against mine was too much. I dropped my hand, and when I stepped away again, he let me go.

SIX

I SMELL TROUBLE

Ryder

STANDING ACROSS THE GRAVEL PARKING LOT UNDER A LARGE OAK tree, I continued doing what I had been doing all day: watching Caroline.

It was hard not to watch her. No matter how hard I tried, my eyes traveled back to her. She was magnetic and beautiful. Especially when she was in work mode.

When Stephen and Miles told me they were getting married, and how tight the timeline was, I knew Caroline would make it happen. That was why I'd sent them her way. They were getting the best wedding planner ever, and she was getting a new, exciting client.

I'd met Stephen and Miles freshman year of college. They'd walked in on me hooking up with one of their fraternity brothers in a bathroom at the frat house. The guy hadn't come out yet, so he very quickly shoved me off him only for my head to collide with the counter behind me.

Miles and Stephen stayed behind to make sure I was okay, and the rest was history.

Now, we were planning their wedding.

On the other side of the parking lot, Caroline was talking to the owner of the third venue, Susanna, and saying her goodbyes. I leaned against her car, waiting for her and thinking about how amazing it would feel to take my damn dress pants off. I'd lost my jacket on the way to the third venue and kept checking to make sure I hadn't started sweating through my shirt.

With graduation imminent and a corporate job calling my name, I had to learn to love a suit and tie. Or at least put up with it. My interview had gone well, and I was one step closer to securing a job after graduation. I had two more interviews scheduled for later that week. One of which would require me to move several states away.

Although I was in the second to last round of interviews, I hadn't told anyone about that possibility. It was the highest-paying position, and they were willing to help me relocate. But I wasn't going to get my hopes up until I had an offer in my hands.

Honestly, I was exhausted. Between preparing for finals, interviewing, and helping plan two of my best friends' wedding, I didn't have a lot of free time. But seeing Caroline made me forget about everything else.

She waved to Susanna and dropped her sunglasses onto her nose. Her long legs ate up the distance between us. Even over gravel, her stride was sure and confident.

"I thought you'd already left," she said, unlocking her car and tossing her papers and bag into the back seat.

I smiled and tilted my head. I knew she was lying. Her eyes had darted in my direction several times while she spoke to Susanna. It was hard to miss when I'd been staring at her the entire time.

"No, you didn't," I said casually, and she flashed me her standard annoyed look I'd grown so fond of. Especially since it often held a little hidden humor behind her blue-gray eyes. "So, it's definitely the last venue, right? It has to be."

Caroline closed the car door and leaned her shoulder

against it. "Yeah, I mean, I have to check with the grooms first, but I think they'll agree. It meets all their requirements and then some. And they have the exact wedding date they wanted."

"You're really good at this," I said, motioning to the venue behind her. Underneath the shade of the tree, she pushed her sunglasses on top of her head and smiled.

"That was nothing. Just wait until the day of the wedding when the pressure is on, and something inevitably goes wrong."

"I'm excited to see you really in action then."

"Yeah, I'm sure you are," she said, ignoring my obvious attempts at flirting. But I didn't want to let her go that easily. Our conversation the other night wasn't enough.

She reached for the handle of the driver's side door I was leaning against. When I didn't move, she shot me a warning look that didn't make me flinch.

"I can't stop thinking about our conversation the other night," I said, intentionally dropping my voice a little bit.

Wide, surprised eyes met mine, but she stayed silent. Her blonde hair fell just past her shoulders in pristine, loose waves and brushed the top of her tasteful cleavage. She was always so put together no matter the occasion—no hair out of place and makeup, if any, flawlessly applied—but the black top, light wash jeans, and heels were particularly perfect.

"And I need to ask you—"

"Ryder—"

"Do you still think I'm dangerous, Caroline?"

She was silent. Her eyes bounced between mine then narrowed as she asked, "What?"

I shook my head immediately. "I know you heard me, but I'll ask again. Do you still think I'm dangerous?"

There was an acute defiance in her eyes before she glanced away. Her jaw tensed, and she shook her head, tightening her grip on the door handle. But I was tired of hearing her deny it. I didn't want her to hide from it.

Taking a risk, I reached for her hip. Like I should have guessed she would, she skillfully stepped out of reach.

"For once, please tell me the truth. If this really is as one-sided as you try to make it out to be, then that's fine. But only tell me that if that's really what you believe."

She stayed silent, unmoving. It was eerie how well she did that. Looking at you, or better yet *through* you, with expression-less eyes that didn't bely any of her thoughts. I tried to be patient, but with each second that ticked by, the more anxious I grew. *Fuck*, maybe I had made a horrible mistake and a gross miscalculation.

My heart was steadily beating faster, and my palms began to sweat. I prepared myself to walk away when she took a breath and straightened. In anticipation for what she might say, I stopped breathing altogether.

"Yes, you're still…trouble."

A triumphant smile slipped across my face, and I stepped forward, only to be stopped by her outstretched hand in the middle of my chest. Fuck, her touch felt good. "That doesn't mean we need to do anything about it, though."

So close, I thought. "Why?" I didn't even think about the question. It was an automatic response.

"Why? You're really asking me *why*? I feel like the 'why' is pretty clear."

I reached up and covered her hand on my chest with my own. It felt good to touch her again, and I was thrilled when she didn't tug her hand away immediately. Concerned she would see my excitement and immediately think better of it, I kept my reaction locked down.

She glanced down at my hand covering her's and furrowed her blonde brows in confusion. Like she felt this strange pull, too, and didn't know how it happened or what to do about it.

"Just give me one legitimate reason why I shouldn't kiss you right fucking now. Especially when my entire body is telling me to do exactly that," I said honestly. The desire was nothing new to me, but naming it, vocalizing it, was something completely different.

Caroline finally tugged her hand away. She grasped it with her other, rubbing them together like she wanted to rub away the memory of my touch.

"Because your mom is—"

"No." I stopped her immediately. "That excuse became mute the moment I found my mom and my best friend in bed together. And don't give me any crap about an age difference either, because a decade is barely any time at all."

"Fine," she said resolutely, doing the opposite of what I expected and stepping closer to me. She was tall, but she still had to tilt her head slightly to look me in the eye. I straightened and uncrossed my arms. She was close enough that her chest brushed against mine, and I could see the few freckles along her nose and cheeks. "Because I can't give you what you want, Ryder. I won't."

I reared back, and she took the opportunity to pull open the car door. She didn't say anything else and closed the door in the next second.

I took a step back out of the way as she backed out and drove off, but I watched her the entire time. Her tires kicked up dust and loose gravel, and I had no clue what to think.

I merely stood in the middle of the parking lot and knew I'd have to set the record straight. All I wanted was her.

SEVEN
SUMMER DAZE

Caroline

THE SUN WAS SHINING, THE BIRDS WERE CHIRPING, AND THE KIDS were screaming—what a beautiful freaking day.

I narrowly avoided one child who sprinted in front of me and another who almost side-swiped me chasing after the first. I gritted my teeth and willed all other children in the vicinity to stay away from me until I could get inside.

I barely made it in the house before another scream erupted followed by a large splash from the pool. I shut the sliding glass door, but it did little to muffle the sounds.

Setting the empty tray of snacks on the kitchen island, I took a deep breath and closed my eyes for a moment.

"Do you need any help, sweetie?" My mom's hand landed on my shoulder, and I startled at the contact.

"No, I'm okay. Thanks, though."

She gave me an unconvincing look and grabbed the tray from in front of me. "I'll help anyway," she said. She opened the fridge and began sifting through the contents, searching for the fruit to replenish the tray.

"Care, do you have extra sunscreen?" My sister, Allison,

appeared from around the corner with my nephew, Thomas, in tow. He was the reason there were twenty screaming children running around outside. Thomas and my niece, Olivia, were the only two people in the world who could have convinced me to let all their friends take over my house for the day.

Especially since it was Thomas's eighth birthday.

"Yeah, it's in my bathroom. The cabinet on the far right."

"Thank you, thank you," my older sister said and ushered Thomas in that direction. He was already sporting little red shoulders, but he had a huge smile on his face.

I thought they were all having a pretty good time, except my brother-in-law, Oliver, and my father who were manning the grill and listening to the kids demand hot dogs and hamburgers along with their parents chiming in with any dietary restrictions.

There was a very good reason why I had willingly and eagerly given up that particular job.

I rounded the island and started opening and arranging the fruit on the platter as my mom retrieved it from the fridge. She sighed dramatically when she noticed me, but it was her fault I had trouble relaxing, I'd gotten it from her.

She saddled up next to me at the counter and began her usual inquisition.

"How's work going?"

"Have you hired anyone else?"

"Have you thought about selling the company yet?"

"Have you thought about selling your house?"

"Are you dating anyone?"

"Do you still have an aversion to love?"

"Mom!" I exclaimed with a huff. "I do not have an aversion to...*love.*"

She scoffed and loaded the container that once held the strawberries into the dishwasher. "You can't even say the word without cringing. It sounds like you're in pain."

"Thank you so much for your thoughtful insight, Mother, but

I'm just fine. I am happy with my life," I said, and for her benefit and to prove her wrong, I added, "I don't need love."

I pretended like I didn't hear the way my voice dipped with the word or how it felt like my throat might close around it. Instead, I shot my mom a sweet, unbothered smile and hoped we'd finished with her questions. I'd answered each of them to the best of my ability—no, I wasn't planning on selling anything, but yes, work was good. No, I wasn't dating anyone, and I had no plans to.

I gave her my usual spiel about not settling on a man and not settling down unless he was exceptional. And how if that never happened, I would be fine.

I had no more answers to give her, so I hoped she would let it all go. My hope was dashed, though, when she started, "Caroline, just because you've had your heartbroken before, just because you've lost someone—"

"Stop," I snapped. And thankfully, she heeded my request. That and my dad appeared beside her. He kissed her forehead and whispered, "Leave her be, honey." My mom sighed and shook her head like the idea was preposterous. What good was coming to my house if she couldn't interrogate me about my life?

He then shifted to me, wrapping a loving arm around my shoulders and kissing my temple. I'd always been a daddy's girl. He'd been there for me through every high school softball game, every late-night study session, and every heartbreak. Even for the ultimate heartbreak my mom so kindly alluded to. The heartbreak to end all heartbreaks. The loss I never saw coming.

But he never came with judgment or opinions, just support. He was the parent I leaned on when I had to. And I was lucky to have him.

He didn't say anything to me—he didn't have to—I felt the love and apology without any words.

He grabbed a drink and walked back outside while I wiped my sweaty palms on my crocheted swimsuit cover-up. But it didn't do much good. Although the fruit on the tray in front of me was perfectly placed, I fiddled with it because I needed something to do with my hands.

"Sweetie," my mom began, gripping my forearm with a forlorn, apologetic look on her face.

She opened her mouth like she was going to say something else, but voices, new voices, echoed from the entryway. And I'd never been so excited for an interruption.

Especially since I would have recognized that voice anywhere.

"Natalie!" I exclaimed. Eager for the interruption, my voice was a little higher pitched than normal, and Natalie clocked it the moment I walked out of the kitchen to greet her. Her eyes were wide with confusion, but I hugged her anyway.

"What—" she began to question when I pulled back, but she quickly stopped. She spotted my mom over my shoulder and nodded. "Ahh," she said instead.

Swallowing down any lingering frustration, I looked behind my best friend. "Hey, Theo. Thanks for coming."

Theo gave me a tight-lipped smile and glanced skeptically toward the backyard. When he'd begun living with my best friend, before they realized they were in love, the lack of desire to be at parties such as these was how we bonded. Theo always acted like he hated being around people, but as long as Natalie was there, he was perfectly content.

"I promise there's only—" *a few kids,* I was about to joke, but my ability to speak suddenly disappeared when the front door swung open, and Ryder stepped inside.

Wearing his standard wide grin, he pushed a hand through his disheveled black hair and brushed a few stray pieces off his forehead. "Thanks for waiting, guys," he said, striding farther into the house and toward our group.

My mouth went dry, and I forced myself to blink and look away when he stopped in front of me.

"Hi, Caroline," Ryder crooned, and my traitorous eyes bounced to his. "Thanks for the invite."

With other people around, I managed to bite my tongue until he threw me a smirk that I couldn't resist.

"Funny, I don't remember inviting you, Ryder."

His smile only grew wider, and he ran his tongue across his perfectly straight, white teeth. "Really? I thought it was an open invitation."

I returned his shit-eating grin. "You're right. So run along, the other kids are in the pool."

Next to me, Theo snorted, but Ryder wasn't fazed by my jokes. "Oh, Caroline, you wound me. You know, I'm a big kid now."

"No more diapers or anything," Theo chimed in.

"Exactly!" Ryder exclaimed, clapping his best friend on the shoulder.

Out of the corner of my eye, I watched Natalie shake her head right before she clapped her hands together and proclaimed, "I need a drink."

I ushered everyone into the kitchen and toward the fridge, ignoring Ryder's presence I could feel at my back.

I'd done everything I could over the past week to ignore the thought of him. Actually, it had been a year and a half of trying —and failing—to ignore him and every other feeling he managed to conjure within me.

But it felt a little pointless. Although he'd been silent for most of the week, I knew he hadn't let it go. He was busy with graduation and finals and searching for a job. But if I knew anything about Ryder, he was stubborn and enthusiastically pursued every interest. Me telling him that I couldn't give him what he wanted wouldn't stop him. Little would at this point which was making me wary.

I served Natalie a drink and let the guys fend for themselves as we joined the party outside. I was keen to get as much distance between me and Ryder as possible.

"So, Ryder told me that he's the best man in his friends' wedding that *you* are planning," Natalie said as we took a seat on the bench under a large tree toward the back of my yard. It was the perfect, shaded spot that kept us far enough away from the crowd but close enough that I could keep an eye on everything.

I took a long sip of my drink and tugged my sunglasses down from where I had them propped on top of my head. "Yup," I confirmed. "The couple are really sweet, and I'm excited they chose me. They had an unlimited budget, really, so they could have gone with anyone else."

"Well, they picked right," she said, nudging my shoulder and wiggling her eyebrows. "But he said since they don't live local, that he's going to be helping you plan it?"

I nodded. "That's what they wanted. Although I told them it wasn't necessary."

"I can't imagine Ryder helping plan a wedding." Natalie laughed. "I had to help him match his clothes until he went to college and decorating his room when he was younger was…rough."

Across the yard, Theo slipped out the glass door with Ryder right behind him. They quickly found my sister and brother-in-law and took a seat at their table. Ryder set his drink down and leaned back in the chair, propping his ankle on his other knee and falling into what I could tell was easy conversation with my family.

With the sun beating down, he fished his sunglasses from his pocket and donned the black aviators. Frustrated with how good he looked, I took another hearty pull of my drink and pointedly stopped staring across the yard.

"How was your mom?" Natalie asked, and I appreciated the topic change. Although my mother wasn't necessarily a topic I loved to discuss.

"Same old, same old," I muttered. *"How's work going? Are you going to sell your house? Why can't you find a nice man and settle down?"* I pitched my voice in a dramatic imitation of my mom's. "I know she loves me and wants what's best for me, but her version of that and mine are always radically different."

"I don't get it. I mean, I'm not one to talk, my own parents kicked me out when I got pregnant with Ryder, but as a mom myself, I can't imagine constantly questioning Ryder's life choices. First," she began, lifting her hand and ticking off each point with her fingers. "Because that's exhausting. Second, because he's an adult, and third, because he's happy. And you seem pretty damn happy to me."

"I am. It's just...the way she's always been. Allison did everything *'right'*—she went to college, got married, had children, stayed at home. And that's what my mom wanted for me, too."

My mom would never agree with my life choices. No matter how happy or successful I was, and unfortunately, I had come to terms with that. Although that didn't keep my friend from wanting to go to bat for me.

Even when she didn't know the entire story or why my mom was so relentless. Which I still felt guilty about. I hadn't kept it from Natalie for any good reason because I knew she would be supportive. I just didn't like talking about it. Like I said, I was happy and content, and I wanted to keep it that way.

Noting my discomfort with the topic, Natalie easily pivoted topics. She cleared her throat and said, "So, tell me the whole story with your new girl at work. What happened with her boyfriend?"

"Oh, Addie, yes! Her boyfriend came by the office," I said excitedly, turning to face her, so I could watch every one of her facial expressions. But in my periphery, I caught Ryder watching me. Not that I could see his eyes behind his sunglasses, but I could still tell.

Not listening to the conversations happening around him, all his attention was on me. And I would never admit it out loud, but I enjoyed it.

EIGHT
BEG

Caroline

"I'M JUST GOING TO RUN TO THE BATHROOM," I SAID OVER THE deafening volume that had not waned the entire day.

"Okay, I'll get everyone out of the pool, then we can cut the cake. It's in the fridge in the garage, right?"

I nodded and gave my sister a thumbs up as I headed down the hallway toward my room. My nerves were fried from little kids tugging on me and screaming and constantly wanting things. I wasn't used to the chaos, and I just needed a moment of silence.

And even amid the insanity, I hadn't missed the feeling of Ryder's eyes on me. I could feel him watching me throughout the day, which only made my already anxious state worse.

Pushing open the double doors to my bedroom, I took an immediate right into my bathroom. I swung the door closed behind me but whirled when it opened less than a second later.

"What the—"

Ryder stepped inside and closed the door behind him. His fingers brushed the lock then turned it slowly. The click echoed through the room.

"What are you doing in here?"

He shrugged nonchalantly, leaning back against the door and crossing his arms. His fitted white T-shirt stretched across his chest, the sleeves of which tightened around his biceps. Dark jeans hugged his thighs, and I watched his ankles cross, too.

A smirk completed his unbothered persona.

"You looked a little overwhelmed."

I snorted and shook my head, tucking my hair behind my ear. "So, you decided to follow me rather than give me a second to collect myself?"

Another shrug.

Closing my eyes, I took a deep breath and considered the possibility of him leaving without this going further.

"You should go."

"Why?"

I turned and motioned to the toilet behind me. "I need to go to the bathroom. Because we are in a bathroom, if you couldn't tell."

Ryder was shaking his head, a few dark strands spilling forward before I'd finished speaking. He wasn't believing any part of my lie.

"No, you don't. You went to the bathroom less than a half hour ago, and you haven't had anything to drink since. So, unless you've developed a very tiny bladder in the past hour, I think you're lying."

My jaw went slack, and I narrowed my eyes at him. "That is so weird. You've been watching me?"

I didn't expect his chuckle, but I felt it low my stomach all the same. He was so unashamed by the fact that he'd been keeping track of me. It made me feel things I hadn't expected.

"Don't pretend like you haven't noticed. You've been watching me, too."

Uneasy with the entire interaction and how out of control I felt, I mimicked his nonchalance as best I could. My ass hit the sink behind me, and I crossed my arms over my chest. Tilting my head to the side, I appraised him. His little smirk grew wider.

"I can't help if my eyes happened to land on you. And if they did, I promise you it was wholly unintentional."

He licked his lips and pursed them like he was considering my words, and his response, carefully. "I see. You're saying it's just a reflex then, to find me when I'm in the room?"

I groaned and tilted my head back to stare at the white ceiling. The sun shining through the window above the sink reflected rays of sharp light across it.

"Oh my gosh, I hate you."

I looked back at him just in time to witness his wide smile and watch his throat bob with a hearty laugh. "Good, it turns me on."

My entire body tensed, and I could see in the way his smile dipped and his eyes remained steadfast on my face, that he was being completely truthful.

We were in uncharted territory. Standing on the precipice of something neither of us fully comprehended.

"You should leave," I said quietly.

"Not yet." He straightened, and I pushed back against the sink. I couldn't get farther away unless I ran into my closet which seemed childish, but I kept the option tucked away just in case. "Tell me what you think I want."

Sighing, I braced my hands against the sink behind me for extra support. I knew this would come up again. Ryder didn't quit, and he didn't give up. "I don't *think*. I *know* what you want."

"Sorry to burst your bubble, but you don't know everything about me, Caroline. But just so we're on the same page, why don't you tell me what you *know*?"

"A relationship, Ryder. And I don't do—"

"Who said I wanted a relationship?"

I ground my teeth and tossed my hands out to my sides in exasperation. I was starting to do that a lot around him. "You would eventually. And starting…*something* knowing that will eventually be an issue is idiotic, pointless, and a waste of time."

For once, he appeared frustrated. Unfolding his arms, he leveled me a very serious look behind his startling blue eyes. "I never said I wanted a relationship," he said, each word slow and deliberate. "I don't think I've ever told you exactly what I want."

I stayed silent for a moment, knowing that the next words out of my mouth were only going to make matters worse. Even so, I said, "Fine then, by all means, enlighten me."

Without missing a beat, he said, "To start, I want to know what you taste like, and I'm not just talking about your mouth."

There weren't many moments in my life where I could remember being shocked beyond words. I didn't often trip over them or struggle to find the right thing to say. By all accounts, I talked too much. But around Ryder, especially when he said things like that, I couldn't seem to speak.

He took the invitation of my silence to take a step forward, then another. With a few feet between us, I could smell the woodsy spice of his cologne mixed with the sunshine clinging to his skin.

His stubble-covered jaw tensed, and images of those cheeks pressed against my inner thighs, scraping against my skin as he did what he wanted, made it hard to swallow.

"I just want a taste, Caroline. I'll take whatever you're willing to give me."

Two more steps, and he was directly in front of me, bracing both of his hands on the counter behind me. I followed the movement and watched his fingers curl over the lip of the sink. Slowly I dragged my eyes back to his and tried to control my quick breaths and chaotic heartbeat.

Sharing the same air, I could feel the heat of his chest against mine and the strength in his lean, taut muscles. He maintained eye contact as he leaned forward and brushed his nose and then his lips against my cheek. He lifted his hands and swept my hair off my shoulder. The shiver that whipped down my spine was swift.

Like a wave, the memory of the last time he did that washed over me. Standing in my kitchen over a year ago, he got that close, eager for more. Only this time, I didn't have the where-withal to stop him. And unlike last time, his lips touched my skin. It was the smallest graze, yet I could feel it everywhere.

"I don't think you understand, Caroline. I would do anything for it." His voice was a low vibration against my neck. One that I enjoyed immensely. "I'm not above begging."

I tilted my head and nudged his face with my chin, raising my hands to push lightly at his chest until he caught on and pulled back. Not enough to give me any sort of room, but enough that he could see my face.

"If you're going to beg, you might as well do it on your knees."

NINE

BEST SECOND OF MY LIFE

Ryder

MOMENTARILY SURPRISED BY HER WORDS, I DIDN'T MOVE. ONE simple sentence had rendered me utterly useless and incapable of thought.

But I wasn't going to pass up such an immeasurable opportunity. So, I stepped back and dropped to my knees.

A perfectly placed rug cushioned my landing, protecting my knees from the hard tile floor. But I would have kneeled on broken glass for the woman staring down at me. It had been second nature to heed her suggestion even if it hadn't been totally serious.

My eyes slowly roamed up her body. Her toes were a perfectly painted shade of light purple, and her legs were remarkably smooth. I refrained from reaching out and touching them just yet as I continued my perusal of her body. I'd glimpsed a peek of her blue bikini beneath the black crocheted cover-up that hung almost to her mid-thigh. Little holes all throughout the material were like a tease of what was beneath. Just enough to allow your imagination to run wild with the knowledge but not enough for a full picture.

The fabric hugged her hips and trailed down her arms to her similarly manicured fingers. Higher yet, I eyed the curve of her breast and licked my lips at the sight of her heaving chest. I dragged my eyes over her jaw just like I wanted to with my lips and decided that I would die if I didn't get my mouth on hers and soon.

Her slightly parted, plump lips were begging to be nipped and kissed.

"Better?"

She tilted her chin slightly and ran her tongue over her bottom lip. No words left those lips, but she did hum her approval which was more than enough for me. Trapped by her blue-gray eyes, they darkened as her pupils dilated. I held that intense stare and lifted my shaking hands, skimming my fingers along the smooth skin of her muscular calves and slipping them higher. Her gasp was soft, barely audible from where I kneeled before her, but I noted it. With a light touch, I grazed the backs of her knees and continued a cautious ascent.

The fabric of her cover-up brushed the backs of my hands, and I devoured each one of the minute changes to her expression. The higher my hands climbed, the harder it was for her to contain her reactions. Her fingers gripped the counter behind her, and her muscles tensed beneath my touch.

My heart was pounding a merciless beat, and every second that ticked by, when she was allowing me to touch her, was the single best second of my life.

Holding my breath, I moved one more inch and barely caressed the perfect crease of her ass, where the top of her thighs curved into two round cheeks. But any further exploration was quickly stopped. Caroline's hand snapped forward, fingers tangling in my hair and tugging my head back.

There was a sharp bite of pain then pleasure that speared directly to my cock which throbbed in appreciation. Apparently, I liked pain. I hadn't ever experienced that before, and I wasn't sure if it was because it was Caroline inflicting it, but I didn't have time to truly examine the foreign feeling.

She swallowed slowly, keeping her grip tight, and said, "I thought you were going to beg."

"Please." The word tumbled from my mouth before I could contemplate it. But her reaction was instant. Her fingers tightened in my hair and tilted my neck farther back. "*Please,*" I said again.

"Come on, Ryder," she said. "We both know you can do better than that."

The smooth, honeyed tone of her voice washed over me, and I smiled at the invitation. Her eyes narrowed on my lips, and I shifted my hands to her hips, gripping them beneath her swimsuit cover-up. Squeezing her like she was my hair, I groaned when she tugged once again.

"Please, *please* let me really touch you," I said through a quick exhalation. "You're so fucking incredible, so perfect. I want just a taste of that perfection. I'll take whatever you want to give me."

Watching her eyes dance with intrigue, her hand in my hair loosened. I licked my lips and leaned forward. She let her fingers run through my hair as my forehead met her hip.

"I want to touch and taste every inch of you. I want to press my tongue into your perfect cu—"

A sharp knock on the door made us both freeze, and abruptly quieted my words. It took everything in me not to groan in frustration. I was making such good progress; I could feel her walls crumbling with each second that passed.

"Caroline? Natalie sent me to come get you," Theo called out from the other side of the door. "They want to cut the cake, and I think the kids are planning a riot."

"*Fuck,*" Caroline cursed as she slipped from my grip. "Get up."

I did as she instructed, but I was much less worried about Theo than she was. My mom might have been Caroline's best friend, but Theo was mine. And he wouldn't say anything.

She took a deep breath and smoothed her hands down her swimsuit cover-up, although nothing was out of place. "Okay, this is what's going to happen," she said. "I'm going to go out there, and you're going to stay in here for at least two minutes. Then you'll come out."

She was panicky and very serious while I was...not. I casually readjusted my erection and stuffed my hands in my pockets, biting my cheek to keep from smiling.

"Okay?" she asked when I didn't respond to her very well thought out plan.

I nodded. "Yes, ma'am. Whatever you want."

She rolled her eyes, but they lingered on me for too long for her to actually be annoyed. Unable to suppress my smile any longer, my lips curved, and she blinked slowly before turning and shaking her head.

What I wouldn't have given to read her mind.

Quickly, she slipped out the door and shut it behind her. I didn't give it but half a second before I was opening the door and stepping out as well. Caroline stopped mid-sentence and halfway to her bedroom door. Theo was right behind her, and turned to look at me with wide, surprised eyes.

He glanced from me to the bathroom door then back to Caroline. He didn't say anything, he didn't have to. The look on his face was enough to tell me exactly what he thought.

Caroline shook her head, but didn't say anything either as she strode from the room, firmly shutting the door without looking back.

Theo stared at the door for a long second then looked back at me. I gave him a shrug and a grin, but he also just shook his head. "Do I really want to know?"

"No, probably not."

"Great. I'll see you out there then." He walked out the door, and I decided to wait the two minutes Caroline had requested. Especially when her scent still lingered around me which meant

it was more like five minutes before I had control of myself again
and eventually left the room.

TEN

LATE NIGHT SWIM

Caroline

IT WAS THE CALM AFTER THE STORM. ALL THE CHILDREN WHO invaded my house had left, and I'd spent the last hour and a half getting everything back to the way it was.

Natalie, my sister, and my sister's family had stayed around to help me clean, which I appreciated, but I was happy to have an empty house once again. I liked the quiet.

For the first time that day, I slipped off my swimsuit cover-up and took advantage of my pool. With the sun nearly below the horizon, the night air was several degrees cooler, but when I dove in, the heated water was the perfect temperature.

I swam the length of the pool, back and forth, until my muscles grew tired, and I floated on my back in the middle of the water. My house was too close to the city lights to see any stars, but a few winked into existence as the sky grew darker.

My eyes slowly closed, and I took a deep breath, letting each of my muscles relax. Until I heard a sound, and I quickly righted myself. I spun in a tight circle, surveying my surroundings and slowly beginning to panic. I whipped back around to face the house and that was when I noticed him—Ryder—relatching the back gate.

"What are you doing here?"

I dipped farther down into the water until it was just beneath my chin as Ryder turned and strode toward the edge of the pool. Motioning to the item in his hands, I didn't recognize what it was until he said, "My mom asked if I would bring this back to you on my way home. She said she already fixed whatever was wrong with it."

"Oh, okay," I muttered. It was a dress I'd wanted to wear the next day that had a small rip from where the tag had been removed. And of us two, Natalie was much better at sewing. I knew it would take her less than a few minutes to fix it whereas I would have stabbed myself six times just trying to thread the needle. "You can just put it on one of the chairs."

Ryder nodded and set the dress on the arm of a chair. Slowly, he turned and began unhurried, measured steps around the pool until he was standing just at the edge, peering down at me. With his hands in his jean pockets, he appraised me. The low lights in the pool and the water cast shadows that danced across his face. His eyes scanned my face before they dropped lower. Everything below my shoulders was distorted by the water, but I knew he could still see the shape of my blue bikini and the rest of my bare skin.

After our *incident* in the bathroom, I hadn't stopped reliving those moments for the rest of the day. The image of Ryder on his knees, making dirty promises that I knew he was eager to keep would forever be burned into my brain.

A muscle tensed in his jaw, and I watched his Adam's apple bob as he swallowed. Even in the warmth of the water, goose bumps appeared down my arms and over my legs under the intensity of his stare.

Although he was silent as he watched me, his expression was loud. All the desire he'd expressed to me before was simmering and churning, apparent in every subtle dilation of his eyes and twitch of his muscles.

Then he shifted and toed off one shoe. It wasn't until he started on the other and tugged off the flannel he'd tossed on over his white T-shirt that I found my voice.

"What are you doing?" I spluttered.

Ryder didn't stop. He pushed his shoes to the side and let his flannel drop on top of them.

"Getting in," he said like it was a foregone conclusion. Like it was obvious that he would get in with me.

Shaking my head, I straightened. The cooler air was a stark difference to the heated water around me, and I immediately felt my nipples harden to little points. Not even the thicker swimsuit fabric could hide the inconvenient evidence of the change in temperature. Quickly, I resubmerged until the tops of my shoulders were exposed.

"Why the hell would you do that?"

He shrugged and reached behind his head for the collar of his T-shirt. "Because it looks…tempting," he reasoned. I swallowed past the excitement in my throat as he clarified, "The water, that is. It's hard to resist."

But the way he said it, in a tone belying all the dirty thoughts in his head, I knew he couldn't be talking about the water.

"Ryder—" I tried to say when he whipped his shirt off and exposed the shallow yet defined muscles of his stomach and the broad planes of his chest where a small smattering of neat, dark hair began. Of their own accord, my eyes followed the path it created until it disappeared behind his belt.

"Yes, Caroline?" he asked, and I whipped my attention back to his face. The cocky little grin titling his lips made me second-guess my inadvertent ogling. "If you really want me to stop, I will, but you have to tell me to. I'll give you ten seconds."

The imaginary timer started, but he didn't stop. He gripped his belt and unfastened it, tugging it open while maintaining eye contact with me. In my head, I counted backward from ten as his fingers brushed against the button of his jeans.

I urged myself to say something, *anything*. To tell him how wrong it was and how badly it would end, but voicing those thoughts was pointless when I'd barely convinced myself. I knew it was frowned upon to desire your best friend's son, and I had no doubt that whatever started—*if* it started—would probably end poorly. But all the reasoning in the world couldn't make me speak before the imaginary timer rang.

Ten seconds later, Ryder pushed his zipper down and stepped out of his jeans only a moment before he dove into the pool. I caught a glimpse of his tight, black briefs before he swam past me beneath the water.

Generally, I was a confident person. In my work and in my everyday life, I was decisive and trusted my instincts. Even when I dated, I was unwavering. Which was why I was unnerved by how hesitant I was of my actions around Ryder. I second guessed every word and every movement.

It was truly unsettling the effect he had on me. Actually, it was terrifying.

And attempting to act like that wasn't the case was growing harder and harder every second we spent together. But still I tried as I stood stock-still in the middle of the pool and subtly glanced in the water around me. Out of the corner of my eye, I caught a glimpse of his moving form, but that didn't keep me from startling when he breached the surface directly behind me.

A few droplets of water hit my back, and I sucked in a sharp breath. He was close, *so* close that I could feel the heat of his body against my back, and his rushed exhale against the side of my neck. Of course, I couldn't see him, but the images my imagination conjured were vivid enough.

Small beads of water stuck to his smooth, tanned skin and were reflected in the new moonlight. There was subtle movement behind me, and I imagined he pushed a hand through his disheveled hair, pushing back the black locks that always fell over his forehead back.

For a second, I thought it was still my imagination running wild when I felt the almost imperceptible brush of his fingers against my arms, but it wasn't. I glanced down to see his hands moving through the water, carefully stroking my skin like he wanted to make sure I was really there.

I took a grounding breath that did little to calm my nerves, and instead, said, "You might as well say what you came in here to say. I know you didn't jump in here because the water '*looked tempting.*'"

He chuckled, and his hands fell away. I pointedly ignored the disappointment that tugged at the back of my mind.

"Hmm…" he hummed. "It does with you in it."

I rolled my eyes and shook my head. I set myself up for that one. "Seriously, Ryder, get on with—"

"I don't want a relationship, Caroline. I just want you in whatever way you're willing."

"How is that fair?" I argued, trying not to remember the similar statement he'd made on his knees in my bathroom hours earlier.

"I don't give a shit about fair. I've wanted you for as long as I can remember. Do you want me to tell you about that Fourth of July party how ever many years ago? That was the first time I saw you. You were wearing a little red, white, and blue bikini with cutoff shorts," he said with a groan I swore I could feel vibrate through his chest. "And the white top you had over it was unbuttoned so I could see your gloriously tan skin. You were so perfect, and you've starred in every single one of my dreams since then."

My throat constricted, and my heart started beating a wild, uncontrollable rhythm. With each word and each second, my walls were crumbling faster than I could reinforce them. The worst was happening, and the longer we stood there together, completely alone under the moonlight, the harder it was to fight it.

"Dreams are very different from reality, Ryder."

He shifted closer, and I held my breath when I felt him brush against my back. "But faced with the possibility of making my dreams a reality, I couldn't pass up the opportunity."

I had nothing left to say. Every argument I had, he handily struck down with little effort. He'd obviously thought through the repercussions and had been thinking about it for longer than I'd realized.

"You know what I think scares you the most?" he asked, energy thrumming off his skin in palpable waves.

"Climate change? Nuclear war? Spiders?" I offered not wanting to hear his answer. But he ignored my suggestions and gripped my waist, guiding me to turn toward him. My mind told me to fight him, but I knew it would have been futile. My body had taken the lead.

With sincerity brimming his blue eyes, he clasped his hands on either side of my face. "I think what scares you the most isn't the fact that I want you, it's that you want me, too."

Wow, very astute, I thought to myself because there was no way in hell I was going to admit that aloud no matter how correct it was.

"You don't have to say anything," he said. "Your silence is just as loud." A smirk, the same one that always made me feel like I was a pubescent teenager with her first full-fledged crush, curved his lips, slow and tempting.

My eyes raked over his face as I tried to steady my breathing. Eyes like a dark-blue sky and a jawline that could cut glass covered in a stubble as dark as the hair on top of his head. Hair that fell in messy, loose waves onto his forehead.

All his attention was on me, and I felt lightheaded beneath his gaze. My eyes dropped to the wide set of his shoulders and like he was following my lead, his hands dropped from my face, the heat of his palms vanishing yet appearing once again against the sides of my neck and over my shoulders.

A shiver I had no control over whipped down my spine as my eyes lowered to his chest. It was intentional, I wanted to see if he would follow my eyes with his hands and was simultaneously pleased and horrified when he did just that. Confident yet light, his fingertips grazed the sides of my breasts, lingering over the skin near my swimsuit. I was no longer breathing. I couldn't do more than one thing at a time, and breathing would require me to think about something other than staying incredibly still and taking in the man in front of me.

Lower and lower his hands fell, dipping beneath the water and finding the smallest part of my waist while I considered what his abs would feel like under my own touch. Finally, at my hips, Ryder's large hands wrapped around me and squeezed hard enough that I had to force air into my screaming lungs.

"*Please*, Caroline," he whispered. "Let me show you how good I can make you feel. How good it can be. Please."

And down, down, down came my walls. My eyes shot back to his, but he was already moving, lifting me into his arms and walking toward the edge of the pool.

"Fuck it," he muttered.

ELEVEN

THREE WISHES

Caroline

MY ANKLES LOCKED AROUND RYDER'S WAIST, AND MY HANDS landed on his shoulders. One second, he was wading through the water, and the next, he set me on the tiled edge of the pool.

I opened my mouth to ask what he was doing, but it was a pointless question. Especially when one of his hands returned to my cheek and tilted my head higher with his thumb, crushing his mouth to mine.

Lightness like I'd never known radiated through me. His lips felt more amazing than I imagined. There was no other way to describe them. They were firm yet soft, and every feeling he'd ever had toward me was communicated in that one single meeting of our lips. It was more overwhelming and powerful than I ever thought possible.

But it didn't stop there. His tongue swiped against my lips, and I knew it would have been a shame not to taste him. My hands on his shoulders banded around his neck and tugged him closer as our tongues tangled. His hands were everywhere all at once, fisting in my hair and memorizing each inch of my body he could reach. It was a brutal, hungry kiss as both of us fought for dominance and control.

It was better than any kiss before it, and any kiss after was unlikely to surpass it. That thought along with the clawing, heady desire settling low in my stomach and burning through my veins, made me pull back.

"Fucking trouble," I muttered, but Ryder wasn't done. He reached behind me and found the towel I'd tossed there for after my swim. He positioned it and urged me to lay back with a hand at the base of my throat.

An uncanny desire burned bright in his eyes, and I couldn't resist it. I wanted to see where he would take this, and fuck, he was right. I wanted him, too.

My head dropped down on top of the perfectly placed towel, and his eyes swept over me. Another shiver, not from the colder night air, and *I* was on the verge of begging the longer he stood there, studying me but not touching me. I'd never begged before in my life, and the words clawing up my throat and poised on my tongue were foreign. It was a feeling I couldn't decide if I enjoyed, but luckily, Ryder's hands interrupted my thoughts.

He tapped the inside of my thighs and stared down at where my little swimsuit bottoms covered my sex.

"Open your legs for me," he requested. "Give me a little room to play."

"Ryder," I said again, but he shook his head and shot me a hardened look.

"The next time you say my name, I want it to be between moans as you're coming on my tongue, okay? Now, open your fucking legs."

I wasn't one to easily give up control. Often, I found myself the more dominant one in the bedroom—or on the edge of the pool—but there was something about his growly, hungry disposition that made me drop my legs open.

He groaned and licked his lips. "Thank you," he said politely, running his hands from my knees up the inside of my thighs until his thumbs brushed against the edge of my swimsuit.

"You're only welcome if you know what you're doing down there."

A cocky smile and the glint in his eyes was his only response. Propping up on my elbows, I stared down my body where his thumb brushed over my swimsuit between my legs. It was the lightest tease of pressure, but it was pointed, sweeping over my slit and swollen clit. It was enough to have my hips lifting off the ground beneath me and searching for more.

"I can't wait to prove to you that I not only know what I'm doing but convince you I'm the best you'll ever have," he stated confidently. And the laugh that leaped from my lips was unintentional yet perfectly conveyed how I felt about his statement.

His eyes shot to mine and rather than dull the confidence I'd noticed before, it seemed to amplify it. I didn't doubt that Ryder would be good, but the best I ever had was a high bar to reach, let alone surpass. A kiss was one thing. But I'd had some really, really good sex. Although I didn't doubt that he would try.

His thumb brushed against me again, and my eyes fluttered closed for a moment until I felt him move. I looked down just in time to see him kneeling in front of me.

"Lucky for you, I also do my best convincing on my knees," he said, leaning forward until I could feel his warm breath between my thighs where the pulsing was growing stronger with each passing second. The spot where he'd decided to set me was at the shallower end of the pool which meant on his knees, he was nearly eye level with my cunt.

The first brush of his lips was against my right thigh where he lingered, tasting my skin and teasing the absolute shit out of me. His eyes caught mine as he slowly moved to the other side and placed a kiss in the same spot on my opposite thigh.

"Teasing me is not helping *convince* me," I ground out.

His chuckle was wry and cruel. He was enjoying the tease,

his attention never leaving my face and examining each of my minute reactions. But he gave in, at least a little and pressed an open-mouth kiss to my pussy. Even over my swimsuit, the sensation was enough that I dropped my head back and moaned.

He'd barely touched me, he'd barely begun, yet I felt like I was already poised on the precipice of release. Teetering on the edge, I looked back down to watch his tongue flatten against where my clit was throbbing behind the wet material. Damp from the water and my arousal.

"Fuck, I'm teasing myself, too," he murmured, reaching for one of the two ties at my hips that kept the swimsuit up. I held my breath as he tugged the little bow, and it fell open. He didn't waste any time switching to the other side. He slipped the tie open and slid his fingers beneath the fabric. In one swift motion, he ripped them from my body and tossed them to the side.

His responding groan was enough to make my toes curl. Reverent fingers ran down my lips and spread me apart, completely exposing my cunt to the air and Ryder's unwavering gaze. With his mouth slightly parted, he stared at me for several long seconds before inhaling a shaking breath.

"Fucking beautiful. I couldn't imagine a pussy this pretty no matter how long or hard I tried. You're perfect, Caroline."

His compliment made my skin warm, and my legs widened of their own accord. I had the fleeting thought—well, more than fleeting—that we shouldn't be doing this. That it was so very wrong, but it felt so, so good. Both sides of my mind warring with each other like the angel and devil on my shoulders, but they quieted when his thumb brushed against my slit.

He fingered my opening and dragged his touch higher until he found my clit. A brush of his thumb against the already pulsing spot made heat radiate up my stomach and settle in my arms and legs.

"Fuck," I muttered, and I was too far gone already to care

about the cocky grin tilting Ryder's perfect lips. Holding me apart with one hand, the other began an enticing rhythm against the needy point.

But I wanted more. And when our eyes connected, it was like he could read my thoughts. He brought his two middle fingers to his lips and sucked them into his mouth. My pussy clamped around nothing knowing exactly what he was about to do with those two fingers. And if he didn't, I think I might have screamed.

Slowly, he pulled them free. The moonlight and soft pool lights reflected against the spit collecting around each digit as he lowered them just as methodically. His fingers poised at my entrance, he pushed inside.

He tilted his head back and shuttered his eyes closed as I sucked in a sharp breath. Every muscle clamped around his thick fingers, and I fell back until my head hit the towel yet again. All the lingering thoughts that what we were doing was wrong vanished with his fingers inside me and his tongue licking his lips like he couldn't wait to devour me.

"I swear, if you don't fucking—" *move*, I was about to growl, but my words disappeared on a needy groan when he crooked his fingers. In one, two movements, he found that spot just a few inches inside that made me see stars.

Then something wet and soft—his tongue—connected with my clit, and those stars began to pulse with a deep, frenetic energy. He flattened his tongue against me and started a rhythm that made me reach forward and bury my fingers in his silky, thick hair. I held him tightly to me and tested his resolve by tentatively grinding my hips. All I wanted to do was bury his face against my pussy and ride his tongue until I screamed, but I didn't know how much he could take.

His responding guttural groan when I tugged on his hair was enough, but then he said, "Yes, ride my face. Show me exactly how you want me to pleasure you then come all over my fucking tongue."

So, I did as he asked and as I wanted. I dug my hand harder into his scalp, and his skillful fingers and eager tongue only worked faster, *better* with the pain.

There was no climb or ascent to ecstasy. The orgasm was swift and brutal. The stars behind my eyes suddenly exploded, and all the pleasure winding its way through my body released in a sudden wave.

Ryder kept his perfect rhythm through the bucking and grinding of my hips even when it felt like I was going to snap his fingers in half or rip out his hair.

My body shuddered in the aftermath, the orgasm waning like the ripples in the water surrounding Ryder. Several deep breaths later, and I was still unsettled by how intense and all-consuming the climax was.

"Fuck, that was the most beautiful thing I've ever seen," Ryder murmured, and I glanced down my body to find his eyes glued to my face. His fingers started up again, grinding against my inner walls which were still tender and swollen from my release. "You must have been really wound up."

That was part of it, but I wasn't going to tell him that. "It's not that hard to make me come, especially not the first time. You're not that special."

"Hmm…" he hummed, leaning down and replacing his lips against my clit. "Then I'll just have to do it again and again until you can finally admit that you enjoy having me between your legs. That I could possibly be the best you've ever had."

He slipped his tongue up and down my slit and lathered my cunt in open-mouth kisses. Any arguments I had died on my tongue as the lingering tenderness dissipated, and my desire stirred. With his free hand, he palmed the inside of my left thigh and shoved it down until it hit the cold tile surrounding the pool. The pressure he applied, holding me in place and wide open, was feeding my need.

Raising my hands, I cupped my breasts over my admittedly tiny swimsuit top and pinched my nipples through the fabric.

Pleasure spiked, and a moan ripped from my lips as I ground my hips against Ryder's face.

"Yes, come on, baby. Let them hear you," he purred.

Through a groan, I panted, "I have neighbors, and don't call me baby."

His tongue still pressed against my most private parts, I could feel the vibration of his laugh against me.

"Okay, pretty girl, but I would still love to hear you moaning my name. Please, Caroline."

Still massaging my breast with one hand, I wound my fingers back through his hair with the other. I tugged hard enough at the root that he had no choice but to rear back. Staring down at him, the sight nearly made me come on the spot. My arousal was dripping down his mouth, collecting around his chin and the stubble that rubbed against my thighs. He licked remnants from his lips, and his blue eyes fluttered like it was the most glorious taste he'd ever experienced. Blue eyes that were unnaturally dark, his pupils blown with his own need.

My thighs were spread indecently wide to accommodate his broad shoulders, and he sat between them like a starving man prepared for a feast.

"Make me come again," I said between clenched teeth. "And I'll scream your name exactly how you want me to. For every one of my neighbors to hear."

"Yes," he panted eagerly. "Yes, let me—" I loosened my grip, he dropped his head forward, and he ate like a man starved.

A few urgent, strong sweeps of his tongue were enough to make me forget where we were, *who* we were to each other. Thick fingers scissored inside me, but the fingers of his free hand trailed up my stomach, inch by excruciating inch, until he cupped my breast.

God, it felt so much better to have his large hand against me rather than in my own. He dipped beneath the fabric and with one swipe of his finger against my tender nipple, my body shuddered in an orgasm just as swift and violent as the first.

"Oh, fuck, Ryder," I moaned into the air around us. And it had nothing to do with the promise I'd made. It was second nature to shout his name. It felt right to exclaim exactly who was making me come.

TWELVE
BLUE BALLS

Ryder

Nothing had ever tasted so good or been so fucking satisfying. Buried chin deep in Caroline's gorgeous cunt was the place I was always meant to be. I'd known it all along, but she hadn't really understood until the second orgasm crested with my name on her lips.

Hearing the glorious sound, I couldn't imagine how anyone had ever willingly walked away from her.

She shuddered and bucked underneath my hands, yet I kept going. Two orgasms weren't enough when I could feel a third sitting on the horizon. Or when I was already addicted to the sight of watching her come apart. All those walls shattering around her for at least a few seconds as the ecstasy took over.

"Ryder, Ryder—" she panted, tugging on my hair while holding my mouth to her pussy. She shamelessly ground herself over my mouth, and my hips rolled in the same motion. She fucked herself against my tongue, and I was fucking, well, nothing.

All I did was displace water and create small waves in the pool. Moving my hips was pointless, but I couldn't stop it. My thighs were tight with the strain of keeping myself from coming. My balls were heavy, and my cock, trapped behind the wet, tight fabric of my briefs, was screaming for relief.

"Come on, baby. One more," I growled.

She tugged my hair harder as I wrapped my free hand—the one that wasn't buried deep inside her—under her ass and tugged her even closer, tilting her ass higher for a better angle.

"Don't call me baby," she argued as I expected.

I chuckled and panted against her cunt. Slipping my tongue over her clit, I poised it between my teeth and bit lightly. And the reaction was a beautiful, new symphony of sounds emanating from her lips. So, I bit harder and sucked the tight bundle of nerves into my mouth. The muscles in my hand began to strain, but I didn't stop. I dragged the tips of my fingers against her inner wall and the sweet spot a few inches in.

Her arousal coated my chin and my tongue. As I added a third finger, a broken, pleasure-laced sob pierced the air, and she bucked hard enough to nearly leap from my hands. But I held on and let her ride my face and clench around my fingers.

Her entire body vibrated as the orgasm ripped through her. I couldn't be certain but the third felt just as powerful as the first, maybe even stronger. I wanted to live in the wake of her pleasure and watch the ecstasy overwhelm her body over and over again. But eventually, her body went limp, and I carefully set her back down.

A faint flush spread over her chest and up her cheeks, and her chest rose and fell quickly, but she laid at the edge of the pool completely sated. A similar satisfaction pounded in my chest. I'd been the one to make her feel that way. So weak from pleasure that her eyes were still closed, and her arms were slumped to her sides.

But there was no satisfaction for my poor, aching erection.

Caroline stirred as I adjusted my soaking briefs. The brush of my hand against the swollen head made my hips jolt, and I groaned at the sensation. There would be no relief until I was deep inside her and not a second before.

Caroline pushed up from the ground and reached for her swimsuit bottoms I carelessly tossed to the side. Not like we really needed them with my head between her legs. With her discarded swimsuit in her hands, she stood and grabbed the towel I'd rested her head on.

"Well, this was fun," she murmured, running a hand through her slowly drying hair as she unfolded the towel and wrapped it around her waist. She scooped up the dress I'd come by to drop off but left the extra towel on the chair next to it. She was halfway to the door before I had the sense to follow.

Without a definitive plan, I braced my hands on the edge of the pool and jumped out.

"Caroline, wait."

She stopped abruptly and turned, holding up a hand, her swimsuit swinging from her fingers. "No," she said. "You're not coming in."

I swallowed and closed my eyes for a moment, willing the blood to migrate anywhere else besides below my waist. Bracing my hands on my hips, water dripped and pooled underneath me.

"Okay, not exactly what I expected. I feel like that was some pretty good begging, convincing…"

"It was," she agreed. "But you said you were willing to take whatever I give you…" she said, and although they were truthful, I knew those words would live to haunt me.

"I did," I agreed and smiled, but Caroline raised one eyebrow and gave me her most withering stare that did little to make me waver. She turned, opened the door, and took a step past the threshold. But before she disappeared inside, she glanced over her shoulder and said, "Good night, Trouble."

I swiped a hand through my hair and readjusted on my feet, imagining all the dirty things we could have gotten up to if she'd invited me inside. "Good night, pretty girl."

Caroline slipped inside, and everything inside me was telling me to go after her. But I figured space was more important. She'd been denying any feelings, sexual or otherwise, for me for years, so I was sure she was overwhelmed.

Me, on the other hand, I think I was in shock. Especially since I couldn't manage a single coherent thought. She'd walked away from me, but I still felt like I was walking on a cloud when I gathered my clothes and retrieved the spare towel from the chair.

Call it overconfidence or cockiness, but I knew that wouldn't be the last time we'd be together. We both wanted, *needed*, more.

THIRTEEN
IN OVER YOUR HEAD

Ryder

"OKAY, YOU'LL LET US KNOW HOW IT GOES, RIGHT?" STEPHEN ASKED as I pulled the door open to the library.

I rolled my eyes and juggled my phone to the other ear as I crossed the crowded lobby toward the back staircase. Finals were upon us, and the entire place was buzzing with stress and anxiety. Luckily, I was headed up to the third floor where it was always less crowded.

"Stephen, you can trust me," I argued, taking the stairs two at a time and dodging people left and right.

"I know, I know. That's why we chose you as our best man."

"Really? I thought it was because of my charm and eye for design."

"That, too!" Miles chimed in somewhere in the background. I could hear waves breaking on the other end of the line along with faint voices and laughter. It sounded amazing and nothing like the terrifying silence of the library.

"Are you at the beach? I'm in the library about to study for finals while you're at the beach?"

Stephen laughed as I tugged the third-floor door open. "That was us last year, man. Let us know if you need anything."

"Caroline and I have it covered. Seriously, you have nothing to worry about."

Stephen scoffed. "You're on a first-name basis with our wedding planner now?"

I stepped into the much quieter third floor and scanned the tables closest to me for Theo. "She's my mom's best friend, Stephen. And I'm the one who sent you her way."

"Oh yeah, that's right. I guess I just didn't think you knew her all that well, too."

I cleared my throat and headed farther into the library, checking each table for my scary, tattooed best friend. Dropping my voice, I said just above a whisper, "Yeah, I know her well." *I know her so well in fact, I can tell you exactly how sweet and heavenly her pussy tastes and how decadent her moans are when she's coming on my tongue.*

But that wasn't something Stephen needed to know. Although he would likely be intrigued to hear about my recent sexual experiences with his wedding planner and my mom's best friend, he didn't need the details.

In the very back corner, I spotted Theo with his head bent over a book and a pen in his hand tapping quickly against the pages.

I said my goodbyes to Stephen and promised to let him know how the food and cake tasting went the following day. Caroline's assistant, Addison, had already texted me to confirm the time. Caroline had pointedly been ignoring me since the weekend before. I was unsurprised that she'd stopped responding, so I hadn't taken it personally.

That hadn't stopped me from texting her as I always had— sending her memes, videos, and music that I thought she would like or reminded me of her.

"I swear, I can see the smoke from the gears turning in your head," I quipped as I slipped into the chair across from Theo. He dropped his pen and leaned back in his seat, dragging his hands down his face. I could feel the stress rolling off him, but I immediately knew it wasn't only related to our impending finals or graduation.

"What's up?"

Theo sighed and dropped his hands against the book still open in front of him then handed me a piece of paper. It took me a second to register what he gave me—the crappy handwriting and the name at the end.

"This is from your mom?" I asked a little too loudly. I threw an apologetic smile to the girl at the table behind us and mouthed "sorry."

He nodded and looked out the window to his left. "Yeah. It's the third one in as many months. I haven't responded to any of them, but she's not getting the hint."

"Fuck," I muttered, shaking my head. I skimmed the letter and was unsurprised by its contents. Simple, surface-level apologies which included no accountability for her actions.

Theo's mom had so many issues. She'd been a chronic gambler who couldn't manage to keep enough cash on hand to pay her debts, and Theo had been her first stop every time. Finally, when he'd told her he had nothing left to give, she'd gone off the rails. She'd set fire to her own house and pointed the finger at him.

The police quickly realized Theo had nothing to do with it, and his mom had taken a plea deal for a handful of crimes. She was supposed to be serving three to five years.

"What are you going to do?"

He shrugged as I handed the letter back. He unceremoniously shoved it in his bag and picked up his pen. I could feel the frustration rolling off him. I hated to see him like that. His mom —hell, his entire fucking family—had put him through shit. Until he met my mom, it seemed like he couldn't catch a break.

"Nothing. Keep ignoring them, I guess. I might try to talk to the attorney or maybe the prison and see if we can keep her from contacting me. She thankfully hasn't tried to call yet. I haven't shown Nat any of the letters either, and I don't really want to."

I nodded and took a deep breath. "I'm really sorry, man. Maybe we burn them? Get rid of all the bad shit attached to them?"

Theo cracked a tired smile and shook his head.

"Why not? I guess it's worth a shot."

Theo glanced back down at his book, and I took the hint—he was done with the subject.

Studying was the last thing I wanted to do, both Theo's situation and Caroline were sitting in the back of my mind and taking up more real estate than I could afford with three finals next week. But I did it anyway. I threw on my headphones and zoned in on the task in front of me. Reading through my notes from the semester and relistening to the recorded lectures, it was two hours before I looked up again.

Theo and I both leaned back in our chairs at the same time. I stretched my arms out to my sides and glanced out the window to see the sunlight quickly fading. The trees and red brick buildings surrounding the library cast in red and pink light.

"I think I need a break. Want to grab dinner?"

"Fuck yes," I sighed, quickly gathering my books and notes, I shoved them in my backpack and stood. Too focused, I hadn't realized how hungry I was until Theo had mentioned it.

Theo chuckled and shook his head as he tossed his backpack over his shoulder and followed me out of the library. Pushing open the front door, we stepped out into the warm night and started walking toward our favorite burger place right off campus.

There wasn't a preamble or discussion, it was our favorite brain food when we were both cramming. The place was fairly packed for a Thursday evening. It was an older building almost as old as the university itself, so the ceilings were low, and the lighting was dim. The line to order was curved around the perimeter, and Theo and I took our place at the end next to the wood-lined wall.

Old metal signs that hadn't moved in decades hung sporadically around the place and the soles of my shoes stuck to the floor with every step. So, you knew the food was going to be fucking good.

The line moved quickly, and after we ordered, the cashier gave us a number, and we found a table in the back room near a few pool tables and old video games.

"So, what's up with you and Caroline?" Theo didn't waste any time the moment we sat down. I was surprised it had taken him that long to bring it up.

I cleared my throat and rolled my lips to hide the smile that was threatening to break free.

"Oh, fuck. What did you do?"

"What do you mean?" I asked without looking up from where I was fidgeting with the label of my beer.

"I know that look. I've seen it at least a few times before, and it's always after you've done something I'd probably consider stupid."

Scoffing, I tilted my beer to my lips and took a long swig. When I looked up, Theo was watching me expectantly. And I knew it was a battle I wasn't going to win. Theo was hardheaded through and through; he would have sat there all night if he had to.

"Nothing happened in the bathroom," I admitted. I had gotten so close, but Theo's timely interruption kept it all PG-13. Or maybe NC-17.

"Yeah, but you left that night after the party to drop something off at Caroline's house. You're telling me nothing happened when you went over there that night?"

I stayed silent, trying not to replay every little detail of that night. But it was impossible not to relive it over and over again. I'd been doing that since Caroline walked back into her house.

From finding her in that tiny bikini in the pool to having her splayed out on the edge, every second had been on instant replay. She monopolized every one of my thoughts, but that was nothing new. She'd been on my mind since the moment I met her.

"Your silence is answer enough," Theo murmured quickly as the waiter dropped our food off and retrieved our order number.

"So, what if something did?" I popped a fry in my mouth while Theo paused with his burger halfway to his mouth.

"If something did happen, I'd say you're in way over your head."

"No way," I argued before taking a hearty bite of my burger and finally feeling my hunger start to wain. "I've been dreaming of this day for…forever. I'm doing exactly what I want to be doing."

Theo nodded, but I could see the argument on the tip of his tongue as he finished chewing. "Without giving me the details, because I seriously don't need to know, how far did you take it?"

I knew what he was asking without him having to explicitly say it: *did you cross a boundary you can't come back from?*

"Far enough. Further than I ever expected to go." *It was the best night of my life,* I thought but didn't admit aloud.

My thoughts drifted once again until Theo's snicker and the reminder of my almost untouched fries brought me back to the present.

"You are one lovesick motherfucker," he stated. My first reaction was to argue, but it would have been in vain. Because I was, and denying it to my best friend was useless. Instead, I smiled to myself and took another bite of my food. Usually a man of few words, I didn't expect Theo to continue, but I stopped when he did. "You're smart, Ryder. Smartest person I know, actually. But in these circumstances, I'm the expert. So, listen to me when I say, don't try to hide this from your mom. She's gonna find out, and if it goes any further, it's better she hears it from you. You know how it feels to figure it out otherwise."

His statement should have been like a cold bucket of water

over my head. But it wasn't. Yes, finding out about my mom and Theo had been complicated and difficult to get my head around, but Caroline and I were different. And there wasn't a guarantee she'd let me anywhere near her again. Although I was optimistic that her resistance was slowly melting away.

It was easy to shut me out via text, but in person, I had a better chance of slipping beneath her shields.

"I've got it all under control," I said with a smile. "It's all under control."

FOURTEEN

JUST A LITTLE TASTE

Caroline

THE ROOM THE RESTAURANT HAD SET UP FOR THE TASTING WAS private and just off the main dining room. Separated by two sliding doors, I could still hear the faint sound of voices and the usual restaurant commotion.

The catering manager dropped off two waters at the table and smoothed the unwrinkled, white tablecloth.

"We're so excited to have you here, Ms. Grant, and the menu we've put together is incredible. I think you'll enjoy what we have planned." The young woman, Kate, had just taken over the position, and I could tell she was nervous and eager to make a good impression. The previous catering manager had burned a bridge that couldn't be mended, but the restaurant had some of the best food I'd found in the city. So, when I heard they hired someone new, I decided to give them another chance.

"I'm sure it will be. You've already gone above and beyond," I said with a smile, motioning to the quiet, secluded room.

There was a quiet knock on the door before a waiter stuck his head between them. "Sorry to interrupt, but Mr. Calaway is here."

I snorted, trying to suppress my laughter which quickly died in the back of my throat when *Mr. Calaway* appeared from between the two doors. My mouth went dry, and my smile fell.

He politely thanked the waiter and greeted the caterer. Giving her his thousand-watt smile, I didn't blame the girl for blushing slightly. But she quickly righted her expression and waved him toward the table I was seated at.

My breath caught in my throat. Those blue eyes turned on me, and I kept very still as they raked over my exposed legs peeking out from beneath the tablecloth. Until I felt his gaze, I hadn't realized the slit in my skirt had ridden almost indecently high up on my thigh. But adjusting it when he was still watching meant showing I was affected by his intense stare, and I refused to do that.

His eyes traveled upward, over the subtle cleavage beneath my satin shirt and along the line of my exposed neck. It was too hot outside to have my hair down for any significant amount of time.

"Hey, Caroline," he said with a smile, pulling out the chair closest to me. He sat, and Kate quickly confirmed that she was going to bring out the first few courses for us to try. She hurried through the door at the back of the room and into the kitchen, leaving Ryder and I completely alone.

Which was exactly what I'd been trying to avoid for the past week. Because I knew what would happen if we were alone again—it was the same reaction I'd had even when he'd texted me throughout the week. My body remembered the way his hands, his lips, his body felt, and it was screaming at me for *more.*

It wanted me to give in to everything I shouldn't, and fuck, I was having a hell of a time remembering why I shouldn't. Especially when he was sitting there in his chair, leaning back like he didn't have a care in the world. One arm slung across the back of the chair next to him and the opposite leg stretched out toward me. The tip of his shoe grazed the bottom of my calf, and I silently pleaded that he wouldn't see the goosebumps that appeared across my skin.

"You look good, Caroline," he murmured in a low, raspy voice.

I glanced over to the door Kate had disappeared through then back to Ryder, whose smugness was written all over his face and found in the tilt of his lips.

"I know," I countered. His eyebrows shot up, and I was pleased with his reaction.

"I'm pretty sure the correct response is '*you look good, too, Ryder,*' but I'll give you a pass."

I huffed out a breath. "I'm not in the business of giving compliments for the sake of stroking your ego. You know you look good," I muttered. Voicing my thoughts made his smile widen, but thankfully, Kate interrupted with perfect timing.

"Are we ready for the first few courses?" she exclaimed, pushing through the doors with plates in her hands and followed by servers holding more plates.

"We were born ready, Kate," Ryder said. He sat up and scooted his chair closer to the table.

They arranged the food in front of us, and Kate took us through each dish. She explained the appetizers that would be passed on trays during cocktail hour, the pre-dinner salads, the main course options, and each side dish.

It all looked amazing, and I was glad I'd put off lunch in favor of the tasting.

"I'll let you both get started and come check on you in a little while."

She exited the way she came as I picked up my fork and surveyed the options.

"I think this is going to be my favorite part of wedding planning," Ryder quipped.

Smiling, I stabbed a shrimp appetizer and popped it in my mouth quickly. The sweet and spicy flavors exploded on my tongue, and my eyes almost rolled back in my head. "It's definitely one of my favorite parts."

Ryder aimed directly for the buttery au gratin potatoes and regretted it immediately. His fork clattered to his plate as he fanned his mouth. He reached for his water glass, and I covered my mouth to keep from spewing shrimp all over the table and to suppress my laughter.

"I can see the steam rolling off those potatoes from over here," I said when I finally managed to compose myself.

Ryder took several long sips and slumped back in his chair like he'd just run a marathon. "I obviously missed that. They're really good, though, from what I could taste between the scalding heat and now second degree burns on my tongue."

"Poor guy. I think you'll be okay."

"Hmm," he hummed as he sat forward and leaned closer to me. On high alert, I straightened and kept my attention on the table and the chicken I spooned onto my plate. "A kiss would probably make it better."

Reflexively, my eyes shot to his, and the smirk sitting on his lips made my scowl deepen. I dropped the spoon in my hand and let it bang loudly against the dish. Ryder didn't even blink.

"I can't help it, baby. It's almost been a week, and I feel like I'm going to die if I don't get another taste."

My hands clenched, and my throat went tight. "We are in public, Ryder, and I'm working," I said, then added, "And don't call me baby."

His lips twitched, and I took a deep breath, hoping the palpable energy between us would fizzle out long enough for me to focus on the food. I blinked and looked back down at my plate. But even when he was silent, all my attention was on him. Like my body was begging to feel his again.

I just needed to make it through the next half hour. Thirty minutes was manageable.

I hoped.

"Are you ready for finals?" My random question was my

attempt at changing the subject to anything that wasn't sexually charged.

Ryder chuckled and ran a hand through his disheveled black hair, but there was no humor behind his laughter. He reached for a serving spoon and shook his head. I could see the exhaustion in his eyes and in the circles beneath them.

"Honestly, my brain hurts from studying so much. That's pretty much all I've done this week. This was a good break. If I spent one more second in that damn library…" His voice was laced with weariness, too, and I fought the urge to reach out and take his hand in mine.

"Which finals do you have left?"

"Two of my engineering classes, one of which is my senior seminar, so that one is going to suck. And the other is a US History class." He truly laughed the second time, and I narrowed my eyes. "Yeah, it is a class I should have taken freshman year but put off until the very, bitter end."

I shrugged and popped a mushroom into my mouth. "I'm sure it helped lighten up your schedule, though. Broke up some of those more difficult classes, so they weren't all in your final semester."

He nodded and lifted his glass of water to his mouth. When he pulled it away, my eyes were fixed on the small droplets of water clinging to his lips and his tongue that peeked out to collect them.

Completely clueless to my gawking, Ryder set his glass back down and continued, "Yeah, it was nice to have a class that was simple and straightforward, especially with job hunting and interviewing, too."

"Any news on the job front?"

When Ryder didn't say anything, I looked up to see him shrug. "I…umm…I've had a few interviews. Several, actually, and I think there are a couple contenders. I have two offers so far, and they've been generous enough to let me wait until after graduation to decide."

"That's really exciting," I said, my enthusiasm completely genuine. Ryder had worked so hard, I knew he wouldn't have a problem finding a company that would kill for his talent.

"It is," he agreed, but his voice was quiet, and his tone was closer to somber. He stared down at his plate and nudged a green bean around with his fork. I lightly nudged his hand with my own fork and drew his attention to me. With a sigh, he sat back in his chair. "One of them is here. It's at a local engineering firm, and honestly, it's exactly the job I was hoping to find. But the other is...it's not local. It's across the country, and they're willing to pay me more. They'll even help me relocate and add a bonus on top of my salary for the first year to help cover any other transitional expenses."

My reaction wasn't what I expected it to be. I was supposed to be supportive and push him to take whichever would be the better opportunity for him, but instead, I wanted to do anything I could to make him stay.

I couldn't remember life without Ryder.

"Wow," I managed to say through thick emotion. "That sounds incredible."

He was silent again for a beat, and I watched every emotion flit across his features in the span of a second. "It is incredible, but the idea of leaving doesn't sound entirely appealing."

"Why?" The question was out of my mouth without a second thought. Ryder's stormy blue eyes flashed to mine. We held each other's stare for several seconds before I finally found the power to look away, and Ryder cleared his throat, readjusting in his seat.

"How the hell did our conversation get to this? This was supposed to be a distraction," he said, waving to the table still full of food. "I'd prefer to talk about anything but finals or work."

The door at the other end of the room swung open, and Kate stepped into the dining room, wringing her hands in front of her as she strode to us. "How's it going? Any thoughts?"

"Everything is amazing," I said, and she beamed with pride.

"That's so good to hear. What about you, Mr. Calaway? What do you think your friends would like?"

I suppressed my giggle with a hand over my mouth, and Ryder—excuse me, *Mr. Calaway*—nudged me with his leg under the table.

"I think we go with all the appetizers except the one with the avocado—Miles's mom is allergic. We should probably avoid it for the entire night. Then I think they'll want—" When Kate realized Ryder wasn't going to stop, she took out her phone and started furiously taking notes. "Three choices for the entrée— beef, salmon, and the veggie. As for sides, I like the potatoes, although they get really freaking hot, and—"

Kate's eyes widened. "Oh no, were they too hot? I'm so sorry. I—I—"

"No, he's fine," I said. "He burned his tongue a little, but it obviously didn't impair his ability to speak."

"Or do other things," Ryder whispered suggestively and only loud enough that I could hear him. I made it a point not to look at him. Kate appeared flustered enough, I didn't want to make things worse.

"She's right. I'm fine," Ryder continued, "The potatoes are great as are the green beans and whatever that one is—" he pointed to a dish that I also couldn't identify, but it was amazing, nonetheless.

Kate nodded and typed furiously on her phone. "Yes, we can absolutely do that." The waiters came in and cleared the plates while we confirmed all the details. Kate left with a promise to bring the cake and dessert options.

"I hope you're in the mood for something sweet!" she said before scurrying off.

At least that time Ryder waited for her to be well out of earshot before making his suggestive remark. "I am in the mood for something sweet. And although it's in this room, it's nothing that Kate is going to set on this table."

Slowly I dragged my eyes up from my phone to Ryder. "You have an uncanny ability to make anything a sexual innuendo, you know that, right?"

He braced his hand against his chest and smiled. "Wow, thank you so much."

I rolled my eyes and shook my head. Kate was back in less than a minute followed by waiters carrying more sweets than we could ever possibly consume. As she had before, Kate explained each dish. "Enjoy. I'll be back in a few."

"I'd enjoy it more if—"

The cutting look I threw his direction was enough to cut his words off but not enough to curb his crooked smile.

"Be good," I warned.

Ryder picked up a cookie and inspected it before taking a large bite. He chewed for a moment then said, "That goes against everything I believe in, Caroline. There's a reason you call me Trouble, right?"

Narrowing my eyes, I tried to renew my depleted willpower. The longer I sat there in his space, remembering the way his stubble scratched my inner thighs and the ecstasy he drew from my body, the more likely I was to give in. He sat with his ankle crossed over his opposite knee, and the image made my brain short circuit.

"You are fucking trouble," I said quietly, choosing a brownie that was covered in caramel and chocolate sauce. I took a bite and set it back on my plate.

He leaned forward and reached toward me. Before I could react, his hand was wrapped around the leg of my chair so he could tug me closer.

A very girly and uncharacteristic squeak left me but was concealed by the scrape of the chair across the hardwood floor. Inches away, I could smell the chocolate on his breath and feel the heat radiating off his body. The electricity arching between us was almost too much to bear. It was hard to ignore when we were so close.

"You know you like it—the trouble, the danger. I think you *love* the fact that it's dirty and wrong. But it didn't feel wrong when you were coming all over my tongue. Even though you want to avoid it, which I'm sure is why you've been ignoring me all week."

The room disappeared around us the longer he held my stare. The melodic background music and the noise filtering in from the main dining room vanished. My world narrowed to the look in his eyes.

"Denying how much I like it seems meaningless at this point," I admitted before I could consider the statement. My pulse quickened, and my heart collided with the inside of my chest. My willpower was fading fast, and lying to myself wasn't doing me any good. My brain was losing the fight with my heart and the rest of my body.

And watching Ryder fight, witnessing how much he wanted it—wanted *me*—made it feel pointless and impossible to win.

"Which is exactly why we should do it again," he said, reaching forward to brush his thumb over the exposed skin of my knee. The only sliver of skin peaking from between the slit in my skirt. My eyes dropped down to follow the movement, and I fought the need to shudder. "I'm not opposed to more begging or convincing. Even right here in the middle of the restaurant. Tell me to get on my knees, Caroline. Right here and now. Right where anyone could see."

I simultaneously loved and hated how out of control I felt. And watching him get back on his knees and beg for anything I would give him would give me back that control. But I couldn't risk it.

"Be on your best behavior while we're here, and I'll consider it."

Ryder immediately straightened and sat back in his chair, trying and failing to hide his triumphant smile. "Anything for you, pretty girl. Literally, anything."

FIFTEEN
CRAWL TO ME

Ryder

I KNEW WHEN I WALKED INTO THE DINING ROOM AN HOUR AND A half earlier that I would be going home with her.

My confidence in the outcome wasn't the result of cockiness or some toxic, masculine bravado. Before the doors had opened, I was worried she'd throw me out of the room altogether. That she'd rather call Stephen and Miles and tell them she refused to work with me than spend another second alone together. I hoped that wouldn't be the case, but with Caroline and her steady silence, I didn't know what to believe.

No, what had changed my attitude from hopeful skepticism to excited certainty was the look in her eyes when she saw me. Her own excitement was skillfully hidden but plain as day to me. Years of studying the woman sitting at the end of the table gave me invaluable insight.

Her blonde hair swept up in a clip, it showed off the long line of her neck and the subtle cleavage beneath her lilac satin top. The first few buttons were open, and I wanted to undo the rest with my teeth, taking my time to tease and taste her skin. But it was the fucking skirt that made me want to drop back to my knees and crawl to her if I had to.

When I said I'd do anything she wanted, I meant it.

Which was how I ended up parking my car in her garage as she'd instructed. The door quickly closed behind me, and the room was pitched into darkness but for the dim overhead light.

I wouldn't have needed to park in the garage and hide my car from my mother who lived down the street if we'd gone to my apartment. But it was inconveniently across town, and I didn't want to make her drive all that way. Besides, her house was the Ritz compared to my one-bedroom.

I stepped out of my car and surveyed the tidy garage as I headed toward the door leading into the house. I reached forward, but the door swung open before I had a chance to try it.

Caroline only stood in the opening long enough to see I was there then she disappeared down the hallway. I hurried inside, quickly closing the door behind me in enough time to see her push open her double bedroom doors and peek at me over her shoulder.

I was already walking toward her, but the bold, wicked glint in her eyes made me move even faster. I stepped over the threshold to see her drop into a dark leather chair on the opposite side of the room near the sliding glass doors that ran the length of the wall behind her.

The late-afternoon sun cast a golden glow across the large cream rug and the king-sized bed. But my eyes didn't linger on the finer details of the room when Caroline reached behind her and unclipped her hair, letting it fall in loose, waves just past her shoulders. She set the clip down beside her and let her eyes settle on me.

I took a step, and she raised her hand. A silent command, not a request, which I heeded.

"If we're going to do this, we're going to do it my way. And to be clear, this doesn't change anything," she said.

I didn't think before I said, "Of course."

Her eyebrows rose, and her eyes slightly widened. "Really? No argument at all?"

I nodded. "When I said whatever you want, I meant it."

Her smile was sweetly devious and made my muscles twitch with the need to move. The desire circling around us was heady.

"Good boy," she purred, and I muttered a quiet curse. I'd never heard those words before, but they sounded really good coming from her lips. I wanted this to be good for her. *I* wanted to be good for her. "Now, stay right there, and take off your shirt. You can ditch the shoes, too."

I dropped my keys on the bedside table and emptied my pockets before I tugged my shirt over my head. It fell to the floor as I toed off my shoes. I watched her watch me as I walked along the side of the bed and stopped at the end where she could see that I'd followed her instructions perfectly, left only in my jeans.

She appraised my appearance then said, "Belt, too."

In a few swift motions, I whipped my belt off and let it fall to the floor, leaving a trail of clothes in my wake. I reached for the button of my jeans, but Caroline shook her head. She crossed one leg over the other, and her skirt fell open at the slit, showing off the length of her smooth tanned leg up to well past her mid-thigh.

"Now get on your hands and knees and crawl to me."

It took several seconds for my mind to comprehend what she'd just asked me to do. Crawl to her. She wanted me to *crawl to her*. Every imaginable emotion made an appearance, but the one that was most potent and sank its claws in so deep I couldn't shake it was the same emotion I'd been feeling all day—an unbearable, unwavering desire.

So, not for the first time with Caroline, I dropped to my knees. Then I planted my hands, and the only sign that Caroline was surprised was the slight widening of her blue eyes.

"Any other instructions?" I asked before I started moving. She shook her head, her chest rising and falling quicker as I began traveling across the rug. The thick pile wasn't necessarily kind to my palms, but the slight scrape against my skin only amplified every feeling and sensation.

My eyes remained trained on Caroline as I crawled across the floor. Every inch closer made my heart beat faster, like I was willingly offering myself to her. The power she held over me was intoxicating. I loved the way she wielded it, and I wanted more. My erection pressed against my briefs and was begging for relief.

I kept a steady pace until I realized there were a few feet left, and I wasn't ready for it to end yet. My movements slowed, and the seconds stretched. The entire time I kept my eyes on her. Her throat bobbed as she swallowed, and she licked her lips, trapping her lower lip between her teeth and finally allowing her attraction to show.

I stopped at her feet and settled back on my knees. Caroline didn't move. I waited for further instruction, but when it didn't seem like she was going to provide any, I lifted my hand. It was torture to be so close and not touch her. My fingers brushed against her knee, and although my intention had been to take it slow, I couldn't resist moving higher. One touch, and I couldn't stop. My hand slid up her thigh where her skirt was parted, and the soft fabric was nothing compared to the feel of her skin.

Goose bumps appeared, and I leaned forward, sweeping my lips over them just inside her knee. A moan lodged in my throat, and I parted my mouth for a taste, but Caroline quickly said, "Not yet."

It took a tremendous amount of effort not to kiss her anyway. I took a deep breath and sat back on my heels. She leaned forward in her chair, and her heels hit the carpet. My cock throbbed at the sight of her. Her blue-gray eyes were dark, and she scanned my face.

A small smile slipped across my lips. "Did you like watching me crawl to you, pretty girl?"

Her mouth dropped open, and a similar smile appeared on

her lips I wanted to suck and bite until…no not until. I didn't want to stop.

"Yes, I really did," she said. "Now, on the bed." I stood immediately. My knees were sore, but it wasn't anything I couldn't handle. It was far from the most important thing on my mind.

Spinning, I strode to the bed and sat on the edge, staring out the wide windows.

"Stay there," Caroline said, walking the opposite direction and back toward her bathroom. "I'll be right back."

I glanced over my shoulder and watched her disappear into her bathroom. I gripped my thighs and squeezed. Each second felt like an hour waiting for her to come back. I was waiting to hear the click of her heels again against the tile, but she must have ditched them in her closet because she appeared before me without any warning.

Unfortunately, she was still dressed, but as I suspected, her heels were gone. I eyed her pretty little light purple toes, but then realized her hands were tucked suspiciously behind her back.

"We need to talk about safe words and limits," she said, and my eyes jumped to hers.

"Do you plan on doing something that warrants a safe word or a discussion of limits?"

She shook her head and let out an exasperated sigh. "Whether I *plan* on doing something or not, it's important to talk about anyway. Preferably this conversation would have happened before, but it didn't. So, tell me."

I thought for a moment and ran a hand through my hair. "I haven't found anything that I'm really opposed to. No water-sports or other bodily fluids except spit. And I'm not a fan of extreme pain, but I do like some."

Her eyebrow quirked as did her lips. "I noticed," she whispered. "Anything else?"

I shook my head. "Your turn."

"Also, no watersports. No touching my feet, and I'm not going to touch yours either. Almost everything else is on the table, to an extent. You can pick a safe word we can both use, if needed."

"Lilac," I blurted before I could think about it. It was the color of her top and her toes. She wore it often, and I knew it was her favorite. And it wasn't something either of us would unintentionally mutter during sex.

She rolled her eyes and shrugged. "Okay, now that that's out of the way. Lay down on the bed. Put your head on the pillows."

Without moving her hands from behind her back, she motioned to the top of her bed with a slight dip of her head. Excited about where this was going, I climbed up the bed and fell back onto the white comforter.

"You're so good at following instructions," Caroline muttered as she followed on her knees. Whatever she had in her hands had disappeared because when she reached me, they were empty. She settled next to me and ran her hands down my arm, circling her fingers around my wrist and tugging it upward.

I didn't realize what was happening until a black piece of fabric replaced her fingers around my wrist, and she was velcroing it in place. She slipped her fingers beneath the cuff to test how much room there was then didn't hesitate to crawl over me and reach for my other hand.

I'd never been tied up before or restrained, just like I'd never crawled across the floor. It was an afternoon of firsts for me, but I didn't stop her when she fastened the second cuff around my wrist and repeated the same motion, checking that it wasn't too tight, and there wasn't a chance it would cut off blood flow.

Curiosity got the best of me, and I tested the strength of the restraints. I tugged hard on each but neither budged. If I really, truly wanted to, I could have probably slipped out of them, but it would take some time to wiggle out.

However, I didn't want to. I hadn't expected it, but I enjoyed the idea of being restrained. My arms splayed out and above my head, I was completely at Caroline's mercy. And based on the glint in her eye, I knew I would love each and every thing she had planned.

She threw a leg over my waist and straddled my hips, giving me a sweet flash of the black panties beneath her skirt. The warmth of her cunt immediately seeped through the denim and cradled my cock. My eyes lowered with the sensation, and my hips bucked of their own accord.

"How does it feel?" She dragged her nails down my chest and over my stomach. My throat went dry as I watched her fingers dip beneath my jeans and tease the edge of my briefs.

"Good," I panted. My thoughts weren't on her question. I was more focused on trying to will her fingers to push lower or silently wish her hips would move against me.

But her nails were sharp when they scratched my skin, and I gasped at the pain. "Try again, Ryder. Tell me how it feels to be tied to my bed."

With a breath that did little to calm my racing heart, I looked up at her. She was a goddess, and I was her fucking throne. "Fuck, I like it. So much."

"Good," she muttered. "Just one more thing." She reached behind her back and pulled out a piece of satin cloth. She smoothed it between her fingers and held it up where I could see exactly what it was.

A blindfold.

A wry chuckle jumped from my lips, and I shook my head, looking back and forth from her hands to her eyes. "You're kidding."

She shook her head. "I wouldn't kid about this, Ryder."

"You're going to withhold the view of you from me. That's torture."

A shadow appeared over her eyes, and her smile turned cruel. "Sure, but it's the best form of torture. If you don't want the blindfold, you know what to say."

She ran the fabric between her fingers and watched me

consider her proposal. But there was nothing to consider. Although I'd never been blindfolded, I heard that it enhanced every other sensation and feeling.

"I'm not saying anything, pretty girl. Do your worst."

She didn't hesitate to slip the blindfold over my eyes, and I savored my last glimpse of her on top of me. I leaned my head forward off the pillow, and she tied the ribbon just tight enough that it wouldn't easily slip off.

And then everything was dark.

SIXTEEN
RIGHT ON THE EDGE

Ryder

A SMALL SLIVER OF LIGHT SLIPPED UNDER THE EDGE OF THE blindfold but not enough for me to see anything. That didn't keep me from imagining what she might look like, though.

With her weight on top of me, she pressed her palms against my chest and ground her hips across my pounding erection. But there were too many layers between us.

One more torturous movement of her hips, and she grappled with the button of my jeans. She slipped off my lap and then tugged them down my legs. For a moment, there was nothing else. I could feel her moving next to me, but she wasn't touching me.

God, it was cruel torment listening to the bed rustle without knowing exactly what was happening and not being able to participate.

"Look at this wet spot on your briefs," she purred, her mouth suddenly next to my ear and the tips of her nails scraping against the fabric stretched around my cock.

I sucked in a shallow breath through my teeth and kicked my hips up to meet her touch.

"No, no," she tsked. She kissed the shell of my ear, and her hand disappeared. "Keep your hips on the bed, or I'll tie your legs down, too."

The idea of her completely immobilizing me, using me for her pleasure and to bring to fruition her dirtiest desires, sounded gloriously devious and erotic. When my ass hit the bed once again, her nails reappeared. She circled what I guessed was the wet spot she'd mentioned and caressed the head of my cock.

A grunt left my lips, and she kissed the sound. Eager for more of her mouth on mine, I chased her lips, but she was too far out of reach. Her little tinkling laughter was farther away.

"You're leaking everywhere for me, Ryder."

I nodded, and my mind was foggy from desire.

"You look so good like this," she continued, her voice barely above a whisper like she couldn't believe what she was admitting. Hell, I couldn't believe it either. Every second we spent together felt like the culmination of every dream I'd ever had. It was too good to be true.

"I've been thinking about your cock since…well, for a while now. But especially since last week." She continued drawing torturous patterns against my briefs, occasionally squeezing my shaft through the fabric. I had little doubt that the wet spot was growing immeasurably. My dick was weeping to feel her bare hand, her mouth or even better, her cunt.

She shifted again next to my right side and then there was a new sensation. Something warm and wet, her mouth and then her tongue, kissing my fabric-covered cock. It took everything in me not to raise my hips and search for more. But I fisted my hands and fought the urge which she rewarded me for. She kissed and licked up and down my shaft, sucking on the crown and brushing against my balls.

"Please, pretty girl," I muttered.

"Please, what, Ryder? What do you want me to do?" Her lips migrated up my stomach, peppering quick kisses back and forth across my stomach and over my chest.

"Take my cock out," I pleaded through gritted teeth then I couldn't help but add, "and see what you've been missing."

Her chuckle was wry yet sweet. "You think I'm going to be impressed or something?"

"I'm an eternally optimistic person, so I hope so."

With one final kiss to the corner of my mouth, she moved again, and I held my breath. Mercifully, her fingers slipped beneath the waistband of my briefs, and I lifted my hips as she slid them down.

She was silent, and I couldn't take it. Without being able to see her facial expression, I couldn't begin to guess her thoughts.

"If you're going to run, just make sure you untie me first," I joked, tugging lightly on the restraints so they rattled against the bedframe.

But without words, she made her intentions clear. Her soft palm dragged over me, and her fingers encircled my shaft. One long, hard pull, and I almost came right then and there. Gritting my teeth, I knew holding back would be excruciating. But I didn't know just how bad until she dropped her mouth to the crown.

Her tongue twirled around me, and the hum emanating from the back of her throat vibrated through my shaft. I felt the sound in my balls and down my legs which shook uncontrollably.

"I'm not going anywhere," Caroline murmured. "And I'm not *not* impressed."

Her hand worked up and down in a rhythm that would have made my eyes cross if they were open. Her mouth was back on me a second later, and the combination of the two was incredible. She sucked and licked like her life depended on it. Using the spit collecting around me, she twisted her wrist in sync with her skillful mouth. I couldn't see her, but the sounds she was making were fucking obscene.

"Fuck, you're going to make me come," I panted. The telltale tightening in my balls and pressure at the base of my cock began, and there was nothing I could do. A few minutes in, and I was going to shoot my load into her pretty little mouth.

But at the last second, just before I hit the peak, Caroline stopped. Her mouth was gone, but her hand was still there yet unmoving. "Well, we don't want that, do we? At least not yet."

I shook my head and tried to even out my breath which was coming in short, staccato gasps. I was already wound up, but the blindfold did exactly as I expected, making every other sense sharper and more potent.

Every brush of her hand felt like an electric shock, and every caress of her tongue was...there wasn't a word that could describe the perfection of it. But I needed a distraction, and there was only one that would do. One that made my mouth water thinking about sampling the sweet, intoxicating taste once again.

"Sit on my face," I instructed, then added a desperate, *"please,"* to get my point across. At that moment, I needed her like I needed the air in my lungs and the blood in my veins.

"I thought you burned your tongue," she said, and I could hear the smile in her voice. Her hand picked back up again, the same taunting twist of her wrist around my cock, only slower and more deliberate. She was stretching out my pleasure, and I swore I was going to fall into a bottomless delirium.

"I'm fine," I grunted and reached for her only to be caught by the restraint. A long sigh slipped from my mouth, and I fought to keep any semblance of composure. All I wanted to do was grab her and move her where I wished, but she was in control. And that was just as hot. "Nothing is going to keep me from tasting your perfect cunt again."

Caroline moved, and my heart pounded against my ribcage with hope that I'd feel her thighs wrap around my head.

"Such a dirty mouth, Trouble," she said, and I tried to identify where she was, but I couldn't tell. Closer or farther away, I gritted my teeth until she brushed against my side.

"You love my dirty mouth, pretty girl. Now, sit on my fucking face." The words were barely out of my mouth when I felt her legs brush against my cheeks and smelled the heady scent of her desire. Her knees pressed into the pillows around me, and my mouth was immediately watering.

Finally, Caroline dropped down onto my waiting tongue, and I wasted no time. Using my tongue, I explored her cunt. I licked and feasted on every inch of her until she was dripping down my chin.

Above me, I listened to her little moans and the sound of her breathing to gauge which movements she liked most. My perfect siren loved when I tugged on her clit with my teeth or sucked it hard between my lips. And similarly, she couldn't help but grind her hips and cry out when I pressed my tongue into her opening as far as I could go. She tensed around me and stalled her hips to allow me better access.

My hands itched to grab her ass and help her grind against me, or to let her milk my fingers as she had the other night, but I didn't need them to make her feel good. My tongue would be more than enough.

Her fingers wound through my hair, and her hips began to rock. Leisurely at first, she made sure my tongue touched every part of her, but her movements sped up as she chased her pleasure. Flattening my tongue, I let her use me. And my cock throbbed with the knowledge she was doing just that. She wasn't concerned if I could breathe. Hell, I didn't fucking care either—both of us were intent on one thing.

"Fuck, fuck, *fuck*," she moaned a second before she fell apart. Her legs shook, and her pussy convulsed. Her taste flooded my tongue, and I did my best to collect every last drop. The prettiest sound, though, between each moan and delighted groan was my name falling from her lips.

She rode out her pleasure, and my hips rocked up into the air. Seeing her wasn't necessary when I could hear and feel her body writhing. Several seconds passed, and I worried that I'd come just from experiencing her orgasm secondhand.

She settled back, her ass landing on my chest, and our panted breaths mingled in the quiet room around us. She moaned softly, and her hand unwound from my hair. Fingers brushing down my face, across the mask, she dragged them across my lower lip, collecting what I assumed was remnants of her orgasm.

"Don't let this go to your head, but I love your mouth," she said.

I smiled and nipped at her thumb. "That's all I want, baby. I hope by the time we're done, you'll love every part of my body."

She tugged her finger free, and her weight disappeared from my chest. "Call me baby one more time, and I won't suck your cock again."

I rolled my lips and clenched my hands into fists. I wasn't sure why she had such an aversion to the pet name, and I'd tried to refrain from using it, but I hadn't had much success. Every time I saw her—or felt her—all I thought was, baby. *My baby.*

"I would never risk that, pretty girl. *Your* mouth is the best thing I've ever felt. That would be the ultimate torture."

I felt her moving next to me again and tensed when she ended up poised between my outstretched legs. Her hands clasped my knees and massaged up my thighs. Not being able to see her, I was on edge waiting for her next move. But she slid her hands higher and cupped my balls in one hand while the other palmed the underside of my cock.

"No, torture would be me taking the blindfold off, sitting in the chair across the room, and making you watch as I make myself come over and over again."

She was right, that would be torture, but that also sounded so fucking hot. Watching her sit in that black leather chair with her legs slung over each arm and her fingers buried in her tight, wet cunt.

Caroline laughed and wrapped her hand around me. "Your cock just jumped like you don't hate the idea."

"I don't," I admitted. "But I also think I might die if you don't wrap your mouth around me again."

She hummed and pumped me in long, hard strokes. "You're

so dramatic. Lucky for you, I want your cock in my mouth again." And she did just that. She sucked only the head into her mouth and worked her hand up and down my shaft.

Seconds, all it took was seconds of her merciless, perfect pace to make my balls draw up. But the moment it began, Caroline stopped. She lifted her mouth off me, and I muttered a curse, groaning toward the ceiling.

When her hand started back up again, and she replaced her mouth, I was immediately barreling toward ecstasy again. I planted my heels on the bed and shifted my hips. She removed her hand and let me fuck up into her mouth until I hit the back of her throat. She gagged but took everything I gave her. And the sounds she was making—

"Fuck, Caroline. Don't stop—don't—" I didn't know what I was saying, each word was a mumbled, garbled plea. The need inside me was building, and my ability to make any sense was long gone. All I was thinking about was how badly I wanted to —needed to—come.

But then she stopped again, and I realized what she was doing. She'd tied me up, blindfolded me, and now, I wasn't going to come until she allowed me to.

SEVENTEEN
WHAT HAVE I DONE?

Caroline

MAYBE I WAS SADISTIC, BUT I LOVED THE SOUND OF RYDER'S whimpered pleas.

It had been a careful dance, pulling back at the precise moment when he was about to come and letting the edge quickly taper off. By the fifth time, I thought he was on the verge of crying. His cock was red, the tip nearly purple, and angrily hard. I could see the thick veins pulsing just beneath the taut skin.

His arms yanked against the restraints, and I'd never been worried about them coming free until it was Ryder's wrists they were tied around. He'd crawled across the floor to my feet, let me tie him up, and willingly accepted the blindfold still covering his eyes. Then he'd begged so well while I edged him. Panting and whimpering for more, grinding his hips up to find my hand or mouth, he took everything I gave him and still said "please" when he asked for more.

In my bedroom, we were just us. Two people with an insatiable craving for one another. A craving that I had nowhere near curbed.

Watching a big, tall man submit to my will and desire was a heady feeling. It made me crave him even more.

Poised on my knees between Ryder's shaking legs, his back bowed. He was leaking everywhere, pre-cum slipping down his shaft and collecting around his base.

"Oh, fuck, Caroline," he cried. Similar to the veins wrapping around his cock, the veins down his forearms were bulging as he flexed against the restraints. "Please, let me come. Please, *please*."

He was barely hanging on, and I knew I'd been cruel enough. I leaned over his cock and spit directly on the crown, using my hand to coat the underside. He moaned, and I noted the sheen of sweat across his face and chest and the blush over his cheeks and neck.

God, I'd really tortured him. But I had every intention of making up for it.

I slung both of my legs over his hips and settled directly on top of him. I nestled the underside of his cock between my legs and moaned when his thick crown brushed against my clit.

"Yes, yes, yes," he chanted as I began to move my hips. "Your pussy feels so good, pretty girl. God, you feel so good."

He began rocking in time with me, using my wetness to easily slide his cock between my lips. I braced my hands against his stomach and was overcome by the sensations pounding through me. Edging him for so long and watching his body react to mine was erotic. My stomach tightened with an orgasm that built and built until I was frantically grinding against him.

The head of his cock pressed against my opening and almost slipped inside, but I moved at just the right moment to keep that from happening.

Reaching forward, I didn't think past what I was doing when I tugged the blindfold up and tossed it across the room. Ryder blinked several times, but neither of us stopped moving.

As the sun dipped closer to the horizon, the room wasn't as bright as it was when we started, but it still took him a moment to reacclimate. When he did, his dark, desire-filled eyes raked over my naked body, taking in the view of me slipping over his cock. My breasts bounced with the movement and all the muscles in my stomach tensed as the orgasm neared.

Lower yet, his jaw went slack when he saw the head of his cock peek out from underneath me. "Fuck, that's a good view," he muttered. "Are you going to come all over my cock, pretty girl? I want to watch you fall apart. I can feel you tightening on top of me. Come on, beautiful."

Two more jerks of my hips, and I shattered. I tipped my head back and dug my nails into his stomach. The cries that fell from my lips were unhindered as my entire body relented to the pleasure.

A deep contentment fell over me, and my hips slowed. But Ryder was still rock hard and urgently thrusting against me. He was so, so close, and I had no intention of edging him any longer.

In one swift move, I was off his lap and kneeling between his legs once again. Only this time, he could see the view of me wrapping my hand around his dripping cock and sliding my mouth over the tip. I'd been edging him for so long, I knew it wouldn't take any time, but what I didn't expect was for him to explode the moment I started.

The volume of his cries rivaled mine, and I was happy my neighbors weren't in earshot. Every muscle in his body tensed as he unloaded against my tongue. I swallowed it all and moaned at the taste of our combined releases.

His orgasm went on for so long my jaw ached, and what I couldn't manage to swallow dripped down the sides of his thick cock. Saying it to his face wasn't likely, but I couldn't help but think how perfect and pretty it looked. I'd never thought a dick looked pretty before—it was a fine appendage that had its uses. But fuck, he was making me second guess everything I'd ever thought.

With a pop, I released him and went to work licking up the

excess dripping down his shaft. His eyes devoured the sight of me, and my skin was warm with his attention.

"God, you're so fucking hot. I want a taste," he panted, and I licked one last drop beading at his tip before crawling up his body. He leaned up as far as he could and met my lips. Our kiss was instantly intense, tongues dueling for dominance as he invaded my mouth. His moan was sweet, and I could feel it down to my toes.

I couldn't remember the last time someone had called me hot, but I really liked the honest, unfettered compliment.

Eventually, we parted, and I rested my forehead against his. My hand dropped to his chest, and I could feel the frantic beat of his heart against my palm. It matched mine almost perfectly, and I was soothed by the rhythm.

I wanted to linger there longer—in the moments after when everything was quiet, and it was just us.

That was why I couldn't sit there another moment. I sat up and ignored the confused look marring Ryder's features as I quickly untied one wrist then the other and slid off the bed.

"I'll be right back," I called over my shoulder. I hurried into the bathroom, closed the door, and slumped against it.

What the fuck did I just do?

I wasn't prepared for the torrent of emotions that suddenly surfaced. "No, no, *no*," I muttered to myself, dropping my face into my hands. It was so easy to give in with Ryder. I was a full-grown, adult woman with my own business and house and life, yet when he turned that stupid charming smirk on me and said the first thing that came to mind, my willpower disappeared. It was becoming a problem, and unfortunately, I didn't have a solution.

And the most terrifying part wasn't that we'd done something I swore to myself I'd never do, it was that I'd loved every second of it, and all I wanted to do was make sure it happened again.

Consequences be damned.

Then there was the reality that he might be leaving and that somehow made everything even worse.

With a frustrated groan, I pushed off the door. Nothing was going to get solved in my bathroom while Ryder was still in my bedroom. I simultaneously wanted to go back out there and stay in the bathroom forever. He would have to leave eventually, anyway.

I used the restroom and proceeded to search for my favorite robe for way too long. It wasn't in its usual place hanging on my closet door.

I flipped through every single piece of clothing I owned until I remembered I'd left it in my bedroom on top of my dresser. Closing my eyes, I took a few deep breaths and braced my shaking hand on the bathroom door.

EIGHTEEN
CARO-LICIOUS

Ryder

THE BATHROOM DOOR CLOSED, AND I TUGGED MY HANDS FREE. When I'd made the joke before about Caroline running and leaving me tied up, I didn't expect it to almost be a reality.

I sat up and stared at the door Caroline disappeared behind as I massaged my wrists. Her expression was serious as she undid the restraints and slid off the bed. But I wasn't surprised by her reaction. The weight of what we'd done had slammed down on me as it likely had her. Although my reaction was fucking elation, I guessed hers was a little more complex.

Part of me wanted to bust down the bathroom door and talk her out of her spiraling thoughts. But I knew Caroline, and she processed best when uninterrupted. Nothing I said would be helpful in that moment, and it was better to let her have the space she needed.

No matter how much it killed me to do so.

I watched the door for a few minutes, and when she didn't appear, I managed to slide off the bed. My body was a little sore from being in the same position, with my arms pulled out to my sides and above my head for almost an hour, but the tension in my muscles made me smile. I would let her restrain me every time if it meant I'd get to experience her again and again. Although I'd eventually go crazy not touching her. But what was a little insanity when I got my dream girl.

Since Caroline was occupying her main bathroom, I walked two feet down the hallway and quickly used the spare to wash up. When I came back less than two minutes later, her bathroom door was still closed.

I found my jeans and slipped them on. When I was reaching for the button, the bathroom doors finally swung open.

Caroline stood in the doorway with her chin high and no evidence of a freakout on her face. She wasn't wearing anything, and I felt my cock give a little kick. A few more minutes, and I'd be ready to go again. God, she was more stunning than I ever imagined. Long legs and supple curves, her lips were swollen, and her eyes were still a little glassy.

I didn't say anything, instead, I finished putting on my pants and found my black T-shirt on the ground as she stepped into the room and looked around.

"Where the hell—" she began to say, but her words quickly cut off. We both stopped and looked at one another. I thought the sound had been in my head, but it was obvious Caroline had heard it, too.

Her eyes went inhumanly wide when a voice carried down the hallway from the front of the house. "Care!"

We both recognized my mom's voice instantly. I should have been nervous, but honestly, it was just fucking funny. What were the chances?

Frantically, Caroline looked around the room, probably searching for something to wear, but there was nothing there for her unless she dug through the drawers. And I could hear my mom's steps echoing like she was getting closer.

Making a decision, Caroline yanked my T-shirt out of my hands and slipped it over her head. It was large through the middle but only long enough to barely cover her ass. As she hurried out, I stared at the lovely peek I got of the bottom of her ass, but she quickly spun and caught me.

Unbothered about where my eyes had been, she warned, "Stay here and be quiet. I'm so fucking serious."

I raised my hands in mock surrender and nodded. Did I find karma hilarious in that moment? Absolutely. Was I going to make a scene in front of my mother? Hell no.

Caroline continued out the door and down the hallway. From where I was standing, I could see her at the edge of the living room, but hidden by the door, they wouldn't be able to see me. Caroline brushed a hand through her hair and my T-shirt rode up enough that it showed off the side of her hip.

My mom stepped into view, and I caught a glimpse of her confused expression.

As much as Caroline was worried about what my mom would think, because I knew that was part, if not most, of her hang-up, I wasn't concerned at all. Not only would it be hugely hypocritical since she was living with my best friend, but she also loved Caroline. Unless my mom knew something I didn't, I couldn't imagine a world in which she didn't approve.

Other than me, and now Theo, Caroline was her favorite person in the world. We had that in common.

I had to strain to hear, so I positioned myself even closer yet still out of sight.

"Hey—what are you wearing?"

"Just a T-shirt, Nat. What's up?" Caroline said quickly.

"I came by to—" my mom began but whipped her head in my direction. I was already hidden, but I scooted even farther back. "Oh, shit," she whispered loud enough that I could still hear. "I'm interrupting, aren't I?"

"A little."

"Okay, just text me later," my mom said, and there was a lengthy pause before I heard her receding footsteps. I chanced another look around the door and saw Caroline disappear into the entryway. When the door closed, I allowed myself to breathe normally again.

I stepped out of my hiding place and smiled at Caroline's irritation. Her dark-blonde brows were drawn together, and her hands were balled into fists at her sides. She brushed right past me.

"Oh, come on, don't you think—"

She shushed me and walked into her bathroom then into her closet. I followed her and watched her open the blinds of a small window that looked out to the front of the house. Peeking over her shoulder, I watched my mom step onto the porch of my childhood home.

Caroline immediately relaxed and leaned back into me when she disappeared inside. Shocked by the display, I didn't let that impede me from wrapping my arms around her waist and nuzzling into her neck. She smelled delectable, as always, but wearing my shirt, she also smelled like me and a wave of possessiveness I hadn't foreseen came over me.

"That was really freaking close," she muttered.

"Too close."

She was silent, and I worried that she was getting lost in those spiraling thoughts again. So, I did what I could to combat them, brushing her hair over the opposite shoulder and kissing down her neck. Her shoulders started to shake, and I reared back. My first thought was *"oh, fuck,"* and my second thought was that I couldn't imagine Caroline crying. Of course everyone cried, but it felt contrary to what I knew of Caroline for her to display that kind of emotion.

I gripped her hips in my hands and spun her around. She lifted her hand to her mouth, and I quickly realized she was laughing not crying. Her eyes were scrunched adorably, and she was trying to contain her laughter, but eventually it burst free. The sound bounced off the walls in the small room, and I couldn't help but join in—it was contagious.

By the time I was able to stop laughing, my abs hurt as did

my cheeks. I straightened and wiped the few laughter-induced tears gathering beneath her eyes

"I have no idea where that came from," she said, resting her hands on my chest.

I brushed my thumbs over her cheeks and took a deep breath, still trying to catch my breath. "Lots of emotions bubbling to the surface," I guessed. Caroline's smile slipped just enough that I knew she agreed.

But I didn't give her a chance to dwell on it. I leaned forward and slanted my mouth over hers. Sweet, willing lips met mine, and somehow, I managed to keep the kiss chaste even though all I wanted to do was scoop her in my arms and fuck her into her bed.

She licked her lips and stepped back. "Umm...well, I don't know about you, but I'm starving."

Neither of us had eaten enough during the tasting for it to be considered a full meal, and I had missed breakfast. Being edged within an inch of my life also worked up an appetite. "Yeah, I'm starving," I said. "Are you cooking for me?"

"Ehh," she muttered and walked past me, grabbing a pair of shorts from a shelf but not bothering to switch out my T-shirt she still wore. I smiled and followed behind her, shirtless and happy.

She strode down the hallway and beelined for the kitchen. Flipping on the lights, she didn't stop until she opened the fridge. Across the kitchen, I leaned my forearms on the marble bartop and watched her.

"Is this your usual MO? Invite someone over, make them crawl across your bedroom floor, tie them to your bed, edge the ever-loving shit out of them, and cook them a big hearty meal afterward?"

She turned with a few ingredients in her hands and kicked the fridge closed with her foot. "Actually," she said, setting everything on the counter and heading toward the pantry. "I usually kick them out."

My eyebrows shot to my hairline which she noted when she

walked out of the pantry with another few ingredients. "So, I should consider myself lucky then?"

She shrugged. "Yes, but anybody I let in my bed should consider themselves lucky." Arranging the food in front of her, she shot me a smirk that made blood surge below my waist.

"No fucking doubt, pretty girl."

"And," she continued quickly, "for the record, I've never made someone crawl to me before."

I covered my heart with my hand and feigned like I was touched. Although I did enjoy the idea that she'd done something with me that she'd never done with anyone else. What the hell, I felt special.

"I feel so special, ba—babe?" I caught myself before I called her "baby," but the word came out more like a question.

She rolled her eyes, but there was a small smile on her lips. She opened her mouth to say something more but stopped. Reaching forward, she grabbed her phone and looked down at the screen.

"I—uhh—I have to take this. Do you want to start washing the veggies?"

"Yeah, yeah, of course," I said, taking her place in front of the counter as she jogged outside.

"Hi, this is Caroline," I heard her say before she shut the sliding glass doors. While I prepped the veggies, washing them and organizing them as I was told, Caroline paced back and forth across the patio.

I tried not to watch her, but I couldn't help it. The longer the conversation went on the more I could see her excitement fade. Minutes later, she hung up the phone and squeezed it between her hands as she tilted her head up toward the sky.

When she pulled open the glass door and came back inside, I braced myself. But she didn't say anything. She hardly looked at me as she slid her phone across the counter and surveyed the work I'd done.

"Thanks," she said quietly.

My heart hurt seeing her dejected, and I wanted to yell at the person on the other end of the phone.

She pulled out a knife and a cutting board from the cabinet next to the fridge. "Want to talk about it?" I asked.

Her knee jerk reaction was to shake her head, which she did, so I changed the subject. She gave me instructions on how to help, and I chopped vegetables as she started the chicken on the stove top. We cooked in amiable silence for a while, but when I placed the cutting board full of vegetables next to her, she sighed.

"That was the owner of one of the largest companies in the city," she said, flipping the chicken. "He called to tell me that they would be going with someone else to plan their huge fiftieth anniversary party. When I asked why, he said that I was too young and didn't have as much experience as the other event coordinator."

The desire to yell at the dickhead reemerged. Caroline was capable in all things, but she was especially talented at her job. I'd witnessed it firsthand how detail-oriented, efficient, and thoughtful she was. It was a killer trifecta, and that dumbass didn't know what he was missing.

"What an absolute asshole. Does he need a firsthand account of your insane skills and talent? I'd be happy to call him back and let him know all my thoughts. But I'm not sure you want to work with such a lovely person anyway."

She glanced over at me, and I caught the beginnings of a smile. But it didn't stick around long. She turned back to the chicken and arranged the veggies in the pan around it.

"You're right, but it's not the first time it's happened, and I know it won't be the last either. It just sucks because I started my own business and worked my ass off to get where I am, yet it won't ever be enough for some people."

Reaching up, I squeezed the back of her neck and slid my hand down her back. "People suck. You're incredible, and I know it doesn't mean much, but I'm proud of you. You're more than enough."

Her hand holding the tongs froze, and she slowly looked up at me. Deep blue-gray eyes bounced between mine, and the emotion that settled behind them disappeared with a few blinks. Every time she reinforced the barrier between us, my stomach sank a little more.

But lucky for us both, I wasn't easily deterred. And I knew exactly how to find that levity again.

I walked into the bedroom and found my phone on the bedside table. As I headed back down the hallway, I connected to the speakers positioned around the living room and kitchen and cued up the song.

I pressed play and the first notes of one of Caroline's favorite songs reverberated through the speakers. Well, I wasn't sure it was one of her favorites, but I knew it would make her feel better and lift her spirits if nothing else.

Dropping my phone, I smiled and started swaying to the music as Caroline slowly turned around. She braced her palms on the counter behind her and watched me with a raised brow. When I started lip-syncing and grabbed a wooden spoon to use as my makeshift microphone, I caught my first glimpse of a smile.

So, I ramped it up a little bit. I slid out from behind the counter with my free arm in the air and really started to sell it. Dancing and lip-syncing my way over to her, that smile grew. When I woke up that morning, I never imagined my day would lead to me lip-syncing Fergie shirtless in the middle of Caroline's kitchen, but life was funny like that.

She crossed her arms over her chest and rolled her lips to try to hide that smile I was working so hard for. "I can't believe you even know this song." She had to almost yell to be heard over the music, but that was the only way to listen—at a volume that could possibly produce hearing loss.

I stopped and straightened. "Umm…this is a classic. Who doesn't know this song?"

"Okay, well, how do you know that *I* like it?"

"You and my mom have listened to it more than once. Mostly when you're both wine drunk, but that's beside the point."

Rolling her eyes, she pushed off the counter and took a step toward me, narrowing her eyes. "One last question: how old were you when this song came out?"

I chuckled and shook my head. Instead of answering, I grabbed another spoon and thrust it into her hands. "Don't ask questions you don't want to know the answer to," I said. Because she was about seventeen at the time, since I was six, and that wasn't something I wanted to call attention to. Twenty-three and almost thirty-four felt a lot less dramatic.

I didn't give her a chance to respond. The music picked up, and I lifted the spoon to my mouth, pretending to scream sing into it. It took a little more coaxing, but Caroline couldn't resist. She lifted her own spoon and started lip-syncing.

Eventually, the memory of her earlier phone call was miles away. The music and laughter were cathartic and brought a much needed levity. And for a while, we were just *us*.

NINETEEN
GRADUATION DAY

Caroline

"Who the hell decided to have the ceremony outside?" I asked Natalie as we walked through the courtyard. "Because whoever it is, deserves a special place in hell. A graduation ceremony outside in *May?*"

Natalie laughed, but it was lackluster. She was already using her program as a fan too, trying to cool herself off some way, somehow. Luckily, she'd warned me that it was outside, so I'd followed her lead when getting dressed that morning. She was wearing a white sundress, and I was wearing something similar in a darker blue. But it was hot enough that we were bound to be uncomfortable no matter what.

"Yeah, I agree. I just hope we don't see—"

"Natalie?" We both stopped, and Natalie tensed, closing her eyes and probably praying that she hadn't just heard her name although we both knew she had. Taking a deep breath, she glanced at me before she turned around, and I understood the silent request in that one fleeting look. She was looking for support, and hell, that was all she would ever get from me.

"Hey, Mark," she said. Natalie's ex-husband approached

with who I could only assume was his new girlfriend following closely behind.

Their divorce had been amicable a few years ago, but that didn't mean there wasn't some sort of tension. Especially since this was the first time he'd brought this new girl around, and he'd been less than impressed that Natalie had begun dating his son's best friend.

"How are you?" he asked and subtly gave me a tight-lipped smile. There was no love lost between the two of us. I was Natalie's best friend, and they were divorced, so it was obvious where my allegiance laid.

Mark was an average looking guy. Dark hair and eyes, he'd aged well, but he was nothing compared to Theo who was objectively gorgeous with brown curly hair and a myriad of beautiful tattoos. Not that it was her intention, but Natalie seriously leveled up in every way.

"Hot. How are you?"

He nodded and reached behind him for his girlfriend's hand. She stepped up with a nervous smile. "Good, I wanted to introduce you to Jessica. Jessica, this is Natalie and Caroline."

Jessica extended her hand with a shaky "hi," and Natalie, then I, accepted it. "It's so nice to meet you both."

"It's nice to meet you, too," Natalie said. "I've heard lovely things about you. Ryder has lots of good things to say."

It wasn't an all-out lie, but I knew that she wasn't Ryder's favorite. According to him, Mark and Jessica had been together for a while and were getting serious, yet she'd been reluctant to get to know him. But Natalie was trying to be nice which was just her personality.

They kept the conversation light and chatted for a few minutes. I nodded and smiled along, but my mind was everywhere else. Particularly on one of the men graduating who had sent me a cheeky picture of himself wearing nothing but his cap and gown that morning. It was a mirror selfie, with his tongue out and a cute little peek at his toned stomach underneath the bulky gown.

It was stupid. And I'd looked at it about a million times.

"Let's all sit together," Jessica said, and I tuned back into the conversation. Natalie threw me a pleading look, but Mark jumped in before I had a chance.

"Yeah," he said. "That would be great."

True to her kind nature, Natalie agreed and let them lead us toward the rows of seats arranged in the courtyard.

"We don't have to sit with them," I whispered. "I can be the bad guy."

Natalie smiled but shook her head. "No, it'll be fine. I don't want to be rude."

"But that's the thing," I offered. "*You* don't have to be rude. I'll be rude for you. I have no issue doing it."

"Care, I promise, I'm fine. I'm a big girl."

We chose seats toward the center of the crowd and near a large tree that provided some much-needed shade. The campus was beautiful—with tall red brick buildings, impeccable land-scaping, and trees that were older than the country itself. It was much more picturesque than the standard, unimpressive state college I'd gone to. No wonder Theo and Ryder enjoyed being on campus so much.

I sat at the end of the row while Natalie was pressured into sitting between me and Jessica. They continued their surface-level conversation while I watched guests file in and prayed for a breeze.

My phone vibrated in my clutch, and I carefully pulled it out and glanced at the screen.

Ryder: Are you here? Where are you sitting?

Me: Sorry, couldn't make it. Congrats, though!

It took seconds for his response to come through.

> Ryder: Don't make me cry on my graduation day. I'll come out there and find you if I need to.

> Me: We're on the right-hand side of the stage about six rows back.

> Ryder: That's what I thought ;) I can't wait to see you

I caught myself smiling down at my phone and quickly straightened my features. We hadn't seen each other since he'd been at my house a week and a half before. With wedding season in full swing and him in the middle of finals, we hadn't had any time to even try.

My mind was still in chaos knowing what we'd done, and the first time I'd seen Natalie afterward made my gut churn with guilt. I felt guilty for doing it, but even more, I felt guilty because I really wanted to do it again. And I hadn't shut down Ryder's obvious advances.

We hadn't seen each other since that afternoon, but that hadn't kept Ryder from texting me and calling. Or kept me from answering every single time. Butterflies, I felt fucking butterflies when his name popped up on my screen, or I heard his voice.

Jessica excused herself to the restroom, and Natalie turned to me.

"So, you haven't told me about the guy from last week," she said, and I made it a point not to look at her. Instead, I continued fanning myself with the program. She hadn't brought it up before, I wasn't sure why she decided now was the time to do so.

"There's nothing to tell. He was...a man," I said, knowing she wouldn't let it go if I didn't say something.

I felt her stare boring into the side of my face, and I read-justed in my seat. "That's all? You're not going to tell me anything else about him?"

"What do you want to know?" I shouldn't have asked, but the words were out of my mouth before I considered the repercussions. And of course, it would be my luck that she would ask the single worst question possible

"Do I know him?"

I stopped fanning myself and whipped my head in Natalie's direction. Guilt and anxiety slipped through me. Caught off guard by her question, I swallowed before I answered.

"I don't think you've known any of the men I've slept with before," I said simply.

She shook her head. "I mean, have you talked about him before? Do I know *of* him?"

"No, I haven't talked about him before." My voice wavered, but the slight shake was concealed by the music that erupted from the speakers positioned around the courtyard.

Jessica also squeezed past us at that moment which I thought was enough to draw Natalie's attention. But she never missed anything. She cut her eyes at me as she smiled up at Jessica. When she took her seat, Natalie nudged my leg with hers.

"You're acting weird," she said. "Is this one different?"

I didn't answer. Instead, I swallowed and shrugged as the processional began. But that was what I was afraid of, that he was different.

The ceremony was long. It likely wouldn't have felt as long as it did if it hadn't been so hot, but we made it. And were gathered underneath another tree, waiting for Theo and Ryder to find us for the required photo ops.

Mark, Jessica, and Natalie constantly scanned the surrounding crowd for the two of them. But everyone was wearing the same black gown and funny hat, so I leaned against the tree and waited for them to find us.

I pushed my sunglasses on top of my head and looked up at the exact moment Ryder and Theo stepped through the crowd. Theo spotted me then immediately searched out Natalie whom he scooped into his arms and spun around.

Out of the corner of my eye, I saw Mark flinch, but he refrained from saying anything. Instead, he stepped toward his son. But the moment Ryder found me, his eyes didn't move, and a slow smile slid across his lips. My skin flushed, and for once, it wasn't due to the heat.

Intercepted by his father and his outstretched hand, Ryder was forced to look away. He shook his dad's hand and gave Jessica a side-hug. They congratulated him, and he thanked them both for coming, but he couldn't get away fast enough.

I pushed off the tree and bit my lower lip as he tugged me forward and wrapped his arms around me. My hands slid around his waist and across the scratchy graduation robe. Rather than get lost in the embrace like I wanted to, I tried to pull back when the appropriate amount of time passed. But Ryder didn't let me go.

"Thanks for coming, pretty girl," he muttered against my ear.

"Any time, Trouble."

Finally, he stepped back, and his eyes raked down my dress. "God, you look good."

I straightened and tried to appear unaffected by the way his sincerity-laced voice dropped.

"Let's take some photos!" Natalie exclaimed, and both Ryder and I jerked our heads in her direction.

"Whatever you want, Mom," Ryder said, and emotion hit me directly in the center of the chest with the reminder.

They took photos in every combination I could think of— Ryder with his parents, Ryder with his dad and Jessica, Theo with Natalie, Theo, Ryder, and Natalie together. Ryder had even requested one with me and Natalie squeezed between him and Theo.

By the time we were done, we were all drenched in sweat and ready to go.

"I'm going to run to the restroom before we leave," Natalie said, motioning to the bathrooms just on the other side of the tree we were standing next to. As she walked away, Mark and

Jessica also excused themselves to get a table at the restaurant they'd chosen, leaving me alone with Ryder and Theo.

"You're coming to lunch, right?" Ryder asked, and I nodded.

"Your mom wouldn't let me get out of it."

Turning, Ryder nudged Theo's arm and offered him his phone. "Take a picture of me and Caroline, please."

Theo stopped and glanced between Ryder's phone and his friend's face. Then he looked at me, and I wasn't sure what the hell I was supposed to do. A picture was innocent enough. We'd held it together through all the other photos, what was one more?

Theo finally took Ryder's phone and stepped back. With an arm around my waist, Ryder tugged me into his side. We both smiled at the phone as Theo pointed it toward us.

He took one then went to hand it back to Ryder who shook his head. "Take a few more," he instructed. Theo's glance toward the bathroom was almost imperceptible, but I'd noticed it. And it was more than enough for me to realize he knew something. I had a suspicion that it had to do with more than him catching Ryder and I coming out of the same bathroom at my nephew's birthday party.

I wouldn't have put it past Ryder to tell him something. It's what I would have done had it not been my best friend I was keeping it from.

Theo lifted the phone again, and Ryder pulled me closer, tilting his head slightly so his cheek pressed against the side of my head. The position was more familiar, but I continued smiling.

That was until he leaned down and said, "Kiss me."

I reared back and looked up at him in shock. My jaw dropped, and I stuttered over a response as I tried to determine if he'd really just asked me that. There was nothing but honesty on his face.

"Not going to happen."

That didn't keep him from tightening his hold on me and

lifting his free hand to clasp my cheek. His fingers pressed against my skin like he was preparing to tilt my face the way he wanted it. Our eyes locked, I held my breath. All the background noise faded away as I watched his blue eyes darken. He licked his lips, and when my eyes flitted to his mouth to watch the movement, it was enough to break me from my trance.

I stepped back and breathed a desperate sigh of relief when Ryder let me go. Theo was there in a second, stepping almost between us and shoving the phone into Ryder's chest.

"Good timing," he said. "Natalie's coming."

I glanced over my shoulder to see my best friend walking toward us and hoped she hadn't witnessed any of that.

TWENTY
FOOTSIE

Ryder

I WAS THE LAST ONE TO THE RESTAURANT, BUT THE SEAT SAVED FOR me was next to Caroline, almost like it was meant to be.

The air conditioning felt amazing after being out in the heat for hours. But I was a college graduate. *Finally.*

When I sat down, there was already an array of appetizers on the table. I popped a piece of bread in my mouth and was happy to see that my parents and their partners were engaged in friendly conversation. There wasn't much animosity between my parents—there hadn't been even when they'd divorced several years ago, but it wasn't always easy between them either. Which I expected.

Still, it had been a while since we'd all been together, and I was happy to see them getting along.

Caroline readjusted in her seat next to me as she reached for her wineglass.

"You get to sit next to me," I whispered.

She tossed me a withering side-eye that did nothing more than make my cock harden. She liked to pretend that I annoyed her or that she couldn't stand me, but I knew it was only a game.

"Or," she said without looking at me. "You get to sit next to *me*."

Containing my smile was pointless. I let it slip across my face and took a cursory glance around the table to make sure everyone else was still occupied.

"You're right. You are the prize, Caroline."

She swallowed, and I was mesmerized just by her perfect profile when my dad started speaking, and I had to drag my eyes away.

The rest of lunch went well. The food was good, and the conversation carried on as we ate and drank. Although I couldn't tell you one thing that was actually discussed beyond graduation. I was too preoccupied with the gorgeous blonde next to me. Watching all her reactions and movements was mesmerizing.

But being preoccupied with Caroline was nothing new to me. It had been that way since I could remember. Although it had gotten worse now that I knew what her pussy tasted like and how well she fit my cock in her mouth. How I'd managed to study, let alone pass my finals, when she was all I could think about, I didn't know.

Since that afternoon at her house, we'd talked and texted almost every day. But I hadn't seen her in person, and the first glimpse of her I got in that royal blue dress standing under the tree in the courtyard would be forever burned into my memory.

I wanted to kiss her so bad, that was my first thought. While my second had been that I couldn't do that with both of my parents standing there.

Letting my intrusive thoughts win, I widened my legs until the outside of my calf brushed against Caroline's. A quick glance was all the reaction she offered, not skipping a beat in her conversation with Jessica. I just wanted to touch her. Even if I couldn't touch her the way I wanted to, I would take what I could get.

I ate my last bite of food and dropped my other hand

beneath the table. My fingers wrapped around the smooth, exposed skin of her thigh right above her knee. She jolted but hid her reaction by adjusting in her seat. We were close enough together, all of us squeezed around a table made for four people, that it was impossible for anyone else to tell where my hand had landed.

Another quick glance my direction, and I had to lick my lips to suppress my smile.

She didn't try to move away, and I leaned back in my seat, letting my hand casually slip higher as I moved. The fabric of her blue dress caught on my hand and slid with me until it was tucked around her upper thigh. Her hand shot out and covered mine to stop my ascent.

A silent warning that I heeded. I didn't want to stop, but I wasn't dumb enough to push too far while my family was sitting around the table. Although I could feel the heat emanating from between her legs against my hand, and my cock heartily disagreed.

Ignoring my growing issue, my phone buzzed, and I glanced down to see a few new texts with photos we'd taken earlier. I saved them all and found the ones I'd had Theo take of me and Caroline in my camera roll. The first one looked forced, as did the second. But as I swiped through, Caroline's smile relaxed, and she leaned closer into me.

My favorites were the ones where I'd asked her to kiss me. She'd decisively objected to my request, but she'd still looked up at me like she was imagining what my mouth felt like on hers.

All that confusion and desire was captured in the photo.

My phone buzzed again, and a new text flashed on the top of the screen.

Caroline: Remove your hand. Now.

Me: Why, pretty girl? Is it turning you on?

Barely holding back my smile, I looked over to find her

hiding her phone beneath the table like we did in high school hoping the teacher wouldn't catch us.

> Caroline: I hate you.

> Me: This photo doesn't look like you hate me.

My response included one of our earlier pictures. Me looking down at her wondering how I'd found myself to be lucky enough to even be in her orbit and her looking at me with both frustration and craving. It was addictive and undeniable.

> Caroline: You should delete those.

> Me: Not a chance in hell. I will cherish them forever.

She read the message and crossed her legs. Except she crossed left over right and squeezed the tip of my fingers between her thighs. My breath caught in my throat, and I set my phone over my thickening cock, trying to hide the evidence. I caught a glimpse of Caroline's small smile before my dad asked me a direct question.

Shaking my head, I glanced up at him and quickly apologized. "Sorry, I zoned out. What did you ask?"

He licked his lips and glanced at my mom like he was annoyed. "How are your interviews going? Do you have any offers yet?"

I cleared my throat and tugged my hand free as casually as I could from between Caroline's legs. Picking up my glass, I took a sip and rested my elbows on the table.

"They're going, but the job market is pretty rough right now."

The table was silent like none of them really believed me. On my right, Theo nudged my knee under the table and gave me an incredulous look. Theo and Caroline were the only people who knew the truth—that the job market was rough, but I'd somehow managed to secure two offers. One locally and the other several states away.

"It might be rough, but Ryder's done pretty well," Theo stated. I shook my head and blew out a breath.

"Has he?" My dad asked, and my mom perked up, too. "Tell us."

"If you want to," my mom added with a soft smile.

"Sure," I began, still unsure how they would react about the news. But if I did take the job, they'd find out eventually when I no longer lived in the same city. I just hadn't planned to tell them until it was done. "One of them is local, an engineering firm with really great benefits. They've even offered to help fund a master's degree if I choose to pursue it."

There was a chorus of congratulations and remarks about how perfect it sounded. Staring down at the table, I held my breath as I prepared to continue.

"Yeah, it's pretty perfect. And the second one is just as good, only they're offering me a little more money and are willing to pay for me to relocate."

When silence followed, I couldn't help but look up. My dad's brow was furrowed, and Jessica's eyes were wide. Caroline was staring down at her plate, and Theo wore his usual unaffected expression although I knew by previous conversations, he wasn't excited about the idea of me possibly leaving.

It was my mom's expression that rocked me. She was putting on a brave, smiling face, but I could see the tears welling in her eyes. *Fucking hell.* Watching her try to hold it together was exactly why I hadn't wanted to bring it up right then. I'd completely killed the mood.

"Nothing's set in stone yet. I haven't told either of them yes or no. They've been kind enough to give me...time to respond."

"How long?" My dad asked.

"Two more days. Then they go with the next applicant."

More silence, and I could feel it crawling across my skin. It was loaded with unknowns and concern. It was uncomfortable, and I wanted to be anywhere but there.

Until I felt Caroline's leg brush against mine. At first, I thought it was an accident, but when she pressed harder and didn't move away, I realized it was intentional. It was a show of support.

"I haven't made a decision yet," I added.

"But it'll be the second, right? Of course, it has to be if it's more money and a better opportunity."

I was shaking my head before my dad even finished speaking. "The opportunity is about the same, and the money isn't enough to make a huge difference. Besides, I have...reasons why staying here sounds better."

My attempts at being non-specific only worked so well because both of my parents descended into arguments about how I shouldn't *not* pursue an opportunity because of them. The issue was that, although I would miss them terribly, I knew they would be fine. I wasn't worried about moving away and how it would affect them.

I loved them, and I would miss them, but it wasn't my parents I couldn't bear to leave behind.

TWENTY-ONE

LET'S PLAY A LOVE GAME

Caroline

Tightening my coat around me, I questioned for the fifth time since I'd left my house what the fuck I was doing. But none of those questions made me consider turning around.

My knuckles collided with the green front door, and I glanced down the exposed apartment hallway. Luckily, it was empty of curious, prying eyes. I would have looked strange to anyone wearing a trench coat in the summer. Strange and stupid since it was so hot, but I'd do anything for the bit.

On the other side of the door, I heard movement, and I silently pleaded for him to hurry the hell up. I didn't have to wait, though. A second later, the door swung open.

Neither of us said anything, and Ryder froze the moment he saw me. A half-eaten bowl of cereal in his right hand, the other was braced on the door to keep it from swinging shut. His tan torso was bare, and the only thing he wore was a pair of gray sweatpants that were slung low on his hips. His apartment behind him was mostly dark but for the little lamp in the corner and the TV that cast shadows over his skin.

"What—what are you doing here?"

I tilted my head and took a deep breath. The nerves causing chaos in my stomach were new, and I wasn't used to the feeling. I shouldn't have been nervous.

"Currently, I'm standing at your front door where anyone could see me," I said, which made Ryder jump into action.

He stepped aside and waved his bowl of cereal toward the room. "Umm…yeah, come in."

Walking through the doorway, Ryder closed it behind me. He set his bowl on the counter and flipped on the light right above the small bar top. I tossed my bag by the door. The air conditioning was glorious on my warm skin.

"I'm so fucking happy to see you, but what are you doing here? And why are you wearing a coat?"

I spun around and appraised the rest of the room. It was almost what I expected of a twenty-three-year-old guy who just graduated. The walls were mostly bare, but there were photos placed around the room. The couch was one I recognized from Natalie's house years ago, as were the pillows tossed in each corner.

Turning back around to face him, I tucked my hands in the pockets of my coat and glanced down at my white sneakers.

"Are you busy?" I asked, and he shook his head.

He motioned to his empty apartment. "Nope, I was watching reality TV and eating cereal. Are you going to answer my questions now?"

"I'm here to give you your graduation gift."

His eyebrows shot to his hairline, and he crossed his arms over his chest, inadvertently flexing his biceps and showing off his defined forearms.

"A gift? For me?"

I nodded and walked toward him. He dropped his hands to his sides and straightened, readying himself for what I was about to do. I offered him my hand, and he didn't hesitate to lace our fingers together. Ignoring the electricity that traveled from my fingers up my arm at just the smallest touch, I led him over to the couch and pointed to the middle cushion.

"Sit," I commanded. Like I expected, he plopped down without hesitation. I stepped around the coffee table as he braced his elbows on his knees and watched me. On the other side of the table, I toyed with my coat ties and slipped my fingers between the knot at my stomach.

"I had to get creative with your gift," I said. "I wanted to get you something original. Something only I could get you and that you'd remember forever."

He licked his lips as his eyes slowly raked over my coat. "I swear if you have on what I think you do under that coat…"

I smiled and undid the first knot then took my time with the second, maintaining eye contact with Ryder who looked like he was ready to leap off the couch. The ties fell to my sides and all that was left was a single black button.

As much as I was teasing Ryder, I was teasing myself, too.

I'd been contemplating his reaction, hyping myself up for the moment, since we were sitting at lunch after his graduation two days ago. Natalie and Mark both got him gifts, and even Theo had something for him while I was empty-handed. Ryder acted like he barely noticed, but I did. And it hadn't been for lack of trying. I just didn't know what to get when everything had recently changed.

What did I get my best friend's son who I'd started hooking up with? A gift card? Socks?

Nothing felt right. Until I thought of this.

I popped open the button and let the coat fall open. Not wasting any time, it fell down my arms, and I tossed it away. Leaving nothing between Ryder's hungry eyes and the outfit I wore underneath.

The red, white, and blue bikini Ryder couldn't stop talking about, the same one I was wearing the first time I met him, was a little smaller than it was almost a decade ago, but I managed to get it on. Although I didn't think Ryder minded that the triangles covering my breasts were smaller and more of my ass would be on display. At least it would be once the light wash denim cutoffs came off.

"Holy...*fuck*," Ryder groaned, rubbing his hand over his mouth and sitting back in the couch. He stared up at the ceiling and said, "You're gonna have to give me a minute because if I look at you right now, I'm going to come in my pants."

Suppressing my laughter, I readjusted the swimsuit. "Okay, Trouble, take your time."

"Ugh," he moaned. "Don't talk either."

So, I stood silently and tried to refrain from crossing to him. Every time we were in the same vicinity, it was startling how hard it was to fight that pull. Like we crossed that godforsaken line, and my body had to remind me every single time we were together or when I heard his voice.

Staring at the very obvious growing erection behind his sweats wasn't helping either.

"Okay," he sighed and rubbed his palms against his thighs before leaning forward once again. "I think I'm okay."

With one brow raised, I stood there as he slowly, *finally* looked at me.

"As good as you remember?"

He shook his head. "Better. So much better." He stood from the couch and watched me as he stepped around the coffee table. I turned to face him, and he stopped right in front of me. When he raised his hands, I was surprised to see they were shaking.

His exposed chest quickly rose and fell as he pushed my white cotton shirt off my shoulders. The fabric fell down my arms and pooled at the ground below me. When he dragged his fingers down the back of each arm, I fought the urge to shiver.

"You're perfect. This is the best gift ever," he said quietly. He entangled our fingers, and I wanted to sigh. It had been too long since he'd touched me. "I don't know where to start."

Taking his left hand, I raised it to my neck and placed it

against my collarbone. "Start wherever you want," I said. "We have all night, so play out every fantasy you've ever had."

He wrapped a palm around the side of my neck and used his thumb to tilt my head higher. "You know, my fantasies are never ending, but I'm sure we can get through a few tonight." I nodded, and he ran his thumb over my lower lip. "And they include me being deep inside your perfect, little cunt until we're both crying out and begging for more."

My heart pounded double-time, and I suddenly found it harder to breathe. I'd known that was what the night would lead to, but that didn't make it any easier. The two sides of my brain were in a never-ending war when it came to Ryder. One side— the logical side—telling me to grab my coat and run before we were well and truly fucked. While the other side—the one that held my heart and my cunt—said our fate was already decided with the first time I'd answered the phone on his birthday.

What was one more step in that fateful direction?

I wasn't strong enough to deny either of us what we wanted anyway. So, I nodded. Decision made.

"Your gift, your fantasy," I said. "Do your worst, Trouble."

The smile that slipped across his lips was slow and devious. And made my already pounding heart feel like it was about to leap from my chest. His smile didn't linger, though. It couldn't when he was determined to kiss me.

The second our lips touched, I felt my entire body relax. If I'd been in my right mind, that reaction would have scared me. But I was too lost in every graze of his tongue and brush of his lips.

"Bedroom," he whispered, but didn't wait for me to go on my own. He gripped my hand in his and tugged me across the living room. Although he was leading me along, he looked back like he wanted to make sure I was really following. The smile playing on his lips was unencumbered and disarming.

He dropped my hand long enough to flip on a lamp in the corner of the room, and I saw his bedroom for the first time. I was happy to see that his mattress wasn't on the floor, that there was a boxspring and a bedframe. And he even had a green comforter and matching pillows. Similar to the living room, it was a little bare but somehow homey. There were a few knick-knacks and framed photographs like they'd been specifically selected.

A careful finger slid across my shoulders as he stepped around me. His slow, deliberate steps were muffled by the carpet beneath his feet. The pile was a little thicker than the one I made him crawl across in my own bedroom. The image of his muscled back and arms working to propel him across the floor was one I'd replayed over and over again since it happened.

And as much as I wanted to sit on the edge of his bed and demand to see it again, I didn't. I knew he would—he'd immediately drop to his knees and willingly crawl to me. Looking up at me through dark lashes and trying to contain the smile threatening to break free. But tonight was for him. I wanted it to be everything he wanted.

"Anything I want?" he asked as he sat on the edge of the bed. A slight nod of my head, and he reached beneath his waistband. "This may sound strange, but I just want you to…stand there."

I shrugged and let my hands fall to my sides, standing up straighter and watching Ryder tug his sweatpants down just enough to let his cock spring free. At the sight of his swollen, rounded head, I inadvertently licked my lips at the memory of how heavy he felt against my tongue. I hadn't realized I'd done it until I saw Ryder's crooked smile.

But he always appeared cocky. It was nothing new, so I went back to staring at his fist wrapped around his engorged length. Swollen veins so close to the surface peeked out from between his fingers as he slowly slid his fist up and down. He, too, forgot about my outward display of desire at the mere sight of his cock. He was too busy raking his eyes up and down my body, devouring every inch and taking his time doing it.

"It's not often I get to just look at you without distraction. Without worrying that someone else might catch me. Even last time, you took away my view with that damn blindfold," he said through heavy breaths.

There was something decisively erotic about the idea that just the sight of me, in nothing more than cutoffs and a bikini was enough to get him so turned on. That all he wanted to do was look at me and take the image in. Commit every part of it to memory so he could likely replay it later. It was on the tip of my tongue to suggest he take a photo, but I knew well enough that would be a horrible idea.

So, I stood there and let him look for as long as he wanted while he jacked himself off to the sight of me. Each rise and fall of his chest grew quicker as did the pace of his hand. His jaw went slack and the tension in the room climbed higher.

I could see in the way his muscles tensed, and his eyelids began to flutter, that he was close. Just as quickly as the thought crossed my mind, Ryder jerked his hand away and stared down at himself like he was amazed what had almost happened.

Inhaling through his nose and exhaling through his mouth, it was several long seconds before he looked back up at me. Like he was nervous to touch his cock, he cautiously replaced his hand.

"I really want to know what you're thinking as you stroke yourself. As you watch me," I said.

He dragged his thumb over the head and through the pre-cum that was collecting every second. A stuttered breath was followed by a muffled groan, but he was able to collect himself, leaning most of his weight on his free hand propped behind him.

"I'm thinking a lot of things. None of which are coherent at the moment."

"Try me," I pushed.

He licked his lips and captured his lower one between his teeth as I slipped my fingers beneath the ties peeking out from above my cutoffs.

"I'm thinking about how fucking good you look and how much I want you to take off those shorts," he admitted, and I

unbuttoned them and slowly slid the zipper lower as he continued. "When I first saw you at that party, I hoped I'd get to see
you dripping wet. I wanted to know if the white fabric was as
see-through as I imagined."

My short laugh met his smile, and I let the shorts fall down
my legs. Similar to the little triangle top, the bottoms also
seemed to shrink with time. The flimsy material did enough to
cover between my thighs and less than half my ass. That was it,
and I was likely never going to wear it outside of that room
again, but I was glad I'd kept it all those years just to see his
reaction.

"I haven't worn this in a while, so I can't tell you if it is. But I
can go jump in the shower really quick, if you want to know."

He shook his head. "I have another idea," he said and stood,
kicking his sweatpants off. "Another, more pleasurable way to
get you wet."

In two quick strides, he ate up the space between us. His
large hands gripped my waist, and he ducked his head. Licking
over the curve of my breast, he kissed the skin that ran along the
edge of my suit. I tossed my arms over his shoulders and ran my
hand through his thick, unruly hair at the back of his head.

"Fuck," I muttered quietly when he sucked one of my nipples
through the fabric. Pleasure rippled through me in increasing
waves with every flick of his tongue and bite of his teeth. He
switched to my other breast and shifted until he'd wrapped one
arm around my back, holding me impossibly close while the
other hand blazed a path down my stomach.

His movements were intent and directed. He wasn't going to
tease me or draw anything out longer than necessary. And truth-
fully, I loved his urgency.

Dexterous fingers slipped over my bathing suit bottoms and
brushed against my slit. Widening my legs, Ryder's forehead
dropped to mine, his panted breaths fanning over my cheek.

"You're already so wet, pretty girl. Let me play with your

pussy just a little bit more, and I bet I'll be able to see the outline and pink of your cunt through the fabric."

I tilted my head and captured his lips in a heated, frenzied kiss. There was too much fabric for his touch to be truly satisfying, but it felt so good to be touched by him. I could still feel the heat of his fingers as he found my clit and began rubbing it in tight, tiny circles. The brush of his tongue against mine, both of us mercilessly fighting for the upper hand, only amplified every sensation.

Ryder pulled back. "Get on the bed," he ordered with a dominance in his voice I hadn't heard before. I slipped from his hold and crossed to the bed, climbing onto the mattress and turning on my knees in the center.

He shook his head and raised one finger, spinning it in front of him. "Turn around. On your hands and knees."

Rolling my eyes, I spun around and dropped to my elbows, letting my legs spread a little wider, and arched my back. The measly fabric covering my ass pulled to the center, exposing even more of each cheek.

I felt the bed dip, and I peeked down my body to see Ryder behind me. He grasped his cock and massaged up and down his shaft effectively spreading the pre-cum beading at the tip and using it to lubricate each pass.

But so much was leaking from the swollen head, more dripped onto the bed below him and between my legs.

"God, you're making such a mess," I murmured, propping up on my hands to peer over my shoulder. "Is all that pre-cum for me?"

He hummed low in his throat and dropped onto his haunches. One firm lick of his tongue against my pussy, and I fell back to the bed.

"All for you, pretty girl. It's all for you."

TWENTY-TWO

RED, WHITE, AND FUCKING BLUE

Ryder

CAROLINE MADE THIS SWEET SOUND SOMEWHERE BETWEEN A MOAN and a whimper, and I couldn't help but smile against her pussy.

When I woke up that morning, I didn't expect all my dreams to come true.

But there I was, lapping at Caroline's fabric-covered cunt, living them anyway.

When she showed up at my door I was confused, but when she dropped her coat, exposing the bikini she wore underneath, I swore I was hallucinating. A fantasy that only lived in my head until twenty minutes ago. One I never expected to experience.

I couldn't remember the last time I was that happy. Excitement and desire were pumping through my veins faster than I could cope, and the result was me almost coming in my pants or in my hand at least three times since she walked through the door.

I hadn't had such little control over my body since, well, since I met Caroline for the first time when I was only fifteen.

The fabric between her legs was soaking wet. Both from my mouth and her arousal pooling underneath it. Flattening my tongue, I mercilessly licked from her clit up to her opening. Even through her swimsuit, I could taste a hint of her sweetness, so perfectly earthy and mouthwatering.

My own desire sat heavy in my lower stomach. With every stroke of my tongue against her pussy and swipe of my fist over my cock, it grew sharper and more impossible to ignore. My orgasm eager to make its presence known. Hastily, I dropped my cock and let it bounce between my thighs.

Focus on Caroline, I had to focus on her. My now empty hand ran up her thigh from her knee to the delicious part of her ass that curved the bottom of her cheek. Her smooth skin twitched under my touch, and I doubled my efforts between her legs, pressing my tongue against the outline of her clit and upping the pressure as much as I could in the position I was in.

Eating pussy from behind was so underrated.

"Fuck, Ryder," Caroline moaned, and my cock kicked at the sound of my name. It was a wonder what this woman did to me.

"Tell me, beautiful. What do you need?"

She gasped and shifted, reaching down her body and motioning with her fingers between her legs. "Push them to the side. I want to feel your mouth on me."

One final lick and I leaned back to look down at the perfect image of her bent over, ass in the air on my bed. "It is see-through," I said casually, running my finger along the wet spot blooming where the white and blue met. Where I could see the outline of her cunt and the dark pink of her lips. "In case you were curious."

"Your hypothesis was right. I'm so *impressed*." The last word died on a moan as I did as she asked, pushing the bikini to the side and exposing her dripping cunt. I tugged the fabric farther to the side and ran my index and middle fingers along her swollen lips.

She bucked into my hand, and I spread her apart. "Your pussy is winking at me, searching for something to clamp down on. What do you want first, pretty girl? My fingers, my tongue, or my cock?"

Her answer was muffled by the blankets beneath her. "What was that?"

"Your mouth," she said again, louder and with barely restrained frustration.

As usual, my response to her annoyance was a smile. But I was in a giving mood, especially when it meant my face between her legs, so I wasn't going to deny either of us a second longer.

I kneeled and buried my face against her pussy. Placing dirty, open-mouth kisses everywhere I could reach, I teased her clit with my thumb and fucked her with my tongue. She loved it as much as I knew she would, and I felt lucky to have that knowledge. Knowing what made Caroline moan and grind and reach back to tug my hair made me feel like I was flying.

And she did all of those things—she moaned that pretty, throaty moan that sounded almost broken as she ground back onto my face and fumbled to find my head.

"Fuck, Ryder. Right there, right there. Harder."

Yes ma'am, I thought.

She gripped my hair and held me against her as I fucked her harder with my tongue and added pressure to her clit. Her entire body suddenly seized, and she was pulsing against my mouth. My hands gripped her ass and spread her wider so she could use me as she pleased.

Once the orgasm ebbed, and she released my hair, I pushed onto my knees and replaced my tongue in her pussy with two fingers. She jerked forward, still sensitive and unsuspecting, but I wrapped a hand around the place where her shoulder and neck met to keep her still.

"You're not going anywhere until I get one more. I know you have at least one more in you," I said. I crooked my fingers and found the spot that would make her legs shake. "Show me how well you'll strangle my cock once I get inside this perfect cunt. Show me how tight you'll choke me."

The words tumbling out of my mouth were a product of delirious pleasure. I wasn't thinking about what I said except for the fact that every time I spoke, she clenched around me like she was urging me to say more.

Tightening my grip around the side of her neck, she turned her head to the side so I could see the euphoria twisting her features. Eyes squeezed shut, her plump lips were parted. Her blonde hair was in messy waves around her face.

My brutally hard cock nudged her ass, and each unintentional thrust against her soft skin was torturous. Before the worst could happen and I unloaded all over her ass, I shifted enough that my cock was once again hanging miserably between my legs.

"So good, so good," she chanted, and I ran my hand over the curve of her ass where my cock had just been. At first it was a fleeting thought—I wondered what her smooth skin would look like reddened by my palm. But I latched on to it and couldn't let it go until I knew.

The first slap was light, tentative. A way to test and gauge her reaction. Her walls tightened around my fingers, and her hands clambered for the blankets.

"More?"

"Yes," she hissed, and I didn't wait to land the second, much harder slap. Her skin bloomed red, but it didn't stain the way I wanted. So, I landed four more, two on each side.

"Fuck, look at that recoil," I muttered, running a soothing hand over her before doing it again and again.

Her startled cries pierced the air, and I'd lost count of how many times I'd spanked her when she began fucking herself back on my hand and shivering through her release. The way she tightened around my fingers, it was impossible to move them. The muscles in her back flexed, and I rubbed the tender globes of her ass. But it was the orgasm coating my hand and gushing toward me that was a pleasant surprise.

"Oh, fuck yes," I whispered as she stilled and collapsed

down onto the bed. My fingers were sore from how hard I'd been fucking her with them, and the palm of my other hand tingled. But I didn't care about any of it. I was focused solely on the sated woman on my bed, and the wet spot between her shaking legs.

Slowly, she pushed herself off the bed and looked back. "Did I—?" she began, but I was already nodding.

"Squirt? Hell, yes you did." I smiled, and for the first time ever, Caroline looked sheepish and almost embarrassed. It was sweet, but she had no reason to feel anything besides content, happy. "That was one of the hottest things—if not *the* hottest thing I've ever seen."

To prove my point, I glanced down at my fingers, still covered in her, and dragged them across my tongue. She watched me, and all evidence of embarrassment disappeared. With narrowed eyes, she turned completely around and pressed up to her knees until we were inches apart. My fingers still in my mouth, she caught part of my hand and my lips with her kiss.

I let my fingers go with a pop as she said, "You look good with your mouth full."

I smiled and let her find any remnants I'd left behind. She sucked my fingers like she did my cock—thoroughly.

"I know I do," I said, and she grinned around my fingers, baring her teeth just enough to hurt and leave little indentations when I pulled them free. "Dirty, dirty girl."

Shifting forward, I used my body weight and an arm around her waist to push her back onto the bed. "You're about to look really fucking good with my cock buried deep in your dripping cunt."

As if on cue, she reached between us and wrapped a hand around my shaft. I was already so wound up, my eyes slipped closed as I groaned and thrusted into her palm.

"Such big talk from a man who looks like he's about to come from the slightest brush of my hand."

My eyes popped back open, and I was moving in the next

second. Reaching behind me, I yanked open the top drawer of my nightstand and ripped open a condom. I rolled it on and looked back at Caroline. She'd peeled back the little triangles of her bikini and was pushing her tits together, tugging and pinching her hard nipples.

In one quick movement, I tugged her bottoms down her legs and tossed them behind me. It was hot, pushing them aside when I ate her, but I didn't want anything in the way the first time I was inside her.

I did the same with her top, pulling at the flimsy ties around her neck and back until I was able to throw that away, too. And finally, there was nothing between us.

"You act like you're in charge," I said through gritted teeth, leaning over her to plant my hand next to her head. My other wrapped around my cock, and I rubbed the head between those pretty lips and through her wetness. "But you showed up at my front door like a needy little slut. Dressed up in what you knew would make me crazy. An outfit that was guaranteed to get you fucked any and every way I could think of."

Her throat bobbed as she swallowed, but her eyes held that fight, fire, and intensity. She widened her legs and lifted her hands to wrap around my neck. She tugged me down and caressed my cheek as I notched my cock at her entrance.

"You're right," she whispered against my lips. "I'm needy for you, so prove you're not all talk, Ryder."

She kissed me, and I pushed forward. My crown breached, and I didn't stop until our hips were flush and her heat surrounded me. Her rushed exhale swept across my mouth, and I dropped my forehead to hers.

Yes, I was precariously back on the edge, worried that any slight movement would send me headfirst into a premature orgasm. But I was also stunned by the enormity of the moment.

She was everything I'd ever wanted, and being inside her for the first time, it felt like something else clicked into place. Something I hadn't known was missing but was suddenly there.

I raised my head enough to look in her eyes which bounced between my own. The blue much grayer in the soft light of my room, I searched them for any sign of reciprocation. Our breath mixed, and my cock pulsed inside her. And just when I thought I could see a shimmer of something deeper, she blinked, and her nails scraped against my scalp.

An evil smile slipped across her mouth, and her hips circled. Devious, she was fucking devious. But I drew back and pushed back in, happy to watch the smile fade into pleasure. I rocked in and out, back and forth, trying to determine which movements made her eyes roll back and figuring out if I could hold out for at least a few minutes.

Holding back was harder than I expected. A sheen of sweat covered my chest, and I could feel it collecting on my back. But Caroline didn't appear to care. She met me thrust for thrust as I picked up my pace.

Her eyes closed, and a whimper was followed by a sharp moan. I kissed her lips just to try to taste the sound.

"God, I love the sweet little sounds you make."

"Well," she said without missing a beat. "If you're doing it right, they won't be little or sweet."

The words weren't as sharp as anything she'd said before, more like a reflex than the truth. But I wanted to rise to the challenge, nonetheless. I planted my elbow next to her head and ran my hand down her opposite side. Over the curve of her breast and the dip in her waist so I could grip her hip and lift her where I wanted to.

Her jaw slackened with the new angle while I ground my teeth together. With her hips tilted, I was deeper than before, and I could feel myself nudging the warmest parts of her. My fingers biting into her skin, I moved. I focused my energy deeper, my thrusts turning more forceful and raw.

"Fuck, yes," Caroline moaned. She dragged her nails down my chest, through the sparse, dark hair and around my back until she palmed my ass. Each inch of my skin was peppered with goose bumps just at the feeling of her hands against me. It wasn't a feeling I'd soon get over or ever take for granted.

"God, you're beautiful. So incredible," I murmured. Her eyes flashed open, and she smiled.

"Don't let this go to your head, but you are too."

I groaned and buried my face in her neck. My orgasm was bearing down on me with every easy slip of my cock. She was perfectly tight and warm and wet, and fuck, she smelled so good, too. With her hands all over me, and her panted breaths against my neck, I couldn't wait.

"That feels so good, Ryder," she said. Each word was broken by the cruel thrust of my hips. "Such a good boy. I'm almost there."

"Oh *fuck*." The bed rocked beneath me, and our skin slapping together was the most beautiful sound. The heat emanating from our bodies circled around me, and when my orgasm finally barreled down my spine, there was no hope of holding back.

She gripped my cock, wrapping her arms around me and bowing her back with the force of her own release while I pumped every last drop into the condom. It wasn't stars or fireworks behind my eyes, but an explosive ecstasy that had been building for years.

She relaxed back into the sheets, and I fell on top of her, careful not to let all my weight crush her. For several long seconds, we laid there together. Our hearts pounding, neither of us attempted to move. My cock slowly softened, but I didn't try to pull out. If I could extend those moments forever, I would have.

Caroline ran her nose along my jaw, and I felt her chest rise and fall with a deep breath. "That was..." she said, her words trailing off before she could finish the sentence. But I knew what she meant. I also had no words.

"Yeah," I agreed. "It was."

TWENTY-THREE
YOU DIDN'T EVEN GO THERE

Caroline

I DIDN'T WANT TO MOVE. MY BODY WAS SPENT, AND I FELT LIKE I was floating.

Eventually, Ryder pulled out of me and took his body heat with him.

I turned into the blankets beneath me, and he chuckled at my muttled groan. I knew I should got up to pee, but moving from the bed sounded like the worst decision I could make. A few minutes wouldn't kill me or result in a UTI. I hoped.

I heard his quiet footsteps as he padded into his bathroom and the soft click of the door opening. The toilet flushed, and the water turned on, but it sounded far away. I was still happily floating.

The bed dipped, and Ryder's arm appeared around my torso. I didn't open my eyes as he tugged me higher onto the bed and positioned me against his pillows. I did, however, roll over and rest my head on his chest. He covered us both with the blanket draped at the bottom of the bed, and I was wrapped in warmth.

When he kissed my forehead and tightened his hold around me, I suppressed a sigh.

"I've never met this Caroline before," he said. "Orgasm drunk, sated, and cuddly. I like her."

My eyes popped open, and I peered up at him. Licking my lips, I refrained from voicing my first thought. *Most people haven't met her.* And by most, I meant almost no one. In my almost thirty-four years, there had only been two. Well, now three.

"By the pool you ran off, and you did the same thing in your bed last time. This is...nice."

Blue eyes bounced between mine, and he intertwined our fingers that lay on his stomach. Fighting that unparalleled desire to flee, I swallowed around the lump in my throat and ignored the pang in my chest as well as the memories of the last two men I'd laid like this with. Instead, I hummed and did the next best thing, deflected with words.

"It is," I said, looking down at our joined hands. "You shouldn't ruin it with your commentary."

He laughed and brushed his lips against the top of my head. When he took a deep breath, I realized he was smelling me, which was slightly odd until it was followed by a rumble in his chest. Nothing that would have been noticeable if I weren't laying directly on him, but since I was, I could hear and feel it.

Whatever he smelled, likely my dry shampoo and hair oil, he liked.

We laid there quietly, listening to the faint sounds from outside his apartment. A car door slammed, and the people above us sounded like they were playing *Dance Dance Revolution* or rearranging all the furniture in their living room.

I was trying to decipher the noise when Ryder's phone buzzed on the nightstand. He didn't reach for it, instead he continued rubbing his thumb over the nail polish on mine. When it happened again but for longer, like someone was calling him, I lifted my head.

"You can get that," I said.

He shook his head and stared at our hands. "It's my dad."

"You know that without looking at it?"

He nodded and sighed. "He's calling because he wants to know which job I took."

Once again, I struggled not to move or react because that question had also been heavy on my mind since he'd told me about the possibility. I wanted him to do what was best for him, but shockingly, I didn't want him to leave. A feeling I was still struggling with.

I'd tried not to think about it, but the more I tried to ignore it, the more it made itself known. It had been a long time since I struggled with controlling my thoughts like I did around Ryder.

"Today was the deadline," I stated.

"It was," Ryder said plainly, and I waited with bated breath for his answer. If he'd taken that job, he'd probably have to leave sooner rather than later. They weren't likely to let him wait much longer.

Then came the realization that what we'd just done—the mind-blowing sex we'd just had—could have been a goodbye. The first and the last time all at once.

Seconds ticked by, and I'd finally had enough. "And?"

He laughed, and I tried to take my hand back, but his grip was too tight for me to shake. "Is the anticipation killing you?"

"If you don't want to tell me, then you don't have—"

"I'm not going anywhere, Caroline."

I stopped and made the stupid decision to look up at him. Tender blue eyes found mine, and Ryder's customary lopsided smile tilted his lips. There was a flash of his shallow dimple before his smile was too wide to see it.

"I took the job here, so I won't be moving. Well, I will be moving, but just across town instead of states away."

"Why? The other one was more money, right? And more potential for growth?"

Ryder shrugged, and I propped up onto my elbow.

"I negotiated the salary of the position here, so I'm making more than I would have at either. And I don't know, the more I thought about it, the more it didn't feel like the right fit."

Unsure what else to say and knowing I would never ask the question I really wanted to, I decided on, "Your mom will be happy."

"She will be ecstatic, although she'll pretend not to be because the last thing she wanted to do was sway my decision."

"You're right," I said, and the blanket slipped down my chest, exposing my breasts. The cold air hit me, and my nipples immediately hardened. Ryder's eyes darted to my chest, and I slowly covered myself back up so I could see the look on his face for longer. The want stirring behind his eyes and the way he licked his lower lip like he was imagining my nipple in his mouth.

He cleared his throat and looked back down at our hands. "There were other..." He stopped and thought for a second like he couldn't find the right word. "...*factors* to consider anyway."

"It's always wise to consider all factors when making a decision," I said, wondering how long we'd both tiptoe around the topic of what *factor* he was talking about.

He hummed and lifted my hand to his mouth, not kissing my fingers but running the back of them against his lips.

"Especially factors that weren't factors a month ago. Factors that I never thought would be factors no matter how much I hoped."

His hot breath against my hand and the intensity in his eyes, the tension around us wasn't just palpable, it was suffocating. And the longer it lasted, the harder it was to stop.

"I think that's the most times the word 'factor,' has ever been used."

Not what he was expecting me to say, Ryder blinked, and his expression faltered. But only for a second before he recovered and donned that crooked grin. "We'll have to look it up to confirm," he said, and in one swift motion, he let go of my hand and grabbed my hip, flipping me until I was straddling his lap. The blanket pooled around my waist as he shifted higher up the bed, my hands landing on his chest for support. He sat back against the headboard.

"But since I'll be here still," he began, running his hands up my sides and caressing the underside of both breasts. "I get more of this. More of you."

"Ryder," I chastised, but he didn't stop. He pressed against my nipples with his thumbs and teased them both until they were hard. The feeling shot directly between my legs where his cock was cradled, growing harder by the second.

He growled and pinched one hard enough to sting. "Don't *Ryder* me. I'm not asking for anything, Caroline. I just want... this. You just like this. You've made yourself perfectly clear."

The head of his cock pressed deliciously against my clit which made it impossible to speak for several seconds, but somehow, I managed to ask, "Have I? Because I think eventually you'll want more."

"And what happens if I do eventually want more?" He replaced his thumb on my nipple with his mouth and drew lazy circles around the sensitive area with his tongue before sucking it hard.

"We stop," I said, and he hummed against my skin. He wasn't deterred by my honesty. Switching to the other breast, he began the pattern over again—licking, sucking, and biting. My hips began to move of their own accord. Like in my bedroom, his cock slipped between my lips easily, my arousal enough lubricant to ease any resistance.

He let my nipple go with a pop and leaned back to watch his cock disappear underneath me. His jaw was slack and all the muscles in his stomach went taut. Dark hair unkempt from my fingers and lips wet with the remnants of his spit—I committed the picture of him to memory. It was one I wouldn't want to forget.

"Okay," he agreed without looking up. His easy response made me laugh which finally drew his attention to my face. His neck was too large for my hand to fit around, but I tried anyway.

His Adam's apple bobbed against my palm, and I loved the way his pupils dilated, and his cock kicked.

He was such a switch, which was exciting since I'd considered myself one for a while. The flip from submissive to dominant and everything in between was addictive. Especially when I was with someone who could match my energy.

"I don't believe how easily you just agreed to that."

"I told you. I'll take whatever you give me."

I shook my head and tightened my hand. His eyes grew wider, but he didn't stop me. "Eventually, you'll want more."

"Do you want to bet on it?"

I leaned forward and kissed just his lower lip. The one that was slightly larger and so expressive. "Sure. What's the wager?"

"Nothing. Just the glory of being the winner. That's all I'll need."

"Fine," I said as Ryder blindly reached for his bedside table drawer and found another condom. I let my hand fall from his neck so I could shift backward and allow him to roll it on.

Sheathed in rubber, he gripped my hips and guided me down on his waiting length. "There you go," he murmured. "Sit on my cock." One of the biggest and most exciting surprises being with Ryder was his dirty fucking mouth. Dirty talk did more for me in the bedroom than almost anything else. *Almost.*

He stretched and filled me so thoroughly and completely, I lowered myself slowly to feel every fucking inch. My eyes flashed to his phone screen which lit up with another new message, but I was more curious about the time.

"Fifteen-minute refractory period. Impressive."

He smiled and groaned when I was fully seated. "Perks of being with a twenty-three-year-old."

God, and was he fucking right. A man who could keep going was always welcome.

At first, I dragged my hips back and forth over his cock, getting reacclimated to his length and girth. But that didn't last long. I replaced my hand around his throat and lifted my hips until just the tip was inside me. His eyes pleaded for me to keep going, and he opened his mouth like he wanted to voice those desires, but I beat him to it. I let my hips fall, plunging him back into me, and we both groaned in perfect unison.

With me on top, he was deeper than I imagined he could be. Every slam of my hips, he grazed my cervix, and unending desire pulsed through me.

"Oh my god, you're gorgeous. Yes, please, fuck me," he ground out through bared teeth. His fingers found my clit, and he managed to keep pace with me as I fucked him.

"Yes, use me, pretty girl. Use my cock to make yourself come. Fuck me just like you need to."

With our eyes locked, I held his throat just tight enough to restrict the blood flow and cut off his filthy words. Then I came apart in a million splintering pieces.

Ryder quickly followed me over the edge, and I collapsed on top of him.

"Fucking hell, you're amazing," he said, and I preened under his words. I was pretty good, I had no doubt in my skills, but somehow Ryder made it better. The two of us together were nothing like I'd ever experienced before.

"You're not too bad yourself," I admitted.

"I'm fucking awesome, don't downplay it."

I pushed up to a seated position, Ryder's cock still inside me, and laughed toward the ceiling. He groaned beneath me, my pussy inadvertently clamping down on his sensitive length.

"Your ego is almost too big for this room," I said, rolling off him and landing on unsteady legs next to the bed. I really had to pee now.

I stepped into the bathroom and pushed the door closed behind me. It didn't shut completely, so I heard him holler, "Stop having multiple orgasms, and maybe my ego will stop growing."

I peed, washed my hands, and tried to tame the crazy state of my hair before I walked back into the bedroom. The condom had disappeared, but Ryder was back in the same place, blanket casually thrown over part of his legs and his arms tucked behind his head.

"Never," I said on my way into the living room. I found the bag I'd brought next to the door and dragged it back into his bedroom.

Ryder perked up. "Are you staying the night?"

"I don't spend the night," I said, fishing around for the pair of shorts I knew I'd packed. "And I have a workout class in the morning on the other side of town."

"Leave in the morning, then." He tried to reason, but I was already shaking my head as I stepped into the fabric shorts and reached for my sports bra then T-shirt. Like hell was I going back outside in that bikini and coat.

Picking up the discarded swimsuit, I zipped up the backpack and stood. Ryder's eyes were narrowed on my chest, staring at my shirt. I looked down to remember which one I was wearing and why he might look like he wanted to rip it off me.

He rolled off the bed and stepped around me. He headed for a drawer in the dresser on the opposite side of the room and found a pair of shorts he quickly pulled on. "You didn't go to college there," he said.

"No, I didn't," I said, my voice belying my confusion.

"Then where'd you get it?"

I thought for a second, sincerely puzzled by his line of questioning, until I realized where the T-shirt had come from. To lie or not to lie, that was the question. I went with the latter.

"A guy."

He nodded without turning around and reached for another drawer. "A guy you slept with?"

What the hell. "Yes, he left it at my house, and it's become one of my favorite T-shirts. It's soft and worn in all the right ways."

Quickly, Ryder spun back around and crossed the room in three steps. "Yeah, that's not going to work for me. When you're fucking me, you shouldn't wear another man's shirt, before, during, or after." My eyes widened, and he thrust one of his T-shirts into my hands. "Do you want to take this off?" he asked, tugging at the hem of the shirt I was wearing. "Or should I?"

I scoffed and crossed my arms over my chest. "I like this shirt, Ryder. You're being possessive, which doesn't do a lot for your argument that you *'won't want more.'*" I dropped my voice to mimic his.

"So, you want me to take it off then?"

I rolled my eyes and took off the damn shirt before snatching the one he offered out of his hands. It was light purple and just as worn as the other one. It was maybe even softer. Although I wasn't going to tell him that. It was a little big and fell to my mid-thigh. By the time I got it over my head and straightened it, Ryder was picking me up, grasping me under my ass, and hoisting me into the air.

"What the hell are you doing?" I cried, but my question was quickly answered when he dropped me onto the bed. He crowded over me and kissed me hard.

"Five more minutes," he said. I parted my thighs and let him settle between them. His tongue swept between my lips, and I became putty under his touch.

"Five more minutes," I agreed, but we kissed much longer than that. When we pulled apart, our lips were swollen, and he was hard for the third time. But it didn't go any further. I'd missed a good make-out session. One that didn't include strings and a requirement for both parties to get off at the end.

Ryder lay beside me, playing with a lock of my hair between his fingers.

"You said something earlier, and I was curious..." I said, unsure how to proceed.

"Yes?" he prompted, and I ran a finger down the center of his chest.

"You said, 'fuck me,' but would you ever let me?"

His expression was blank, features unmoving, and my

fingers went still against him. Worry tickled at the back of my mind that I'd said something wrong, but I knew better than that. A little smile finally tilted one side of his lips. He licked his lower one and looked down at the piece of hair he was still holding.

It took him a few seconds to speak. "Sorry, I'm just surprised."

"If it's not okay, then that's fine. I wasn't trying to—"

"It's a pleasant surprise, Caroline," he admitted, and my stomach did that weird thing it always did when he said my name. "So, yes, the answer is yes. I'd willingly, *eagerly*, let you in my ass."

My eyebrows shot up, and the images my mind conjured were enough for me to contemplate running out and buying a dildo that moment. Or asking if he had one we could use.

"Don't look so surprised," he said with a laugh. "I've done similar things before, which I'm sure you could guess since I've also been with men."

"I didn't want to assume."

He placed a kiss on the center of my forehead then my hairline. "That's nice, but it's the right assumption. And I have to admit," he said, dropping my hair to tug me closer. We shifted until every part of his front was lined up with mine and the space between us was nonexistent. "The idea of you wearing a strap and palming a dildo you were intent on using on me..." His words trailed off on a groan, and his eyes fluttered shut. To drive his point home, he ground his hips against me. I believed him already, but his thick cock against my thigh really solidified it.

"Great, I'll start planning. What do you prefer? Longer? Thicker? A fun color?"

He laughed, and I smiled up at him. "I'm not opposed to a fun color, but I prefer thicker if I had to choose."

"Good to know," I said as the ideas bombarded me. I'd have to do research on the best brands and anything else I needed to know going into it. Ryder brushed his fingers against my cheek, drawing me back to the present. "I should probably go."

He shook his head and kissed me softly. "Five more minutes."

"It's already been more than five minutes from the last time we said that."

"So what?" he offered. "Please. Five more minutes."

I sighed and laid my head back down on his arm. It ended up being much more than five minutes because next thing I knew, the sun was peeking through the bedroom blinds, and I couldn't make myself move for fear of disturbing Ryder's perfect sleeping form.

TWENTY-FOUR
"HERE'S...SCOTTY!"

Caroline

I WALKED INTO MY HOUSE AND STRAIGHT TO THE KITCHEN WHERE I kicked off my heels and unceremoniously dropped my bags on the floor.

Miles and Stephen's wedding was almost completely planned. There were only a few more things to check off my list. Like finalizing the music selection and hiring additional parking attendants just in case.

A black tie, three-hundred guest wedding with a sit-down dinner and on-site accommodations was a lot to put together on a standard timeline but having only a few months made it nearly impossible. Well, nearly impossible for anyone except me.

It was tiring, though, especially on top of all my other responsibilities and clients, which made me ever the more thankful for the help I'd hired. Addie had taken on two of the smaller parties and the pre-planning for a wedding set for next year. I wasn't sure how she found the time with her other job, but she somehow got it done. And always did so with a smile.

My phone buzzed on the counter, but I didn't check it immediately. I walked to the fridge and pulled out the open bottle of rosé I'd been thinking about the entire drive home. My first thought was to sip directly from the bottle, but I opted for a glass instead.

I poured the remainder of the bottle into the glass and took a sip as I walked back toward my phone. I wasn't surprised to see Ryder's name along with a new message. We'd been texting all day, well, all week really. He'd walked me to my car that next morning and made me promise to text him when I got home since I'd missed my nonrefundable workout class.

I'd let him know I was home safe, and we hadn't stopped talking since.

> Ryder: Do you think squirrels intentionally run out into traffic? It sure as hell seems that way sometimes.

I shook my head and set my glass down to type back a response.

> Me: Did you know you can have a thought and not send it to me?

His response was almost immediate.

> Ryder: Trust me, these are not all my thoughts. I keep many to myself.

> Me: That's terrifying.

At the top of my screen, another text appeared from Natalie. The guilt that churned in my gut every time I saw her or thought about her or talked to or about her was unfortunate but entirely self-inflicted. As much as I hated lying to my best friend, I was more worried about what might happen if she knew. And not seeing Ryder again felt...unlikely. Especially when it was temporary because I knew I was right—eventually he'd want more, and we'd have to stop.

And hopefully the aftermath wouldn't be too disastrous.

Natalie had sent paint swatches for their bedroom and asked my opinion. I texted her back, opting for the green rather than the dark blue, and flipped back to Ryder's messages.

Ryder: You home yet?

Me: Yes...

He didn't respond, and I warily slid my phone back onto the counter. I picked up my glass of wine and went back to the fridge, pulling it open and surveying the contents. What I'd planned to cook—a basic chicken and rice recipe—no longer sounded appetizing. I closed the fridge and grew frustrated with my prospects when I remembered that my favorite Italian restaurant did half-price pasta on Thursdays.

I was walking back to my phone, prepared to call in an order, when my doorbell rang.

I stopped at the edge of the island and peered around the wall into the entryway. It was a stretch, but when I squinted, I could see someone standing just beyond the opaque glass.

Pulling up the front door camera on my phone, I immediately beelined for the door when I realized who it was. I yanked it open and pulled Ryder inside a second later.

"What the hell are you doing here? Your mom is going to see your car!" I whisper-yelled because it felt fitting.

"She won't if I'm in and out of here like I plan to be!" he whisper-yelled back, which made me stop and consider how ridiculous it was.

"Answer my first question," I said in a normal voice. "What are you doing here?"

"What do you mean? You're the only person who's allowed to show up at someone's front door unannounced?"

I shook my head and crossed my arms over my chest. "Don't answer my question with a question. And as I know you remember, I showed up at your door wearing the outfit of your dreams, so unless you have something scandalous under your shirt and jeans, you lose."

He narrowed his eyes and rubbed his stubble-covered jaw. "What would you like to see me in? Special kind of briefs? Maybe a T-shirt with the Superman emblem and Clark Kent-style glasses?"

"An Easter Bunny costume. Now, what are you doing here?"

He laughed but still didn't answer my very pressing question. I opened my mouth to argue as much when he raised a hand and said, "I want to take you somewhere."

"Take me somewhere?"

"Yes."

"No."

He sighed and squeezed the bridge of his nose like I was the irritating one. "Caroline, please."

Why did he always have to sound so sincere? It made it hard to brush him off when his voice dropped, and his excitement ebbed. "Where do you want to take me?"

"It's...a surprise," he said

I shook my head and stood firm. We were inching into date-like territory, and that was more dangerous than anything. "I don't think that's a good—"

"They have the best mozzarella sticks," he said, and my argument died. All substance to said argument was further diminished when my stomach growled louder than it had any right to. "It'll be fun, I promise. I'll even let you pay for something, so it doesn't feel too much like a date."

"Let me?" I questioned, but by his smile, he knew he had me. He closed the distance between us, his hands dropping to my hips, I was greeted by his scent—something deep with a touch of sweetness that I wanted to smell every single moment of every single day.

I didn't let myself linger on that revelation too long. I leaned in as he did, but the second before our lips touched, the doorbell rang again. Both of us stopped, a breath apart, and looked at each other then to the door.

"Are you expecting someone else?"

"Well, I wasn't expecting anyone to begin with," I said. He reluctantly let me go, his fingers lingering against my waist for as long as they could. I stepped up to the door and felt Ryder close at my back.

When I swung it open, I wished I hadn't.

"Scott," I said by way of greeting. His smile was slow as was his voice when he said, "Hi, Caroline."

"What are you—what are you doing here? I didn't know you were in town."

"Last minute business trip in the city, and I have a free night tonight. I figured I'd surprise you. I have a reservation already. It's a new French restaurant downtown."

Two months ago, I would have jumped at his offer. Scott was an executive at an oil and gas company, which required extensive travel. He didn't live in the city, but when he was here, he always called me. And I always answered.

He didn't expect anything more than the one night we usually had. It started with dinner at some very nice, expensive restaurant and ended with us in a very fancy penthouse suite at a hotel downtown. He didn't spare any expense, and it was a good time for all.

Now, I was dumbstruck and not pleasantly surprised.

"I—I see. It's good to see you, but I don't think I can—"

"Hi," Ryder interrupted my stuttering and stepped into view of the open door. I closed my eyes and tried to take a deep breath. I was living a nightmare, but unfortunately, it was my real life. Waking up wasn't an option.

I opened my eyes in time to see Ryder extending his hand. Scott quickly glanced from me to it.

"I'm Ryder. It's nice to meet you, Scott, was it?"

Scott took Ryder's hand and shook it once with a tight-lipped smile. The saying, "you could cut the tension with a knife," wasn't strong enough. You would need a chainsaw or some other gas-powered tool to cut through the tension weighing down the air around us.

"Nice to meet you," Scott said. "I didn't mean to interrupt. I probably should have called first."

"It's not a problem," I said automatically, and I caught Ryder glance at me out of the corner of my eye. I wasn't thinking straight. I didn't know what else to say that didn't involve screaming and running away.

"I'll just call you later, Caroline," Scott said, and rather than open my mouth to cause more of an issue, I nodded and tried for a smile. "Nice to meet you, Ryder."

Ryder waved, and I couldn't get the door closed quickly enough. I shut it, locked it, and leaned against the glass. Deciding that it wasn't a good idea to bang my head against it, I shut my eyes and attempted to recompose myself.

Scott was a man of his word—he would absolutely call me later, and I had no idea what I was going to do when my phone rang. It wasn't my intention to sleep with anyone else—honestly, I wasn't really interested—but doing so would unequivocally prove to Ryder how serious I was about not wanting anything more.

I knew it was an awful thing to do or to even think, but that didn't keep the thought from creeping in and taking root.

I opened my eyes and straightened to find Ryder watching me, arms crossed in front of him and eyebrows raised. Smoothing my hands down my dress, I matched his stance, crossing my arms but trying for an unbothered expression.

We stared at one another for a long while. Long enough that my eyes went dry, and I began to feel uncomfortable with the distance between us. The urge to cross to him was strong. A muscle in his jaw twitched, and I noticed his hands flex from beneath his arms.

Finally, he relaxed and ran his fingers through his hair.

"I know you're hungry, so we should probably get going."

"What?" It wasn't the last thing I expected him to say, but it was definitely low on the list.

"Do you want to change first or…?"

My arms fell to my sides, and I shook my head as I walked past him and down the hallway toward my bedroom. I heard Ryder's steady steps behind me and headed straight through my bedroom and into my closet.

I surveyed the clothes hanging around me and spun around when I heard him enter. He was leaned against the doorframe, arms and ankles crossed, looking better than he had any right to which made me even more frustrated.

"What should I wear?"

He shrugged and glanced around the room. "Something casual. Jeans, shorts, sneakers, that kind of thing."

With a huff, I found a pair of jeans and pretended to ignore the feeling of Ryder's eyes on me as I tried to unzip my dress. Getting it on was easy, but removing it was much harder. Especially when I was amped up.

Before I had a chance to try again, Ryder was behind me. Tender fingers brushed against my neck and lowered the zipper. He didn't linger and stepped back far enough for me to slip the dress off and my jeans on. I grabbed the first top I saw and a white pair of sneakers.

Dressed and ready to go, I turned to find Ryder had gone back to leaning against the doorframe.

"Good?" I asked, walking toward him and motioning to my new outfit. He inclined his head as I stopped in front of him but didn't appear interested in moving to let me pass.

A stare-down commenced. But it didn't last as long as the one in my entryway. Ryder's offset smile graced his face, and I stiffened.

"Why are you mad, Caroline? Because he showed up or because I didn't react?"

I brushed a piece of hair that had fallen from my clip out of my face and cocked my head to the side.

"I'm not mad."

He snorted out a halfhearted laugh and straightened to his full height. "Okay, whatever you say. I just don't think there's any reason for me to be jealous."

"Really? Why is that?"

"Because he left, and you're coming with me. In this scenario, I won. And when he calls you later, you're not going to pick up."

I ran my tongue along my teeth and stuffed my hands into my jean's pockets, searching for something to do with them. I felt raw under Ryder's stare. Like he was seeing too much of me, knew too much of me.

"He probably won't call. I think you did a good job scaring him off."

Ryder laughed, and the sound bounced off the walls of my small walk-in closet.

"He'll call."

"You sound very confident discussing the behavior of a man you don't even know."

He took a step forward, one hand in his own pocket, the other reached for me. I could've stepped back or ducked around him. I had an opportunity to flee the closeness, but I didn't. I stood there as he clasped my jaw and ran his thumb over my cheek. I was frozen as he surveyed my face with a sweet tilt to his lips.

"I know he'll call, pretty girl, because you're Caroline Grant. And no man is stupid enough to let you slip away without a fight."

TWENTY-FIVE

MERCY RULE

Caroline

UNFORTUNATELY, RYDER WAS RIGHT ON ALL ACCOUNTS. SCOTT called, and I didn't answer.

Granted, I didn't hear my phone ring anyway. I was too busy beating Ryder's ass at air hockey and any racing game we could find.

The arcade he took me to had a little bit of everything. In the car, my stomach was making it known how hungry I really was, so we first stopped at the restaurant inside. And Ryder was, yet again, right. The mozzarella sticks were straight out of my dreams. We ordered—and ate—two baskets worth and shared a pizza.

Then we took our drinks and hopped from game to game. Ryder was a million times better than I was at Skee-Ball and basketball, but I had him beat on anything that required driving and my favorite, air hockey.

I looked up at the score and smiled. My cheeks hurt from smiling so much.

Shooting my arms in the air in celebration, Ryder looked rightfully dejected. He'd scored once to my ten. Mercy rules should have applied after eight, but I enjoyed the victory too much.

"We need to switch sides or something," he said, setting his mallet (yes, I had to Google the name of it after I won the first game) down on the edge of the table.

I picked up my margarita and took a sip as I shrugged. "We can switch if that makes you feel better," I said. Ryder retrieved his own drink, and we both walked around opposite sides of the table. "But it's going to be even worse when I kick your ass from this side, too."

He set his drink down on the conveniently placed table and narrowed his eyes. "Who knew you were so goddamn competitive."

I rolled my lips and picked up the mallet and disc. "It's a sickness."

"No, what's a sickness is how much you gloat *after* you win."

I shot him my best *"who me?"* smile and dropped the disc on the table. He fumbled for his own mallet and rolled his shoulders a couple of times, bouncing up and down like he was preparing for an Olympic trial. I rolled my lips to hide my widening smile. He was so serious it almost made me want to concede a few points.

I didn't, but he still scored enough to make it a closer game. When he did score, he always celebrated like he had actually won an Olympic medal—asking passersby if they saw what he had done or jumping up and down while pumping his arms in the air. There were a few whoops sprinkled in there, too.

And maybe part of me would have been embarrassed if I wasn't having such a good time. He was fun and exuded a light that I wanted to experience. It was warm and felt good against my skin.

I won the last point by banking the disc off the side and managing to sink it directly into the goal. Dropping my mallet, I tried not to gloat, as he'd accused me of. I picked up my drink and stepped around the table. Ryder met me in the middle.

I stuck out my hand for him to shake. "Good game."

But he ignored my offering and growled low in his throat as he wrapped his arm around my waist and pressed me to him. Without hesitation, he stooped and kissed me soundly. He was unbothered by anyone else, and I wished I could be that relaxed. But there was a nagging voice in the back of my head that said we were bound to get caught being so affectionate out in the open. Not even the dim lights or pounding music over the speakers were enough to hide us.

I didn't have the strength to pull away, though. Soft yet firm lips brushed mine, and my free hand squeezed his bicep.

We pulled away just before it became too much for such a family establishment.

"Why does your competitiveness turn me on so much?" he asked, and I could no longer ignore the definite hardness pressed against my hip.

"Ryder, I think everything I do turns you on at least a little bit."

His smile widened, and I matched it. "You're right."

"As always," I quipped which earned me a pinch to my side. I yelped and tried to jump back, but he grabbed my hand and laced our fingers together.

"Let's sit at the bar for a while," he said, and I nodded. Both of our drinks were nearly empty, and being the competitive assholes we were, we'd expended a lot of energy trying to beat one another.

We chose two seats at the end of the bar where Ryder swiveled the barstool for me to sit. "You keep doing things like that, and it starts to feel more like a date," I said. He took his seat and waved to the bartender who was headed our direction. He ordered us another round and sat back. I raised one eyebrow at the other obvious example of date-like behavior.

"So, you're saying I need to act like an asshole?"

"Yes, exactly. Let me struggle getting onto the barstool, order my own drinks, pay for my own food."

He took the final sip of his whiskey and leaned back in his seat. His navy-blue T-shirt pulled tight over his chest, and his legs spread just enough to make me want to slip between them.

"Not going to happen, but thanks for the feedback."

The bartender returned with our new drinks and retrieved our empty glasses. I was mid-sip when Ryder asked, "Is that how Scott treated you?"

Tequila nearly came out of my nose at the abrupt change in subject, but I managed to choke it down. It burned, and my eyes watered as I set my glass on the bar top.

"What are you talking about?"

"Did Scott treat you like crap when he took you out? He felt comfortable showing up at your house and asking you to dinner, so I'm guessing you've been out with him before."

Spinning the tiny straw in my glass, I had no idea what to tell him or what he really wanted to hear. "Actually, I've never met him a day in my life. So odd. People are extremely forward these days."

"Caroline," Ryder chided, and my eyes bounced to his. He'd leaned forward in his seat, facing me but with an elbow on the bar. Serious, intent eyes held mine.

With a sigh, I took another sip and turned more toward him. Enough that my knees fit between his.

"No, he didn't treat me any particular way. Every time we went out, he pulled my chair out, bought the meal, paid for my ride home."

Ryder nodded, and I wished we weren't having the conversation at all, but especially not there. The music was loud enough it was hard to hear yourself think let alone speak to another person.

"So, why can't I do it?"

Because it means more coming from you, I thought but didn't say out loud.

"I'll let you buy my drinks if it'll make you feel better," I said instead.

He put his hand against his chest and feigned relief. "Wow, perfect. That's exactly what I wanted."

I tossed my hands in the air and nudged his knee with mine. He dropped his hand and reached for mine, taking two of my fingers between his. My chest loosened a little bit when that easy smile once again found his lips.

"It's not a dick-measuring contest," I said. "Just because he bought me expensive dinners, doesn't mean I expect the same from you."

Ryder's eyes narrowed, and his smile took on a far more devious, calculating quality. I immediately stiffened in my seat and prepared for the next words out of his mouth.

"But if it was a dick-measuring contest…"

My sigh was loud enough to be heard over the music. What a poor choice of words on my part. "I know men don't often believe this, but I promise, size is not always most important when determining if the sex is or will be good."

He nodded and continued stroking my fingers that were resting on his knee. "Fair enough, but my curiosity is killing me, so humor me. Head-to-head, no pun intended, which would you choose? Using whatever factors you see fit to decide."

I took another sip of my drink to give me more time to contemplate my answer. Not that it was really a contest, but I was trying to decide whether the truth was the best option. Fortunately, or unfortunately, I didn't know, there was just enough alcohol running through my bloodstream that my filter had been significantly altered.

"I'm here with you, aren't I?"

When I glanced back at him, Ryder appeared subtly triumphant, and if I wasn't mistaken, there was a blush darkening the apples of his cheeks just above his stubble.

"That you are," he said in a low voice that sent a shiver of desire through me. His fingers against my hand slowed, and his eyes darkened. "You're saying you're not here because of my winning personality and exceptional *not* date choosing skills?"

My eye roll only made him smile wider. "I only tolerate those parts."

"Okay, so just so we're clear. I'm better in bed than expensive-suit-wearing, six-figure-salary, five-course-dinner, Scott?"

Another sarcastic, snippy remark was on the tip of my tongue, but behind the playfulness in Ryder's eyes was something more. Something akin to worry or anticipation for my answer. And the feeling that sat heavy in my chest and my stomach when I was around him made me want to extinguish it.

"You are much better in bed than...Scott." *Anyone,* I almost said but caught myself. It was a step too far. Although I hadn't said the word outright, Ryder caught the change in my voice and tone. Like it wasn't what I meant to say.

Thankfully, he didn't question it further. "We can finish these," he said, motioning to our drinks in front of us. "Then we can go back to your place, or mine, and put my much better, highly superior dick to good use."

I laughed and blamed my blush on the alcohol in my system, not the images that were conjured just by Ryder mentioning his highly superior dick.

"Although my apartment probably isn't a good idea. It's a maze of boxes and other random shit in piles."

"When do you move?"

"In two days. Connor, Theo, and my mom will be there bright and early Saturday morning to help me pack the U-Haul and drive it across town."

Across town, not across the country. And somehow, closer to me. The offices of the engineering firm that hired him were on my side of the city. If he'd stayed in his apartment near campus, he'd have at least an hour commute one way. It only made sense for him to find something new. And the fact that it was closer to me was just a perk.

"Do you need any more help?"

He gave me a toothy grin before he sipped his drink. "No,

we've got it covered, although I enjoy your company, so I wouldn't be sad if you happened to stop by."

"I think I'd need a reason to be there. Not just 'stop by,' but I can help you unpack after."

"Perfect," he said and leaned forward, grazing his lips over mine in a sweet, chaste kiss. "You can put your touch on it, too."

"My touch?" He chased my lips as I leaned back, searching for another. He tugged me forward, and I couldn't resist.

He hummed against my mouth and the chaste kiss was on the verge of something neither of us knew how to stop. We were both just tipsy enough to be happy and carefree.

"Yes, your touch. I think it would be nice to have in my new place."

He wanted me in his space. My touch, as he called it. But I knew what he meant and the way he said it. Like he wanted me to linger there long after I was gone.

"Like when I look around, I can still see you there," he continued, confirming my interpretation.

And it felt good to be wanted that much. It felt…

Abruptly, I stood, nearly stumbling from the chair. Ryder jolted to catch me, but I was able to right myself before falling flat on my face.

"Sorry, bathroom," I muttered. I started walking, but Ryder caught my arm, and my heart stalled.

"That way," he said, pointing the other direction. I spun and smiled as I walked the way he indicated. Around the bar and down a long hallway lined with photos of random people smiling, obviously posed, and playing games.

A woman was pushing out of the bathroom as I walked in, and in my haste, I almost ran her over. She scoffed, unappreciative of my tight-lipped smile and apology.

Unbothered by her annoyance, I continued into the bathroom and found the first empty stall. With the door shut and locked behind me, I finally let out the shaky, labored breath I'd been holding.

The beat of the music playing in the entire establishment was just as loud in the bathroom and drowned out everything else. Except my thoughts, the incessant, stupid thoughts.

I'd been careless. Thinking that we could keep it casual was foolish. Ryder meant more to me than almost any other man had. At least anyone in the last decade, and that itself was already a bad start.

A man that meant that much to me was bound to leave. I knew better, but I didn't seem to care about my rules when it came to Ryder. Around him, the past was nonexistent, and the lessons I'd learned from it were inconsequential.

He made it easy to think that there could be something more.

Running my hands through my hair, I breathed in through my nose and out my mouth. I did that several times, but it was unsuccessful at calming my racing heart. Wherever I learned that supposed technique, they were lying.

We couldn't keep doing what we were, that much I knew for sure. But what I couldn't decide was what I should do about it. Tonight solidified what I already knew. We were both bound to get hurt when it ended. Any faith I had that we could walk away without it had vanished. As had my willing suspension of disbelief.

When I said it would end badly, I didn't want to be right. Breaking Ryder's heart would shatter mine, too.

I used the restroom and stepped out of the stall. Walking up to the sink, I glanced at the mirror. Although I looked the same, I felt completely different. Not that I'd resolved anything, but I could feel and see the resignation hanging over me.

I washed my hands and took another unhelpful breath before I stepped back out into the hallway. The entire walk back to the bar, I braced myself and prepared to see him once again. Still unsure what I was going to do but knowing what I should. I turned the corner and came to a stop.

Ryder was gone. His barstool was empty, but both of our drinks were still there. I continued slowly walking toward our seats and finally spotted him a few feet away from our barstools. He was standing in front of a row of capsule machines. The ones where you paid a quarter and got a temporary tattoo or the world's worst candy.

He was turning the handle when I came to a stop next to him.

"What are you doing?" I asked, but he didn't respond. He leaned down and lifted the metal lid, letting it clang back down after he'd retrieved the little plastic globe holding his prize. A few other plastic containers were sitting on top of the machine.

"You went to the bathroom, and I saw these here. I couldn't resist. I remember begging my mom to let me get something, *anything* when I was a kid," he began, popping open the little container and surveying the contents. "We didn't have a lot of money for a really long time—perks of having teenage parents—but these were cheap, just a quarter, so most of the time when I asked, she said yes."

He must have been excited about his prize because he smiled wide, and my heart did a weird stutter thing that I didn't particularly care for.

"Here," he said. "It's for you."

The prize he'd won was a silver ring with a cute little light purple flower in the center. It was nothing more than nickel with glued on jewels, but it was sweet. Too sweet.

"You don't have to wear it or anything," he clarified. "But it just reminded me of you. It feels stupid now that I'm saying it out loud and watching you hold it."

My heart was doing that stuttering thing again, only more violently. So violently that I thought I was having a heart attack. Then my stomach flipped, and I considered rushing back to the bathroom in case I puked.

Why did he have to be so *good*? Why did he have to make me feel things?

It was a goddamn fake ring, and somehow it made me want to wrap my arms around his neck and press my lips to his.

I'd realized I'd been quiet for too long, clutching the ring between my fingers, when I looked up and recognized the dejection on his face. All at once, everything inside me wanted to fix that.

"Thank you. It's not stupid," I said quietly and tested the ring on a few different fingers before I realized it fit perfectly on my right ring finger. I wiggled my finger and let the light catch the jewels. It was my favorite color.

I cleared my throat and looked back at Ryder. I smiled up at him because it was hard not to. Then I remembered the pile of other, unopened prizes. "Looks like someone left their prizes behind," I said.

Ryder shrugged. "I couldn't manage to get that one," he said, pointing to the ring on my finger. "So, I kept trying."

Realization dawned. "You went through all those prizes because you wanted this one? For me?"

"Yes," he said like it was obvious, and he wasn't sure why I was questioning him.

Too fucking sweet, I thought again. And I let my urges win. I stepped closer and wrapped my arms around his neck. His hands landed on my hips like they were meant to be there, and I simply kissed him.

With every second we were connected, everything else floated another mile away. Any thoughts, feelings, ideas, I might have had minutes earlier were so far in the distance, they were nothing more than an echo.

Because all I could think or feel with Ryder's lips on mine and his arms wrapped around me was, *yes.*

TWENTY-SIX
SOMETHING TO LOOK FORWARD TO

Ryder

I TURNED THE HOMEMADE SPAGHETTI SAUCE DOWN TO A SIMMER AND hoped it would turn out. I made it the same way my mom always did, but nothing ever tasted as good as when she cooked it.

Pulling out the pasta from the pantry, I glanced around at my new place one last time. It was still sparse and filled with all my old stuff, but I'd deep cleaned and made sure it was as presentable as it could be.

That was why Caroline was coming over anyway. After almost three weeks at my new job, I had enough money to buy a few new things for my place and start making it my own. And I wasn't joking when I told her I wanted her to leave her touch. Glancing around my space and seeing her everywhere would be amazing.

My schedule since I'd started had been chaotic. Late nights and weekends were the norm while I was training and getting the hang of things. Although everyone told me it was temporary, and that the work I was putting in now would pay off, it felt never-ending. This was the first Friday night I hadn't been either out with coworkers, trying to be friendly, or working late.

Not to mention, Caroline was in the midst of the summer wedding rush which meant she spent the weekdays preparing for the weddings she coordinated on the weekends.

Between both of our jobs, we'd missed each other at almost every moment. I'd seen her once since our arcade *not* date, and it happened to be at my mom and Theo's, also known as my childhood home.

She'd been drinking wine with my mom and painting their primary bedroom when I dropped by to return their dolly they'd lent me during the moving process. At some point, we found ourselves alone, and I wasted no time pushing her up against a wall—one not wet with paint—and kissing her until the ache in my stomach somewhat eased.

It wasn't nearly enough, but we quickly ran out of time when I heard my mom coming back down the hallway.

That was a week and a half ago, and I was craving her something fierce. All the texts and phone calls and one FaceTime in which I jacked off while she fingered herself in the bathtub, was great but they didn't extinguish my desire.

Lost in memories, I hadn't started the pasta like I planned when there was a knock on the door. I dropped the bag immediately and jogged through the kitchen. I took a steadying breath before I yanked the door open, but the breath did little to help when I saw her.

She was dressed casually in a white tee and light wash jeans with a bag clutched in her hands. Her hair freely fell around her face and just above her shoulders, but my eyes zeroed in on her eyes, grayer in the evening light, and the smile that graced her lips.

It wasn't my plan to jump her—for lack of a better description—but fuck, I couldn't help it when she smiled at me like that or when she greeted me with a low, "Hey, Trouble."

Reaching forward, I ushered her inside and quickly closed

the door. Simultaneously, I flipped the lock and backed her up against the wall in the entryway. It was reminiscent of those few seconds we got in my mom's bedroom, but I didn't care. I just wanted to touch her, feel her under my fingers, and taste her lips.

Her bag thudded to the floor as I slanted my mouth over hers. Automatically she opened for me, sweeping her tongue against mine, I moaned in approval. Her hands ran up my chest, and her arms wrapped around my neck. My hands were everywhere else, running up her sides and over her stomach. I braced them just below the curve of her breasts and felt her heart beating wildly in her chest.

She nipped at my bottom lip, and I growled into her mouth as I lifted her into my arms. Her legs tightened around my hips, and I walked us the few feet into the kitchen. Our kiss was the culmination of three long weeks without much. I sat her on the counter and yanked her to the edge where I could feel the heat from between her thighs against my raging boner. The same one I'd had since she'd responded to my earlier invite.

Schedules that aligned made me hard.

Between kisses, Caroline laughed. "Hi to you, too."

My hands ran down her thighs, and the last thing I wanted to do was step away. But if I got started, we would never eat dinner, and I'd promised her a meal. I also hoped that she'd brought extra clothes and toiletries so she could stay the night.

I'd considered buying her a few essentials I knew she used, but that didn't send the signal that I was okay with keeping things casual. Although I didn't think it made much of a difference, I knew how Caroline thought, and I was doing my damnedest not to spook her.

Even when it required swallowing and hiding all my desires and suppressing my instincts.

"Hi, pretty girl," I managed to say as I pulled away. God, she was fucking gorgeous. But even more so with her hair disheveled and her lips swollen and wet from our kiss. I'd shaved so she wouldn't have any beard burn around her mouth, but I liked that, too. When her skin was slightly red, it was more proof that she'd enjoyed our kiss.

I planned to kiss her so many times while she was here, and I didn't want it to hurt the next day.

"What do you think of the place?" I said, giving her one final kiss.

She giggled against my mouth, and the sound landed directly against my heart. "I haven't seen much of it yet. But your mouth feels just like I remember."

"Fucking hell," I said, dropping my head and pressing our foreheads together. "I've missed you." The words were out of my mouth before I could think about them, and as expected, Caroline stiffened under my palms. Her hands, wrapped around my biceps, loosened and dropped on top of mine where I held her thighs.

I had missed her. I missed her so much every time we went too long without seeing one another. But my plan to keep my cool was harder when I was just happy to be in her presence again. I was out of practice holding my tongue. It was easier over text and on the phone, I had time to contemplate my answers.

I wasn't sure why her urge was to automatically deflect every time the conversation strayed inches deeper than surface level, but it did. And figuring it out required a more substantial conversation that she was dying to prevent.

"Did you miss me, or did your cock miss me?" she purred, letting her fingers trail up my hand and linger over the outline of my dick through my jeans.

Momentarily, my thoughts took a turn. I could think about little else when she was touching me.

"Why can't it be both?" I asked. My eyes fell shut, and she tightened her grip. But only for a moment before her hand disappeared, and she pushed me backward.

"Give me the grand tour," she said, and I helped her off the counter. I took her hand and stepped out of the kitchen.

Waving my hand in front of me, I motioned to the room we'd just been in. "Here's the kitchen."

She shook her head but examined the room, nonetheless. She ran her free hand over the edge of the granite island. "I like it. It's really open," she said.

The kitchen opened directly to the living room which extended out into a patio with double French doors. To the right was my bedroom, which was slightly larger than my previous room, and the bathroom that opened into my room and out into the living room. One day I'd be able to afford something more than a one-bedroom, but I was only one person. I didn't need much more.

It didn't take long to guide her through my little space. But she ooo'ed and ahh'ed, pointing out the upgrades and improvements from my old place.

She didn't point out the picture of us I'd printed from graduation. It was the one where I'd asked her to kiss me, and she'd explicitly said no while her eyes said something different. I knew she saw it, she paused long enough that I was able to follow her gaze, but she didn't say anything.

Knowing she was coming over, I'd moved it from my bedside table to the dresser across the room.

"I'm sorry, I don't have anywhere to sit," I said as we walked back into the kitchen. "Maybe barstools should be the first thing we try to find."

"That and curtains if you want to sleep past seven." I grabbed a pot from a cabinet next to the stove and began filling it with water. Caroline toed off her shoes and hopped up on the counter next to me, in the same spot I'd set her down earlier. Reaching behind her, she pulled her laptop out of her bag and opened it on her lap.

While I started the pasta and made sure the sauce wasn't burning or sticking, Caroline explained her ideas.

"I already bookmarked a few things I think you'd like. These barstools that have a gray cushion and lighter brown wood. They're kind of midcentury modern, but I think they're the vibe you're going for. And I think cream curtains would look best. You also need lamps. Using the overhead lights are horrible and should be avoided at all costs—what?"

She abruptly stopped talking and looked up from her computer. I hadn't realized I'd ceased stirring the sauce in favor of staring at her and watching her animatedly talk about furniture for my apartment.

"Just listening," I said, shaking my head. "So, I need lamps?"

She blinked and licked her lips. She stared at me for a moment like she knew I was lying. Like she somehow managed to learn telepathy and read my mind to figure out I was actually thinking thoughts similar to, *I like you in my space. I want you in my space. Please stay.*

Maybe not those exact thoughts, but something very similar.

"Yes, you need lamps," she continued, and I made it a point to keep cooking as we talked. I started the garlic bread and cooked the chicken, again just the way my mom did.

Caroline turned her screen every once in a while to show me a piece she thought would look good or to explain why it wasn't going to work. By the time I had plated the food and was arranging it the best I could on the coffee table—the limited furniture I did have—we'd ordered most of the things I needed and planned to thrift the rest.

She curled up on one side of the couch, and I sat on the other.

"This is amazing," Caroline complimented. "Don't tell your mom this, but I think this is better than hers," she said around a mouthful of food that I found oddly endearing.

I chuckled around my own bite. "I won't say anything. She would not take kindly to that information."

"So, how have your first few weeks of work been?"

I nodded. "Good…"

Caroline glanced up from her food with her eyebrows raised,

her incredulous look spearing right through me. She made me cave without a word.

With a sigh, I said, "It really is good. I like the company and my coworkers, but it's a lot. Moving and starting a new job, I needed a night off already."

She reached for her wineglass and took a long sip. "Welcome to the next thirty plus years of your life! Aren't you looking forward to it?"

"Working until I die?"

"Yup."

"I couldn't think of a better way to spend my life."

Her smile widened, and she took another bite. Humming around her fork, she shut her eyes slowly like she was savoring the flavor. "If you want some unsolicited advice," she began, looking back at me. "It will get easier. You'll figure out whether you love your job or not, and then you'll make a change if you need to. Just don't spend your life doing something you hate."

"Is that how you started your own business?"

She shrugged. "Sort of. I wanted to start a company that was inclusive to anyone and everyone. No matter who you are or what your budget, you deserve to have the event of your dreams. So, when the right...investor came along, I jumped. I also realized that although I work well with others, I like to be in charge."

I slid my empty plate on the coffee table and settled back with my glass of wine. "I know you do," I said with a smile. "Did you always know you wanted to be an event planner?"

"Yes, I came out of the womb wanting to plan elaborate parties and gorgeous weddings." She slid her empty plate onto the coffee table and clasped her wineglass with both hands, propping feet up on the cushion between us. My couch wasn't too large, so the tips of her toes almost grazed my thigh. "I knew in college, and after I graduated, I got a job at a wedding planning company. My first wedding, I knew it made sense for me."

"So, you still enjoy it just as much now as you did then?"

She tipped her glass back and took a sip. Her tongue darted out and ran over her lower lip, collecting the excess wine and making me consider what she'd taste like right then. I bet the wine would taste even better on her tongue.

"I enjoy it more now than I ever did back then. My first job didn't…" She cleared her throat and glanced to her left. The only thing over there was the TV, but it wasn't on. She looked everywhere but back to me. That was until she swallowed and took a shallow, forced breath. "It didn't end well, so yeah, I like it much better now."

There were so many follow-up questions on the tip of my tongue. I knew Caroline so well, but her past, she kept close to her chest. Even in the time I'd spent with her family, they didn't spare many details aside from the occasional high school story or anecdote from childhood.

I wanted to know everything about her. The good, the bad, and everything in between.

But she didn't give me an opportunity to press. Not that she would have answered any of my questions anyway.

"So, what about you? Did you pop out of the womb wanting to be an engineer? Actually, I distinctly remember when you were probably sixteen, your mom told me you wanted to be a teacher."

With a sigh, my head fell back onto the couch cushion. "Yeah, I'm not entirely sure why. I thought maybe I could coach either baseball or swimming and teach, too. I haven't completely put aside the idea of one day teaching, but I think I'd get my master's and become a professor instead. Teaching children, even high school, sounds terrifying."

I finished off my glass and slipped it onto the table next to my plate. I was enjoying our conversation too much to get up and clean. It would be there until I did it and that was fine with me. I liked the little bubble we were in.

Caroline tracked the movement. When I leaned back, her partially lidded eyes followed me.

"I really am glad things are going well," she said, touching the edge of her glass to her lower lip.

"Me too." My voice was softer because all I could think about was her goddamn mouth. One small movement, and it was like she had me in a trance. A fucking siren singing a song made specifically for me.

"Do you want more wine?" she asked. Her eyes darted back down to my empty glass, but I kept watching her.

"Maybe in a little while."

She hummed and pushed up to her knees. My breath hitched, and my pulse was pounding in my neck and farther south. But I didn't move as she crawled toward me skillfully managing not to spill the red wine on my couch. When she reached me, she slung her left leg over my hips and settled on top of me.

TWENTY-SEVEN
SHARE LIKE A GOOD BOY

Ryder

I MASSAGED MY WAY UP HER LEGS, FROM HER KNEES UNTIL I PALMED that beautiful bend in her hips where her ass curved. Her fingers dug into my hair, dragging through it with care and tenderness. My eyes fell shut as her nails scraped my scalp. But they flew back open when she gripped it at the root and pulled back.

My head hit the back cushion, and I was staring directly up at her. Her blonde hair was hanging around her face, and her eyes were dark and intent on my face. She leaned forward and acted like she was going to kiss me, but at the last second, she turned, leaving me chasing a kiss she never planned to return.

Instead, she leaned down until her mouth was level with my ear, and I could feel her hot breath against my cheek and her breasts against my chest. My grip on her hips tightened.

"Don't move, Trouble," she instructed.

She didn't require an answer from me. I wasn't going to move when she was sitting on top of me making demands I was more than okay with. She leaned back and ran her hand over my jaw, trailing her thumb over my lower lip and dragging my mouth open.

Whatever she wanted, I was going to give it to her.

She kept her thumb beneath my lower lip, silently requesting that I keep my mouth open. A pleased smile tilted one side of her mouth before she turned and tilted the wineglass to her lips. She took a large sip then looked back down to me.

When I didn't see her throat bob, I realized what she was doing, and my cock responded in kind. I stuck my tongue out to prepare for her offering. Her eyes glinted brighter as she watched me eagerly awaiting what I knew she was about to give.

Thankfully, I didn't have to wait long. She wasn't moving slowly, but the seconds felt more like minutes. I sat there and watched her with my mouth open, offering myself to her and waiting for anything she planned to give me.

Finally, she leaned over, poised her mouth above mine, and fed me the wine. My hips pressed up to meet hers, and a little moan caught in my throat as the fruity, tart flavor hit my tongue.

She let the last drop fall onto my tongue and wrapped her hand around my throat. Her hand wasn't large enough to make an impact, to reduce my airway or decrease blood flow, but it was enough to reinforce the power dynamic.

"Swallow," she instructed in a low, soft voice. So, I did. Her gaze bounced between my lips and my eyes as she felt and watched me swallow. "Good?"

I licked my lips and nodded, still not moving my head. "It tastes so much better that way."

She smiled and took another sip. The moment the edge of the glass touched her lip, I opened my mouth. She slipped her fingers through my hair and spit into my mouth as she ground her ass over my cock.

I swallowed quickly, not waiting for her direction a second time, and muttered out a low, "fuck," before I leaned forward and slanted my mouth over hers. It was a long, thorough kiss that I felt everywhere. My tongue swept against hers, and she managed to surrender a fraction of control.

"Hold on," she murmured against my mouth. Pulling back, she swigged the last of her wine and twisted to set it on the table. While she turned, I let my hands wander up and down her body. Not in any specific direction or with a purpose in mind except feeling every part of her I could.

The desire simmering beneath my skin was at the brink of boiling over. I'd never felt need so carnal and consuming. My hands shook with restraint, and when Caroline righted herself, I couldn't get my mouth on hers quickly enough. She gave as good as she got, and I trailed my lips over her jaw and down her neck. She let loose those gorgeous sounds I loved.

"Yes, you're right," I mumbled into her skin. "My cock missed you, too. My entire body missed yours."

I said the words but realized how dumb they sounded. Caroline seemed to understand, though, because she moaned out the prettiest, "yes" I'd ever heard.

"Show me," she said, and it took me a few seconds to register her request.

"Show you?" I finally asked.

She clasped my cheeks and tilted my head back to look down at me. But her hips kept moving. A taunting, slow pace that made me buck up against her not of my own volition.

"I know we just talked about how much I like control, and I usually do, but the way you're looking at me right now. It's like I can see all the dirty things you want to do to me. Like I can feel you holding back. I don't want you to hold back. I want you to show me how much you missed me."

Desire clouded my thoughts, and my brain felt like it was working at half its normal speed.

Caroline knew what she was doing, though. "Come on, Ryder. Be a good boy, and fuck me like you want to."

And my restraint snapped. I stood, and Caroline gasped. She didn't even have time to wrap her legs around me because I dropped her back on the couch in the spot I'd just vacated. Her eyes widened, but I didn't stop moving. I had one intent, one purpose, and it was to get her naked and my head between her legs as soon as possible.

"Take your shirt off," I demanded as I worked the button of her jeans open. I slipped them down her legs and tossed them across the room. When I saw the light-purple lace panties, I didn't wait to drop to my knees.

I pressed my palms to the inside of each of her thighs and eyed the matching bra. Her tits spilling over the lace cups, and she looked fucking delectable nestled in the corner of the couch. "I knew this was your favorite color," I said, running my tongue over her panties. Her salty, sweet taste exploded on my tongue.

"How did you know?" she panted.

Another firm lick of my tongue over her center, and she bucked her hips. My smile was hidden by her perfect legs. "You wear it all the damn time. You paint your nails this color, and your phone case is the same."

"God, I didn't know you watched me so much. It's a little creepy, don't you think? I'm nervous that you're—"

I cut her off with a growl, wrapping my arms around her hips and yanking her ass up off the couch. "Shut the fuck up and let me eat your perfect pussy."

She had nothing left to say after that. All words and arguments forgotten when I pushed the fabric to the side and buried my tongue in her cunt. God, I wanted to stay there forever. I'd die a happy man with my head between her legs.

I spread her wider and drew tiny little circles over her clit, taking two fingers and thrusting them inside her. She was wet and my fingers easily slipped in. She moaned and tried to buck when I crooked both fingers. It was easy enough to find that soft, pronounced spot just a few inches in.

My life was complete now that I knew Caroline Grant's pussy inside and out.

I sucked her clit between my lips and then bit down just hard enough to amplify every sensation. The muscles in her legs and stomach tensed, and I knew she was close. I looked up her body, at the glorious sight of her, and watched the pleasure ripple across her features.

Lips parted and eyes set on me, her brows were scrunched together, and pink had stained her cheeks and chest. I pushed my fingers deeper, fucking her harder. I laid her back down on the couch and let her ride my face while I reached for my belt and button of my jeans with my free hand.

With a choked cry, she strangled my fingers and coated them with her orgasm. I couldn't wait another second. Before she'd finished coming, I was tugging her off the couch and around to the side. I pressed her stomach to the arm and bent her over until her face was in the cushion and her ass was pointed up at me.

I ran my palm over her ass and gripped my cock before I slid inside her in one swift thrust. I tugged my shirt over my head and enjoyed the view of my bare cock in her tight cunt.

That was when I realized my mistake.

"Fuck." I stopped and took a deep breath. "I forgot a condom."

Caroline lifted her head and tossed her hair over one shoulder to peer at me over the other. "I—I did, too. I don't think I've ever forgotten before."

"Me neither," I said and caught her eyes, watching the count-less thoughts flit behind them.

It fucking killed me, but I started to pull out. Inch by inch, I gritted my teeth and kept going. Her pussy was gripping me, doing its damnedest to keep me inside, and halfway there, her hand whipped backward and covered mine.

"Stop." I did. "I'm on the pill, and I've recently been tested. My results were clear. What about you?"

"Yeah, same," I said through a strangled breath. "Well, about my results, not the birth control. Although if I could take some of that burden I would. I don't like that you have to—"

"Ryder," she cut me off with a growl. "Can we talk about that later? I really need you to put your cock all the way inside me again."

"Mmm..." I hummed and dropped my jeans, managing to kick them and my briefs off without pulling out of her. "Yes, ma'am," I said. I smoothed my hands over her ass and slapped each cheek, spearing back inside her.

Without worrying about the lack of protection, I stared down at where her pussy stretched around my bare cock. I pulled out and watched the thick veins reappear until the mushroom head was stretching her entrance.

Caroline lay back down on the cushion, her face turned to the rest of the room and where I could watch her expression as I slowly pushed back in.

"Fuck," she cried. "I love the way you fill me. God, you feel so..." Her words broke off in a moan, and I joined her as I bottomed out.

"Come on, baby. Finish your sentence. What do I feel like?" I picked up my pace and wrapped my hands around the smallest part of her waist. Pushing her harder into the couch and the pillows beneath her stomach, I found a new, deeper angle.

She tried to speak again but couldn't find her voice between brutal thrusts.

"You got it. I believe in you, baby. Tell me."

She gritted her teeth and tried to push back into me, but the couch was *just* tall enough that she couldn't stand flat-footed and get the leverage she needed.

"You feel fucking perfect, and don't call me baby."

I licked my lips and smiled. I pressed harder, and she finally gave up her fight, stretching her arms out above her head and taking what I gave her.

"I thought I was in charge," I stated. "At least I know I feel perfect. Fucking this perfect cunt with this perfect, fat cock. You're so lucky, pretty girl. I'm so lucky."

Nudging the inside of her legs, I spread her wider and enjoyed the way my balls slapped against her clit and hood. I leaned forward and slowed to a deeper, more measured stroke that intentionally grazed every millimeter of her inner walls. I wanted to hit every nerve ending and pleasure point imaginable. Even the ones we hadn't yet discovered.

By the time she was falling apart again, I wanted tears in her eyes.

My body folded over hers, and I ran a tender hand down her spine. She shivered, and I weaved my fingers through her hair at the base of her neck. One hard pull and her back bowed, head craned backward. She propped her elbows beneath her and let her arms hold her weight.

My hold in her hair, my grip on her hip, and my thrusts were all unforgiving. I wanted her to feel me for days.

"Please, Ryder," she pleaded.

"What do you need, beautiful? Tell me."

She whimpered as her nails dug into the cushions. "More. Just...more."

A million different glorious ideas flashed behind my eyes. All of them included some version of *more*. But one stuck out.

My hand on her hip slipped around her stomach and made its way up her front until I wedged it in the small space where her bra had pushed her tits together. Then I wrapped it around her throat.

Using my grip on her throat and in her hair, I wrenched her head back. She stood, and my plan momentarily went out the window. With her sarcastic, sweet mouth so close, I couldn't help but kiss her. The kiss soft and tame compared to the relentless pounding her pussy was taking.

I pulled back, and the first shiny tears collected in her eyes. It made my cock throb and my balls draw up. Her lips were wet, and I removed my hand from her throat to shove my thumb in her mouth.

"Suck." One word and she closed her mouth around it. Caroline was nearly undone—a limp mess of desire and pleasure. But she still sucked my thumb like it was my cock, and like she'd receive a reward for being the best.

When I'd had enough, and I could feel the sensation of her

tongue through my entire body, she released my finger with a pop, and I shoved her back into the cushions. The pad of my thumb, wet thanks to the beautiful woman impaled on me, circled her ass, and she scrambled for something to hold onto.

"You don't want this, tell me now. We both know the word" —*lilac*, I thought but didn't say—"say it once or tell me no, and I stop."

She shook her head. "Fill me up. Finger my ass as you fuck my pussy."

"Fuck, you and your filthy mouth," I murmured as I teased the outer ring of that second hole. She pushed her ass harder into me as much as she could. Leaning over her, I spit onto her hole and spread it around with my thumb as I barely pushed inside.

My thrusts stuttered, and I had to force myself to keep moving as I worked my thumb inside her tight hole. She moaned, and her back tensed like she was struggling to keep herself still. But her body eventually gave into me and accepted my thumb.

My jaw went slack, and I dropped my head back to stare at the ceiling rather than where her body took me. A few deep breaths, and I wasn't any closer to control, but I had to do something.

Glancing back down, she was even more wet, and my cock easily slipped in and out of her. My thumb pulsed inside her other hole, and I ran my free hand down her hip. As my thrusts picked up strength and speed, I held onto her tight enough that there would possibly be bruises the shape of my fingers against her skin.

But she didn't seem to care. Both of us were lost in the plea-sure-filled haze. Our skin slapping and our combined sounds filling the space, I worried we'd break the couch. But I'd buy a new goddamn couch because I couldn't—*wouldn't*—stop.

"Please," she moaned, which turned into quiet, simple begging. "Please, please, *please*."

My balls drew up, and my cock thickened as my orgasm

made itself known. I tangled my fingers back into her hair and gripped it hard, shoving her face onto the couch and keeping her exactly where I wanted her. Her surrender was so beautiful.

A few more thrusts, and she was clenching around my cock and my thumb, milking both with an intense orgasm. An orgasm that triggered mine. It barreled down my cock, and I pumped inside her. I kept coming and coming until I couldn't believe there was anything left.

I stilled inside her, trying to control my breathing as I peered down at where I filled her. Her ass pulsed around my thumb, and her pussy squeezed the life out of my cock. I could feel my warm cum mixing with her arousal, and by some miracle, my dick kicked. The idea of pumping her full was too fucking erotic.

So erotic that I slowly pulled my thumb and then my cock free. Caroline groaned, and I dropped to my knees. Eye level with her swollen cunt, I ran a thumb over her each lip then spread her open.

"Push my cum out, pretty girl. Let me see it spilling out of you."

Her cunt constricted then relaxed, and slowly my release dripped down toward her clit. But I didn't let it get that far. I lapped up the cum seeping out of her and tongued her opening to capture as much as I could.

Fuck, we tasted so good together.

My legs shook as I stood, but I pushed through the weakness and reached for Caroline. Although she was limp and sated, she clambered off the couch and straightened in front of me. Her hair was rumpled, and her skin was flushed. She looked up at me through bleary eyes. A stray tear fell, and I tracked its progress down her cheek. It disappeared against her neck just above her collarbone.

The sight of that pretty little tear made me momentarily lose track of my intentions.

Fisting my hand in the back of her hair, I tilted her head back and eyed her lips. Like she knew exactly what I planned, and the cum I'd collected, her eyes sparkled.

"Are you going to share like a good boy?" she asked and opened her mouth, offering me her tongue.

Leaning over her, I dropped the mixture and proof of our pleasure onto her waiting tongue. She happily took every drop, and I bracketed my hand around her throat as she swallowed like she'd done to me earlier.

Then, because I couldn't stand not to, I kissed her, running my tongue against hers and giving her another taste. She leaned against me and wrapped her arms around my stomach as I cupped her cheeks. She was tired and pliable and so fucking sweet.

I kissed the corner of her mouth, her nose then her forehead as she tucked her face into the curve of my neck. She took one deep breath, then another.

"I missed you, too," she admitted in a quiet voice I barely heard in my silent apartment.

My heart beat a furious pace. In awe of her admission, I wanted to do anything but stand there. I wanted to lift her into my arms and make her repeat it over and over again until her voice was hoarse. I wanted her to keep going and admit that everything between us was already so far from casual that it was impossible to ignore.

I wanted her to admit that she was already mine, and I'd admit that I'd always been hers.

But none of that would happen. The realization was a punch to the gut if I'd ever felt one. I'd fucked her mercilessly and made her cry. That was how she'd come to confess one tiny feeling.

If that was what it took, I had to wonder what I'd have to do to make her admit the rest.

TWENTY-EIGHT

LILACS

Caroline

"Let's discuss the Peterson wedding on Monday. They have some...interesting ideas that are going to require more brain power than I have on a Thursday afternoon after a long week."

Addie smiled at me from across my desk and closed her laptop propped on her lap.

"Yeah, I reviewed their questionnaire. They want hot air balloons?" She tucked a piece of her blonde hair behind her ear and stood.

I shook my head and saved the document I'd been taking notes on. Out of the corner of my eye, I saw my phone light up. I picked it up just to make sure it wasn't work-related. It wasn't.

Ryder: Whatcha doin'?

I typed out a response to Ryder while I explained to Addie that was exactly why I couldn't handle it until the following week. I needed sleep and extra caffeine if I was going to discuss balloons filled with hot air flying through the sky. And all the safety requirements that go with them.

Me: Finishing up a meeting and hoping I don't fall asleep at my desk.

"Caroline?" Addie prompted, and I jerked my head up.

"Yes? Sorry, I was—"

"Smiling at your phone," she said with a smile of her own. "You don't have to give me any details, but it's nice to see you so happy."

My phone vibrated in my hand, likely with Ryder's response, but I didn't look down at it. I'd been caught once. I wasn't going to have her find me smiling at my phone again.

"Are you saying I'm not usually happy?" I joked, pressing my elbows to my desk and narrowing my eyes.

Addie took my joke in stride and waved me off. "Of course, you're rainbows and sunshine all the damn time. But recently, it's like you're, I don't know, floating on a cloud made of cotton candy."

Her description of my attitude took me off guard, and I choked out a surprised laugh. Getting dick on the regular would do that to a person. Especially when it was platinum, A+ dick.

"I don't think anyone has ever described me that way. Usually, it's workaholic or blunt, but I like the picture you paint better."

She shrugged. "Last question—is it the same guy who sent the flowers?"

She pointed to the bouquet of mostly light purple and pink lilacs sitting on the table in the middle of my office. They'd been delivered that morning, and I'd quickly hidden the card tucked inside them.

Lilac is my favorite color, too, pretty girl.

They were beautiful flowers, and the gesture made me smile. I would have hidden the bouquet, too, if it were possible and if everyone else in the office hadn't already seen it.

Realizing I wasn't going to answer, she straightened her pink skirt and white blouse. Turning for the door, she stopped halfway there. When she pivoted back around, worry creased her brows and hung across her features.

"Oh, I meant to tell you, I will be about an hour late to set up for the company party tomorrow night. I already talked to Sarah about it, and she said she'll make sure the caterer and staff know where to go."

"Sure, that's fine. I'll probably stop by after I finish with the Russell's rehearsal dinner. Everything okay?"

With my question, every indication that something was wrong disappeared, and her smile slipped back into place.

"Yeah, absolutely! Just…family stuff." She didn't wait around to provide more of an explanation. She reached for the glass door and pulled it open, stepping back into the hallway.

I was always concerned for my employees and their well-being, but Addie was special. She somehow managed two jobs, family issues I wasn't privy to, and a boyfriend who, for lack of a better description, was kind of an asshole.

As her employer, I did what I could without stepping on her toes or invading her privacy. Which meant I eavesdropped occasionally and watched for changes in her mood.

Remembering my unread text, I looked down at my phone.

Ryder: Sounds like you need coffee. I'll be there in three minutes.

My eyes went wide. The text had been sent more than three minutes ago. I furiously started typing back a response, telling him that he should by no means come to my office, especially right—

"Hey, pretty girl."

I didn't look up. I didn't need to. I set my phone down on my desk in front of me, my now pointless text staring up at me, and took a deep breath.

"What are you doing here?" I asked, standing from my desk and crossing to him. He stepped into my office, and I peered down the hallway before shutting the door behind him. Addie was probably about to leave, but I think we were the last two left.

Ryder held up the drink carrier with two coffees. "Bringing you coffee like I said I was."

He plucked one out and handed it to me. I took a tentative sip. An iced vanilla latte—my favorite. I turned and walked back to my desk, needing the distance between us.

Ryder had told me about his meeting downtown, so I wasn't surprised to see him in a dark-blue suit and a white button-down shirt. That didn't keep my body from reacting, though. His black hair was windswept and slightly messy, and his cheeks were flushed from the June heat. He looked damn good, thus the required distance between us.

Safely on the opposite side of my desk, I set my coffee on the edge and turned back to find him unabashedly staring at my ass. My ass did look better than normal in the fitted black dress, so I appreciated he noticed.

"You gave me the coffee. Now, unless there's something else…"

Completely ignoring me, Ryder set the carrier on the table next to the flowers and retrieved his coffee. He took a long sip and walked around the table, gazing at the flowers.

"I'm glad you got the flowers," he said with a coy smile he hid behind his coffee cup. I stayed silent and watched him watch me.

"You can't be here, Ryder," I said.

Like usual, he wasn't dissuaded by my bluntness. If I wasn't mistaken, his smile widened. Similarly, I didn't let his lack of reaction stop me.

"Your mom is going to be here any minute, so you should probably go." I pointed to the door and crossed my arms over my chest.

Ryder's eyebrows shot to his hairline. "My mom? Natalie?"

I nodded.

"What is she meeting you here for?"

Rolling my lips, I reached for my coffee and considered what I should tell him. What she was really meeting me for wasn't something I wanted to share with her son.

"We're going shopping," I said simply.

"Just shopping?"

I rolled my eyes and groaned. "You are so freaking nosy."

Ryder began walking toward me, and I had to quickly decide whether to keep the safe distance between us and head around my desk even though it would certainly show weakness. Or stand my ground and try my best not to react.

I chose the latter and held my breath as he came to stand in front of me, placing his coffee down near mine.

"I just don't believe you," he said. "I think you're coming up with excuses to make me leave."

"Although I wouldn't put it past me to do something like that," I admitted. "That's not what's happening now."

He stepped closer and reached for my waist before I had a chance to pull back. He gripped right above my hip and tugged me into him until it was just my crossed arms between us.

"So, you're just shopping? That's a little vague."

"You want to know what we're shopping for?" I asked, my patience and ability to bite my tongue gone. He didn't stop me, so I continued, "We're going shopping for lingerie, because she wants to—"

His hand appeared over my mouth, effectively cutting off my explanation. He grimaced, shaking his head and screwing his eyes shut, and I had the fleeting thought that his horrified expression was kind of cute.

"You're right," he said without opening his eyes. "I didn't need to know that."

He dropped his hand, and I smiled smugly. "Say that again."

He slowly opened and narrowed his eyes. His fingers tightened around my waist, and I had to work hard not to let him hear or see my breath catch or let my smile wobble.

"Tell you that you're right?"

I inclined my head and held his stare. He licked his lips, and my eyes inadvertently darted to them, watching his tongue slowly slip across his lower lip.

My ability to think straight was wholly compromised by his presence, let alone his proximity and how good he smelled and felt.

"You're right, Caroline." He dropped his voice, and I swallowed down my arousal. "You're so smart, brilliant, really, and driven and successful, and *so* fucking gorgeous it makes it hard to think straight."

With my folded arms still between us, that didn't keep Ryder from cupping the side of my face and running his thumb over my cheek. The moment his blue eyes landed on my lips, he leaned in. And I lost my mind for a second, because I dropped my arms to my sides and let him tug me closer as he pressed his mouth to mine.

A little grunt escaped his lips when my hips brushed against his cock, and I felt lightheaded. His urgent tongue swept against my mouth, and his palm flattened against the small of my back. That slow-churning pull in my gut that I always felt near him was at an all-time high. Not so much slow as it was consuming and impossible to ignore.

I slipped my hand over his that was still against my cheek and tilted my head to the side to deepen the kiss.

"Fuck, Car—" Ryder muttered against my mouth. But his words were cut short by a sound out in the hallway.

Instantly, he dropped his hands, and I stepped back, glancing over his shoulder to identify the noise. Not seeing anything, I took a labored breath and moved around the desk. I leaned to the left and peered down the hallway to see Natalie stooping to pick up her phone she must have dropped on her way to my office.

"It's your mom," I whispered. My heart was pounding. "So, you better fix *that*." I glanced quickly down at the outline of his noticeably hard cock pressing through his tight dress pants.

Ryder didn't look as horrified as I was that we'd almost been caught by his mother. But he did smooth a palm over his problem and readjust his slacks while I sat in my desk chair and logged into my computer that had long gone dark.

"God, I cannot stand you sometimes," I muttered under my breath, attempting to type my password for a third time. Shaking hands made the process difficult.

Ryder groaned and dropped his head back. "I told you, you can't say stuff like that to me. It just turns me on."

My retort fell dead on my tongue when the door opened, and Natalie stepped inside.

"Oh, Ryder, hi. I didn't realize you...what are you doing here?"

God, we were lucky. *So* fucking lucky that we had a built-in excuse for Ryder being in my office.

"We had a few last-minute things we had to talk about for Stephen and Miles's wedding," I said casually. Or at least, that's what I was going for.

"And I had a meeting in the area, so I thought it'd be easier to just drop by," Ryder added smoothly. He was so much better than I was at lying to his mom. Likely from years of practice, but also because he was less concerned about her reaction if she found out about all the sneaking around we did behind her back.

Guilt made me nauseous just thinking about it.

"That's convenient," Natalie said as she crossed to Ryder. They hugged, and I wanted to puke. "How was your day?" she asked her son, and I tried to entertain myself by responding to emails that could have waited and randomly clicking around on my home screen to appear busy.

I used the length of their short conversation to try to get my mind right and to push away the guilt at least for the time being. Not that I could do much more than that—it always came back.

"Care?" Natalie called my name, and my head popped up. I could tell by her tone—and Ryder's barely suppressed smile—that she must have said my name several times.

"Yeah?"

Natalie was across the room and standing in front of the very large, purple bouquet. "Who are these from?"

"A client," I said quickly.

She raised her eyebrows, and her smile broadened. I knew immediately she didn't believe me. She tucked a piece of dark hair behind her ear and leaned forward to smell the flowers. "A client or a man?"

"What do you mean? I—"

"I mean, I don't believe you, but that's fine you don't have to tell me."

Somehow, I managed to keep my expression neutral even with Ryder's eyes burrowing into the side of my face. "Fine, it was a man. Are you happy?"

Natalie's smile widened. "Is there a card?"

Fuck, fuck, fuck, I thought.

"I didn't see one either," Ryder piped up. Slowly, I turned toward him and gave him my most menacing look that he, for some reason, seemed to enjoy. It didn't have its desired effect, but at least he knew that I didn't appreciate his commentary.

"There wasn't a note," I said. "The delivery guy dropped it on his way up. But...I know who they're from. A card wouldn't have been necessary." I knew I had to give Natalie something, otherwise she wouldn't drop the topic. And with Ryder in the room, I was feeling pressure from all sides.

She pursed her lips and nodded. But I knew that look all too well—she'd descend into a million questions later, and I had to prepare for each of them. I began compiling answers as we stood there.

Fuck Ryder and his gorgeous bouquet.

"Okay, well, should we go? Unless there are other wedding

details you all need to discuss?" Natalie clutched her bag in one hand and looked between me and Ryder.

"Nope," I said quickly. "We're done. Let me just grab my bag, and we can go."

"I guess I'll head out as well. Bye, Mom, love you," Ryder said, stooping to hug his mom once again. He stuffed his hands into his pockets and strode toward the door. But before he walked out, he glanced back at me over his shoulder. I hoped Natalie didn't note the way I tensed when his eyes landed on me.

"I'll talk to you soon, Caroline."

He left, and I finally felt like I could breathe again. Shaking away the lingering feelings, I grabbed my purse and shut down my computer, stuffing it into my bag.

I could still hear Ryder's footsteps on the tile floor in the hallway when Natalie asked, "So, who's the guy?"

"Just a guy."

She scoffed, and I pushed my chair underneath my desk, straightening a few things before I looked up at her. She gave me an incredulous look.

"Whattt?" I asked, drawing the word out and slumping my shoulders. "What do you want from me? He's just a guy, Nat."

The words felt wrong the moment I said them. They didn't just sour on my tongue. They made my stomach turn and my head hurt.

"The way you just said that. I don't believe you," Natalie said. I hadn't thought to control my voice. I didn't think that it would shake over the words. "But, whatever. If you don't want to tell me, you don't have to."

"Nat, I—" I began, stepping toward her, but she waved me off then reached for my hand. She wrapped her fingers around mine and squeezed once. Her soft smile hit me directly in the heart.

"I'm serious. You don't have to tell me everything, although that won't keep me from being curious and wanting to know. I just...you can tell me when you're ready. *If* you ever are ready or *if* it becomes something worth telling."

TWENTY-NINE
SUPER SLY

Caroline

MUSIC CARRIED INTO THE BALLROOM FROM THE SMALLER SPACE JUST
down the hall that was being utilized for the rehearsal dinner. It
was a room that wasn't as grand but was just as beautiful and
looked out onto the courtyard as well.

White bulb lights were strung from tree to tree over the gray
stone, highlighting the pristine, recently manicured garden.
Wisteria that the owners were careful to take the best care of
climbed the ivy-covered walls and delicately wrapped around
the windows. I'd stood next to the fountain earlier in the night as
the sun was setting and stared up at the beauty and grandeur of
the home.

Now, I was staring longingly at the beautiful doors and wall
of windows looking out onto the courtyard while standing in the
reception hall, trying my damndest to make sure it was perfect
for the next day.

"What do you think?" Addie asked, interrupting my
yearning thoughts.

I turned to find her across the large, circular table we'd been
working on. The centerpiece, minus the flowers which would be

added the following morning, was in the center—the candles, the greenery, the table numbers—were all there and perfectly placed.

"It looks amazing," I said, straightening the tablecloth and pushing in one of the cushioned chairs.

"Only twelve more to go," she said. Addie smiled—I rarely ever saw her without a smile—but I could also see how tired she was beneath it. We were both exhausted.

We'd been decorating and coordinating all day. Greeting the wedding party and family when they arrived and ushering them to their rooms, then organizing the rehearsal dinner and ensuring more guests found their way to the party.

All the while, we prepared the reception hall and made sure the day of the wedding went as smoothly as possible. My checklist felt never-ending, but we were slowly ticking away at it.

I mustered the best smile I could and readjusted the bun I'd messily thrown my hair into.

"The rehearsal should be over soon, then Sarah and everyone else will be able to help us."

"Did someone say help?"

I startled at the voice. I hadn't heard any of the doors open, so when I spun, the last person I expected to see was Ryder striding toward us. He had his hands in the pockets of his slacks, and he was missing the tie I'd seen him wearing earlier. The top button of his shirt was undone, showing off the column of his throat and tan skin.

An easy smile spread across his face, and I felt it down my arms to the tips of my fingers and all the way to my toes.

"You're the best man, you should be enjoying the rehearsal dinner," I said. "Making sure the grooms are happy and stress-free."

Ryder stopped in front of me, and I caught his eyes flitting down my body. I wasn't much to see in a mostly shapeless black dress and sensible shoes. It was something that both looked nice for when I was helping with the rehearsal and was easy to move around in while setting up the reception. But from the way Ryder looked at me, you would think I was wearing that bikini again.

"I've done my part. It's Theo's turn. So, put me to work," he said, stretching his arms out to his sides like he was an offering.

Like she could feel my hesitation, Addie chimed in, "We do kind of need the help, Caroline. I can feel myself fading, and I know you are, too."

Since that afternoon in my office when we'd almost been caught by Natalie, I'd been extra careful. Ryder and I both had been. We didn't spend any extensive time at my house. Instead, I went over to his new apartment and parked far enough away from his unit that even if Natalie did randomly show up, she wouldn't see my car. He also didn't show up at my office unannounced anymore or try to sneak a quick kiss when we were both at Natalie's.

The two times we had been there at the same time, it had been hard to resist, but we managed.

And being together in the reception hall while his mom was down the hall as Theo's date was not a good idea. I just hoped Addie would be enough of a buffer.

"Okay, you can help."

On the other side of the table, Addie used her last bit of energy to clap and jump up and down. "Great! I have heavy stuff you can lift."

Ryder dutifully removed his suit jacket and tossed it over one of the chairs before rolling his sleeves up. Addie walked back toward the front doors, motioning to the boxes I knew she wanted help with and giving Ryder instructions over her shoulder. He wasn't listening, though, and frankly, neither was I.

My eyes were glued to his newly exposed forearms. The lights were lower in the ballroom than they were elsewhere on the property. I was getting a headache, so I'd turned them down earlier. But I could still see the dark hair dusting his skin and the muscles tensing beneath it.

It had been two days since I'd felt his arms around me. Two days, and I was going mad with the need to feel them again.

I swallowed and blinked away the sudden rush of arousal. When I looked back up, Ryder caught my eye and had noted where I was staring.

"Keep looking at me like that, pretty girl, and I don't care who else is in the room. I'll throw you down on that table right now."

I rolled my eyes and crossed my arms over my chest. "Don't touch that table. It took us at least twenty minutes to put together."

He glanced around the room and pointed to one of the tables we hadn't gotten to yet. "That one okay?"

"Yes, perfect."

"Ryder?" Addie called. He turned toward her, but his eyes lingered on me as he walked away.

And they didn't move from me for the next hour as we worked. We finished the tables and every other piece we still had left including the seating chart and the arches around the two main entrances to the room that would be strung with flowers the next day.

Ryder and Addie were finishing up the final touches as I sat on the floor and proceeded to lay down on the cool wood. Every part of me was exhausted, but it was mostly done. Only a few things were left and then the actual wedding itself. But I wasn't worried about that—it would be perfect.

I stared up at the elegant, painted ceiling and tried to relieve some of the pressure in my back. I had taken to trying to awkwardly massage some of the tension as Ryder plopped down next to me. I looked to my left and saw his dress shoes.

Propping up onto my elbows behind me, I peered over at him. His cheeks were slightly flushed, and his hair was a mess. Addie had been right, too—his help was much needed.

The sounds of the rehearsal dinner had quieted the later it

got. The music was still echoing down the hallway, and every once in a while, we could hear laughter or raised voices.

Ryder nudged my arm with the tip of his shoe, and I glanced over at him. His little smirk was on the verge of becoming an all-out grin.

"I still like watching you work," he said. I was too tired to control my facial expression, so my surprise was written all over my face. He shook his head. "You're just so good at your job. You're creative and authoritative but not too controlling. And you had a vision from the start—taking what Stephen and Miles wanted and making it even better. It turned out…perfect, Caroline."

The unrestrained sincerity in his voice made my chest tighten. I sat up so I was eye level with him. "Thanks," was all I could manage to say around the lump in my throat.

"I think—" Ryder began, dropping his eyes to my hands that were fidgeting in my lap. But we were interrupted by both Theo and Natalie.

"This place looks phenomenal," Natalie complimented. I smiled up at my friend who looked gorgeous in a blue and white floral dress. She tapped Ryder's leg with her foot. "I was wondering where you went."

"Found a few wedding planners who needed help," Ryder said.

Natalie looked back at me and grimaced. "You okay?"

"I will be after I take a shower and lay down in that comfy bed upstairs."

Ryder stood and then offered me his hand. If I didn't take it, I would look rude, instead of like I was trying to prevent myself from reacting to his touch like I actually was. I slipped my hand against his and ground my teeth against the shock that rico-cheted up my arm at the slightest, most innocent touch.

I groaned like I was twice my age as I stood, and even as I straightened our hands lingered together. Ryder's thumb brushed the back of my hand once then twice before he reluctantly dropped it. Both of us watched our hands fall apart and quickly looked away.

I rubbed my palm against my leg and took a step farther away. Theo was glancing between us, from me to Ryder and between us where our hands were linked a moment before.

"Is there anything you need from us?" Natalie asked, leaning into Theo's side. He wrapped an arm around her but didn't drop his quietly incredulous look.

"Nope, we're done. And the clean-up crew will start on the rehearsal dinner in the next few minutes."

Natalie smiled and tapped Theo's chest. He finally looked away from us and down to her. His expression immediately softened, and an uncharacteristically sweet smile slipped over his lips.

"Okay, then, I vote we go to bed. My feet are killing me." Theo nodded as Natalie squirmed and bounced from foot to foot.

Theo nodded. "Go ahead. I have to talk to Ryder really quick."

Natalie said good night, but Theo didn't begin speaking until she was out of earshot. He watched her walk away then turned back to us.

"You two are not as sly as you think you are. If you don't want Natalie to know you're fucking, then you're doing a shitty job."

I straightened and dropped my arms to my sides. Immediately, I whipped my head toward Ryder who was shaking his head and scrubbing a hand over his jaw.

"Seriously, Theo, why—"

I smacked Ryder's side and angrily whispered, "You told him?"

"No, he didn't," Theo answered. All my frustration dissipated in one swift rush. "After I caught you leaving the bathroom together, I asked him, but he didn't give much up. Then the photos at graduation. I've also just watched the two of you together ever since, and it's hard to miss whatever"—he motioned between us—"this is."

Nervous energy swam through me and churned my gut. Theo turned to walk away, and I had to know for sure. I reached out and grasped his forearm.

He stopped and slowly looked back at me. "She doesn't know?" I asked quickly.

He shook his head and tucked his hands into his pants pockets. Seeing Theo dressed in a suit was a strange sight, although he hadn't altered his usual all-black attire.

"No, but I also don't like lying to her. You should think about telling her. I think we all learned that secrets only make things worse." He glanced at Ryder, and I let go of his arm. Without any other context, we knew what he meant. Maybe the situation would have gone smoother if he and Natalie had told Ryder earlier about their relationship instead of waiting for it to blow up.

Theo followed the same path Natalie took out of the room and to the right where the curved staircase would take him to the second floor and the guest bedrooms.

Ryder and I were left in the middle of the room, silently standing side-by-side.

"He won't say anything," Ryder said.

I scoffed and tugged the hair tie out of my hair, running my fingers through the tangled strands and massaging my tender scalp. Exhaustion was creeping in, and I couldn't think straight when I was worried about keeping my eyes open.

"He might not say anything, but if he's noticed, it's only a matter of time before Natalie does, too."

"We could tell her," Ryder said like it was asking her to grab something at the grocery store or reminding her of an appointment. Like it wasn't something that could possibly irreparably change my friendship with her forever.

"And how do you think that conversation would go?" I asked. "Something like, '*Hey, Nat. Ryder and I have been sneaking around behind your back for a few months. We're just fucking, so don't worry about me becoming your daughter-in-law or anything. Hope you don't hate me now.'"*

When I looked back up at him, Ryder's blue eyes were filled with a vulnerability I yearned to erase.

"Let's...I don't think this is the time for this conversation," I said and began to walk past him. But I didn't make it far. Ryder's arm shot out and caught me around the waist, effectively stopping me mid-step.

He bent his head, and I could feel his breath against my cheek. He was so close, his nose brushed my hair. Suddenly, everything else disappeared, and all I could think about was how much I liked when he touched me or when I felt the heat of his body. My focus was solely on his fingers gripping my hip and his forearm pressing into my lower stomach.

"Don't walk away like this, Caroline," he whispered. "We should talk about it."

I tilted my head in his direction, and his lips brushed my forehead. "Not now," I said, remembering myself. I straightened and scanned the room. We were alone, but for how long, I wasn't sure.

"I'll come find you tonight."

He let me step away as I choked out a disbelieving laugh. "Your mom and Theo are in the room between us. Sneaking into my room is tempting fate."

Ryder shrugged and retrieved his jacket from the chair he'd tossed it on an hour earlier. "I'll get creative, but tempting fate is worth it when it comes to you, pretty girl."

THIRTY

A TWELVE-FOOT DROP

Ryder

IT WAS ALMOST TWO IN THE MORNING, BUT THE THOUGHT OF GOING to sleep alone, in my own bed when Caroline was only two doors down, seemed impossible.

I tossed my wet towel over the shower door and ran a hand through my damp hair as I stepped back into my room for the weekend.

I didn't know places like this actually existed. Especially in our part of the country.

Each room, although not as elegant or elaborate as the rest of the property, was decorated with antique finishes and every detail in mind. I wasn't an expert on interior design, but it was feminine and pretty. And I was nervous about touching anything.

I glanced around the room at the lighter green accents they'd chosen and headed for the door. My hand landed on the silver knob, but before I turned it, I pressed my ear to the dark wood and listened.

Even early in the morning when we all had to be wedding-ready a few hours later, there were still voices up and down the hallway. They weren't loud, but they were there. Which meant I had to either wait for them to eventually go to sleep or find another way to sneak into Caroline's room.

And I refused to wait. Spinning, I took one look at the patio doors and strode across the room. I didn't hesitate to push open one of the French doors, but when I did, I pretended to be interested in the courtyard below and the gardens in the distance rather than look immediately to my right. I had to fake nonchalance in case Theo or my mom was on or near their own patio.

When I didn't hear anything or see anything out of the corner of my eye, I chanced a look toward their room.

Nothing.

I stepped as close as I could on the little stone balcony. The curtains were drawn and there wasn't any light from behind or around them. I waited a full minute before I felt confident that they were asleep and the coast was clear.

One balcony further—which should have been Caroline's room—was illuminated by the soft light inside.

There was a fleeting moment where I wondered if what I was about to do was ridiculous, but the thought was gone as quickly as it appeared. Yes, I was crazy enough to hop balcony-to-balcony and climb across the exterior of the house to get to Caroline's room.

It was worth it even if nothing happened. Even if I only got to glimpse her beautiful scowl at my somewhat absurd antics, it would be worth the possibility of falling twelve feet onto the unforgiving stone patio.

The distance between each patio wasn't more than several feet, and as long as I shimmied across the little ledge between them, I would make it. Hopefully.

I didn't think about it too long. I braced my hands on the edge of the patio railing and hoisted myself on top of it. The stone was sturdy enough to hold my weight as I crouched and reached for the brick, ivy-covered wall.

Holding on for my life to an imperfection in the wall, I placed one foot then the other on the very small, much less sturdy ledge. My heart was attempting to escape my chest as I shimmied across. And I almost fell once but managed to make it to Theo and my mom's patio.

My landing was louder than I hoped, and I cringed as I waited to see if either of them heard me. When no sound emanated from their room, I crept across their patio and didn't hesitate to find the ledge on the opposite side. Having done it once, the second time was much easier.

My landing on Caroline's patio was even less graceful, though. I tumbled down from the railing and landed on the floor with a resounding thud. Gripping my hip and knowing there would be a bruise the next day, I was writhing when I noticed the curtains move and Caroline peeking out between them.

I sucked in a breath through clenched teeth and ignored the pain radiating from my hip. I stood and waved at Caroline. She was wearing a pair of tiny sleep shorts and an oversized T-shirt. My T-shirt I'd lent her more than a month ago. Suddenly, the pain in my hip was forgotten.

Her hair was damp from the shower, and she was wearing light purple frame glasses.

"Want to let me in?" I whispered and mimed for good measure, pointing to the door handle and pretending to open it.

She rolled her eyes and threw her arms out to her sides in an obvious exasperated gesture. She shook her head and said, "I can't." Not that I could hear her, I just read her lips.

"Why not?"

"It's stuck," she said and made a show of unlocking the door and tugging on it. Sure enough, it didn't move, and my heart sank.

Glancing back and forth across the patio, I spotted a window on the other side just beyond the railing. I motioned to it, and Caroline's eyes followed. Her eyebrows shot up, and she looked at me like I was crazy.

But still, she turned and walked into her bathroom. A few

seconds later, the light turned on, and she was pushing open the window.

"You are insane," she said.

I was already climbing back on top of the railing for the fourth time when I smiled. "Insane for you. Now, watch out."

She groaned and stepped back. I hopped onto the ledge and swung one leg into the window. Thankfully, I had long legs and could reach the floor as I slipped through the opening.

It was more graceful than my other two landings, but I still managed to almost fall against Caroline. I caught myself on the counter with her wedged between me and the marble surface. I grunted at the impact and stopped my forward trajectory before I could hurt her.

"Hi," I said with a smile after I'd steadied myself.

She scowled up at me, and I proved that yes, seeing her annoyed expression—the furrow between her brows and down-turned lips—was worth it.

"Hi," she managed to say back as she crossed her arms over her chest. "Why on earth would you do that? You could have seriously hurt yourself."

I shrugged and lifted my hands to toss her damp hair over her shoulders and clasp each side of her neck. "To see you, and it was worth it."

She didn't try to pull away when I fitted my lips against hers, and I felt her body relax as the seconds ticked by. Her arms dropped to her sides, and her mouth opened as I coaxed her lips apart with a quick brush of my tongue.

Her hands dropped to my waist, and her fingers dipped beneath my shirt, teasing my skin and sending goose bumps up and down my torso. Every swipe of her nails and subtle moan against my lips eased any lingering anxious energy I felt any time I was away from her.

I didn't voice that thought, though. I just lost myself in her.

"Ryder," she muttered my name against my lips and pressed her palms against my chest. I took the cue and leaned back. "It's two in the morning, and I have to be up at seven. I'm exhausted. I don't think I can do this tonight."

I nodded and kissed her once more. "Okay, we don't have to do anything. I'd still like to stay, though."

In the faint bathroom light, her eyes darted between mine. She was so hard to read, but it was almost like I could see the myriad of thoughts bouncing around her mind. We hadn't stayed the night unless it had been preceded by carnal, uninhibited sex. I knew she was considering what it would mean if I spent the night in her bed and we didn't have sex or fool around in any way.

I took a breath and opened my mouth to further plead my case when she surprised me.

"Fine," she said and pushed harder against my chest, slipping from between me and the counter.

Although I expected her to put up more of a fight, I wasn't going to question her answer. Instead, I followed her out of the bathroom and shut the light off behind me. She dropped her glasses on the bedside table and crawled across the bed. I couldn't help but appreciate the curve of her ass peeking out of the bottom of her shorts as I toed off my shoes and slipped off my shirt.

She shut off the light on the opposite bedside table, and the room descended into darkness. The only light that remained was from the moon streaming in through the window and partially open curtains.

I lifted the sheet and slid into the bed. For a place so old, the air conditioning worked incredibly well. The bed was cold, but it was more of an excuse to curl up against Caroline. I wrapped my arms around her, squeezing one beneath her head and tossing the other over her hips, until every part of her back was pressed against my front.

She adjusted the pillow, so it was wedged between her head and my arm and burrowed farther into the blankets, tucking them beneath her chin.

"You're such a cuddler," she mumbled, and I laughed as I kissed behind her ear. I nestled my nose into her clean hair and breathed her in. She smelled clean and warm and safe.

"You can pretend you don't like it, but I know the truth."

"And what might the truth be?"

My hand flattened against her stomach, where her T-shirt had ridden high enough to expose her skin, and I tugged her closer into me. She couldn't have gotten any closer no matter how hard I tried. I drew random patterns around her navel and up and down her stomach. When she shivered, I smiled.

"That you actually love it. I know that every time you tell me you hate me or I'm annoying, you don't really mean it," I said, and she pressed her ass harder into me, grinding against my obvious erection. "It's part of that hard exterior you try so hard to keep up. Why do you do that, Caroline? Is it all for me? You don't have to protect yourself from me."

She didn't respond, and I knew better than to expect her to, no matter how much I wanted to hear her tell me why she wouldn't let me in. My mom, our age difference, it was trivial. They were obstacles we could easily overcome.

My questions hung in the air around us. The only sound was our quiet breathing and the occasional noise emanating from beyond the window or rustle of the sheets. Even the sounds in the hallway had died down. She scooted away from me, and I tensed, prepared for her to demand I leave. The shameful walk— or climb—back to my room would be torturous knowing what and who I left behind.

But she didn't ask me to leave, and suddenly, my body was tensing for a whole other reason. The little bit of space she'd made, she used to slip her hand between our bodies and palmed my cock through my sweats.

"I thought you were too tired," I groaned.

"I changed my mind," she retorted quickly, slipping her hand beneath my waistband and swiping her thumb through the pre-cum collecting at the tip.

Another groan stuck in my throat as I pushed my hips up into her hand. Even in the awkward position, with her hand twisted behind her and her fist upside down, she skillfully worked me into a reasonable frenzy.

"Your cock pressing against my ass is hard to ignore," she said. "And an orgasm would help me sleep."

Nudging her shorts down, she slipped them off her legs and allowed me to tug her closer once again. My cock wedged between her ass cheeks, I lifted her leg and propped it on top of both of mine. The change allowed me more room and the ability to slide the head of my pounding erection against her dripping slit.

"Are you saying I have a big dick? Too big to ignore?"

I tossed the pillow she'd wedged between her head and my arm away and tightened my forearm around her upper chest, pulling her toward me. She sucked in a sharp breath. I reached down and grabbed the base of my cock, running it back and forth as best I could. But she quickly took over, canting her hips over my length and getting me nice and wet.

"Would it really give you that much satisfaction for me to compliment your cock?" she asked in a breathy, low voice.

"Mmm...yes," I answered honestly against her neck.

"Thankfully for you, I'm feeling generous." She reached between her legs and found the underside of my cock, pressing it harder against her cunt as she rode me. "You have the prettiest cock I've ever seen, Ryder. And the things you do with it make me want it all the time. It's big and thick and perfect. And—"

One thrust and her words disappeared on a whimpered gasp. I was perfect? Her cunt was the epitome of the word. Warm and soft and tight and better than anything else. I didn't have to experience another damn person to know there was nothing better out there.

"You know how much I love when you praise me or call me a good boy," I said when I finally caught my breath and started a slow, rolling motion. "It shouldn't be a surprise that I like compliments."

I tightened my hold around her chest and wrapped my other arm around her stomach, effectively holding her in place as I picked up the pace.

"Fuck, yes," she moaned a little too loudly.

I smiled into her hair and nipped at the shell of her ear. "My mom's in the next room, pretty girl. You don't want her to hear how much you love her son's cock, do you?"

Her pussy fluttered around me, and her arousal made it easy to slip in and out. "You like that?" I asked.

"No," she said automatically.

I chuckled and hoped the bed didn't start squeaking. It was one thing to pretend like my mom would hear us, it was another for it to actually happen.

"You can lie, but your pussy can't. I think you like the idea that this is forbidden. That you're not supposed to be fucking me."

She growled, and I felt the sound emanate from low in her stomach, vibrating up her throat with increased intensity.

"You're so fucking chatty tonight," she said. She shifted and wrapped her hand around mine, moving it until my palm was against her throat. "You want to be my good boy? Don't hold back. Shut up and fuck me."

As she requested, I tightened my hand around her throat and fucked her harder. My hips bounced against her ass and the delightful sounds that came with it were music to my ears.

"Yes, right there. Fuck, Ryder, you're such a good boy. You fuck me so well. I can't wait to return the favor."

The visions her words produced were enough to make my orgasm bear down on me. The thought of her naked, wearing a strap-on, and bossing me around made my balls draw up and my brain short circuit. All control disappeared in an instant and being quiet was the furthest thing from my mind.

I rolled over on top of her and let her take most of my weight.

My hand wrapped around the back of her neck, and I shoved her face into the pretty white sheets. Any cries that escaped her lips were muffled by the blankets beneath her. Her T-shirt was pushed up, showing off the planes of her back in the dim moonlight, and I ran my free hand down her exposed skin until I reached her ass that bounced with each of my movements. I spread her cheeks apart and gaped at where my cock disappeared inside her cunt. Where it wrapped around me and sucked me in deeper again and again.

"Deeper," she moaned, and my eyes rolled back in my head as I made the adjustment. With her legs pressed together beneath me, she was tighter than anything I'd ever felt.

"Fuck, you feel so good. Your pussy is incredible. I want to live and die between your legs, baby."

I didn't know what I was saying. Words were tumbling from my lips as my orgasm churned.

Caroline's body tensed beneath me, her noises becoming more frantic as her own orgasm materialized. She slammed her hand over her mouth as her pussy seized my cock and milked me dry.

Her beautiful face contorted in pleasure, and I forced my eyes to stay open as bliss overwhelmed my senses. I didn't want to miss a second. I wanted to experience every sensation with her.

"Holy shit," she mumbled, dropping her hand and letting her eyes fall closed. She was breathing hard, and I dropped down next to her, also trying to catch my breath. I rolled to my side, and she came with me. She reached back and rested her hand on my forearm, squeezing once.

"Don't," she said. "Don't pull out. Not yet." My slowly softening cock was sensitive, but I did as she requested. She wanted me inside her longer. And I didn't mind staying there forever, feeling every aftershock or inadvertent tightening of her cunt. Each time, it was like an electric current running up my shaft.

We lay like that for a long time. Our intertwined fingers rested on top of her exposed thigh, that was when I noticed the ring around one of her fingers. Subtly, I looked down and saw the purple rhinestone flower glinting in the moonlight filtering in through the windows. I hid my smile against her neck as I lifted my other hand to run my fingers through her hair. I enjoyed every second as her body relaxed and her breathing evened out.

The tightness in my chest expanded until I thought it was going to burst. Until I thought I'd never experience calm and contentment like that ever again.

"It's not just for you."

Her voice was barely above a whisper, and she'd been quiet for so long I'd thought she'd fallen asleep.

"What isn't?" I asked in a similarly low voice, still raking my fingers through her hair.

"My hard exterior, as you called it."

My fingers faltered, and I had to swallow before I asked, "It's not?"

"No, it's for us," she whispered and squeezed my fingers where our hands were still intertwined against her thigh. I squeezed back. "To protect us both."

The tightness in my chest morphed from calmness and contentment to apprehension and doubt. I had nothing to say. I didn't know how to respond or what words she wanted to hear. Protecting herself, *us*, was noble, but I had no idea what she was protecting us from. From the outcome of what we were doing?

None of the thoughts bouncing around my head were coherent enough to voice, so the silence eventually filtered in once again. I slipped my arm beneath her head and wrapped the other back around her, trying to convey the torrent of emotions by touch alone.

Like she felt everything I wanted her to, she sighed. "Because without it, I'm worried about what will happen."

THIRTY-ONE

YOU'RE A HEARTBREAKER

Caroline

"Seriously, go eat," Addie said as she pushed me toward the corner of the room where my food had been sitting for an hour. "I had one of the caterers heat it up, and if you don't go now, you're never going to eat."

With a huff, I begrudgingly handed over my iPad and took the earpiece out of my ear.

Addie smiled and gave me one last push. "Good girl," she said as I started walking away.

I waved her off and eyed the plate of food. My stomach growled on cue, and I couldn't deny I needed some calories.

The day had gone off without a hitch. I wasn't one to gloat or brag, but that was why my clients hired me—my attention to detail and preparedness were unmatched. They were guaranteed a good—if not perfect—outcome.

The ceremony had been perfect, and even the elements I couldn't control—like the weather—had cooperated for the most idyllic sunset vow exchange I'd ever witnessed. The cocktail hour had run smoothly as had the dinner service we'd wrapped up about a half hour ago.

I sat down at the little table and scooped a huge bite of potatoes into my mouth as I looked across the dance floor. The smiles on Stephen and Miles's faces were proof enough that I'd done my job well.

I lived for those smiles.

I bent my head, and with little grace, I began shoveling food into my mouth. I promised Addie I'd take a break, but I didn't specify how long that break would last. I planned to be done in five minutes until someone slid into the seat beside me.

"This wedding is beautiful," Natalie said. I nodded and mumbled a "thank you" around a mouthful of steak. "Is this the biggest one you've planned?"

With a guest list of over three hundred, it was close but not quite the largest. I swallowed my food and shook my head as I sipped the glass of red wine sitting in front of my plate.

"Almost. The largest, and priciest, was the Timothy wedding last year. Four hundred people not including the wedding party and vendors. *That* was the biggest."

Natalie nodded slowly and sipped her own nearly empty glass of wine. "Oh, and did you see Beckett is here? Apparently, he's friends with Stephen's dad? It's a small freaking world."

Beckett Crawford, Natalie's boss, owned the law firm she worked for. His father had started the firm when he was Beckett's age and had retired a few years ago, leaving his son in charge. Beckett had worked with his father since he graduated law school, so he was more than prepared for the promotion.

Natalie tried to set us up at one point, but it hadn't gone anywhere. Not because he wasn't amazing or drop-dead gorgeous, because he definitely was. I just wasn't into sleeping with my best friend's boss. Her son, on the other hand...

I shook away the thought and took another long gulp of wine, refraining from searching for Ryder across the room. Not that it would have taken much searching—he was in the middle of the dance floor with his friends. They were jumping and singing to the beat of the music that echoed around the ballroom.

But I didn't look up. I kept my eyes glued to my plate and listened to Natalie discuss the possibility of the company opening a new office in Chicago. I didn't think about how good it felt to wake up next to Ryder that morning. Or how he conned me into laying there with him for an extra thirty minutes by rubbing my back and playing with my hair.

I also made it a point not to think about what I'd divulged in my softened post-orgasm haze the night before. Vulnerability did not come easy to me, yet every time I was around him it became easier to show parts of me I didn't think I'd ever let anyone else see again.

I'd done it twice before and both times had permanently changed me. Shattering pieces that could never be repaired. A third time might break me altogether.

The song changed, and Natalie and I descended into a comfortable silence. I finished eating, and she sat with me, watching the crowd, as I did. Theo brought her over a new glass of wine, brought us both cake, gave her a quick kiss, and then returned to the table he was sitting at with a few of his college buddies.

Nothing was out of the ordinary until I caught Natalie out of the corner of my eye chug half of her glass in almost one swallow. It was very out of character, and I was immediately on alert.

"Is every—" I began to say, but she beat me to it.

"It's Ryder."

My fork stopped mid-air, and I froze. "What?" I asked around my sudden panic.

"The guy you've been..." She stopped and thought for a moment like she was unsure what word to use next. "...*seeing* that you won't tell me about."

A litany of curse words, ones I hadn't even thought of or used before, crossed my mind as my panic began to suffocate me. My stomach dropped, and I set my fork down on my plate. It more like clattered to the plate unceremoniously and loudly even over the music.

"Should I skip the *'what are your intentions with my son'* speech?"

"Natalie, I—" I began, but she waved me off, turning in her chair to face me completely.

"Just let me say something really quick before you explain."

She waited for me to acknowledge her request, and I managed to nod my head as I prepared for my best friend to justifiably berate me. But I should have known better. I wasn't sure Natalie had berated anyone in her entire life or even considered it.

"You're my best friend, and I love you more than almost anyone in the entire world. Except for maybe the moody guy over there," she said, motioning with her head to Theo. "And Ryder. I know it would be hypocritical of me to be upset since I did sleep with, date, and move in with his best friend, but I'm still a little concerned."

"You're not upset?" I wasn't sure how she heard me over the music, but she did.

She began to shake her head, the dark curls from her updo framing her face brushing against her cheeks, but like she thought better of it, she stopped and shrugged. The music faded at that moment, and I could hear her loaded sigh.

Anxiety made my stomach churn, and the anticipation of what followed that sigh made me want to puke.

"You're going to break his heart, Care."

"No," I said immediately, *vehemently*. "It's not...serious. We both know it's not."

Her dark brows shot up, and her expression was the very definition of incredulous. She reached forward and clasped my hand in both of hers. "Okay, now, once more with feeling."

"Nat, I'm serious that we're *not* serious," I said. "And I'm not going to break his heart. I don't want to do that."

"You might not want to, but you're powerful. Your heart-breaking ability isn't something you can entirely control. I've seen you break them without batting an eye."

Shaking my head, I squeezed Natalie's hands and glanced down at where they sat in my lap. "I didn't—we didn't—" I groaned and took a breath through my nose before I could continue. Words were hard even when Natalie was being so kind and understanding. Talking about my feelings didn't come as naturally to me as it did to her, but she was my best friend and gave me a moment to collect myself and find the words.

"I didn't mean for this to happen," I finally said quietly.

She nodded, and I looked up to find a small smile on her pink lips. "I know, babe. I can't imagine that you meant for any of this to happen."

"You shouldn't be mad at Ryder either. He wanted to tell you, and I just…I couldn't. I didn't want to disappoint you or fuck anything else up. Especially when it was just supposed to be—"

Abruptly, I stopped talking. The realization only hit me toward the end of the sentence that I was about to tell Natalie something she likely didn't want to hear about her son.

"Just supposed to be, what?" she asked.

I rolled my lips and shook my head. Natalie proceeded to roll her eyes and lean back in her chair, dropping my hands and picking up her wineglass. "Supposed to be fun?"

I momentarily closed my eyes and tried to figure out how I'd gotten myself into such a fucked-up situation. I was careful and mindful and intentional. I had a purpose for everything I did— whether that purpose be business-related or pleasure-centered— I thought things through. I considered all possibilities and identified the repercussions. Which was why I didn't date, and I rarely slept with anyone—at least anyone who lived nearby —regularly.

Except for Ryder. It was always except for Ryder. He radically disrupted the rational side of my brain by doing nothing at all.

"Yeah," I said, finally answering her question.

"You're sure he knows that?"

"Yes, of course. We made that very clear from the outset."

Natalie looked from me to her wineglass, then to the dance floor where Ryder was still in the middle of the chaos. A carefree smile gracing his lips and his once perfectly styled hair falling over his forehead and into his eyes.

"He might have said that, but did you entirely believe it?" Natalie asked without looking back at me. I ran my finger around the bottom of my wineglass and also continued staring at Ryder. Even from that distance, I could feel that pull in my chest. The anxiety and panic from before morphing into something else the longer I looked at him.

I swallowed around the emotion and pushed it to the back of my head. "I had no reason not to believe him."

Natalie took a sip of her drink and finally looked back at me. Seeing her head turn out of the corner of my eye, I was finally able to look away from Ryder.

"He's had a crush on you forever. Everyone knows that. I mean, I thought it was like a teenage crush that would eventually fizzle out, but obviously it didn't. And knowing that, I think he's in the perfect position to really get hurt. Especially since you're not the most *open* person with your feelings or love."

I tried to hide my reaction by taking a sip of my wine, but apparently, I didn't do a very good job. Natalie huffed out a laugh and shook her head.

"See, you just cringed when I said the 'L' word. I know you both very well, and if you ask me, whatever you think the rules or boundaries or agreement is, he likely thinks something different."

Thoroughly uncomfortable with the topic of conversation and gobsmacked at the turn the night had taken, I readjusted in my chair and looked around the room until I spotted Addie. She was in the opposite corner, tapping away on the iPad in her hands, and talking to one of the venue staff.

"I should probably get back, but I need to know," I said. "How did you find out?"

"Hmm...well," she hummed. She leaned forward in her chair

and set her glass down, propping her elbows on the table she appeared deep in thought with her eyes narrowed. "I'm not blind, for one. The two of you are not as slick as you think. And you not telling me about the guy you were obviously dating— sorry—seeing was a big indicator. But that was only on top of catching you two making out in your office."

The fact that wine didn't come out of my nose or mouth was a miracle. I coughed for several seconds and took a careful sip to quell the burning in my throat before I croaked out, "What?"

She shrugged and acted like it wasn't a big deal. "I actually walked up to your office door about ten seconds before you thought I did. When I caught you two, I wasn't sure what to do —I wasn't going to call you out right then and there—so I walked back down the hallway and made a noise. You know the rest."

My jaw was permanently in the dropped position. She'd acted completely normal. I had no idea she'd known which was impressive on her part and awful on mine.

"And all of that would have been enough to figure it out if I hadn't noticed you were wearing his shirt when I showed up at your house that day three months ago."

THIRTY-TWO

RING THE ALARM

Caroline

THANKFULLY MY MOUTH WAS ALREADY OPEN, SO IT SAVED ME THE energy of dropping it once again.

"What? How? I—what?"

"You're not the only person who requests that I repair their clothes. The shirt you were wearing, Ryder had asked me to fix the hem a week before which I wouldn't have noticed except when I repaired it, I didn't have any black thread to match. All I had was this thick white thread that definitely stood out in the few places I used it."

The DJ said something over the microphone about something...I wasn't paying attention. I was still trying to comprehend everything Natalie told me. When the DJ cut off the microphone and the music changed, I could finally speak.

"I'm so sorry, Nat. I'm so, *so* sorry."

"I know," she said without an ounce of anger in the words. "And I accept your apology. Just...keep me in the loop now. I don't want to know everything, but the highlights would be nice."

For several seconds, I just looked at my friend. We were sleeping together, that's all it was, so what would the highlights be? "Also, and I know you're going to hate this, but I'm going to say it anyway. I don't think you believe it either. You thought I'd be mad, maybe angry enough for it to seriously change our friendship, but you did it anyway. And the Caroline I know wouldn't do that if it was just *fun*."

Lucky for me, I didn't have to respond. Not that I would be able to form words anyway. The music changed to something much slower, and Theo appeared on the other side of the table. He offered Natalie his hand which she took without a second thought. She gave me a smile before Theo led her onto the dance floor. I was too busy watching the two of them and thinking about relieving Addie that I didn't see Ryder next to me until I stood and almost walked straight into him.

"Oh, shit," I muttered, halting my momentum with my hands against his chest. As I stumbled, he reached forward and grabbed my waist before I could knock him over. All the breath rushed from my lungs the moment I felt him against me.

He chuckled, and I righted myself. Smoothing my hands down the front of my black dress, one of his hands stayed firm on my hip.

"Dance with me," he said. Not a request, but a statement. My eyes flicked to his, and the blue captured me as it always did.

Alarm bells were going off in my mind. Blaring and warning me against getting closer or crossing another line. But those same alarms that were screaming only a few months ago, had slowly grown quieter. It was more like a quiet, annoying beep when a smoke detector's batteries were low.

It was annoying but manageable. And once you got used to it, you barely heard it at all.

"Okay," I found myself saying. Ryder's smile widened, and a part of me felt lighter knowing I put that smile there.

He led me onto the dance floor, and although no one was

paying attention to us, I felt like everyone was. Except for Natalie who caught my eye across the floor and smiled softly as she laid her head against Theo's chest.

We weaved between a few couples, and Ryder spun me once before his arm wrapped around me and settled against my lower back. The other found my right hand as he guided us around the dance floor.

"When did you learn how to dance?"

"My mom taught me a while ago."

"I had no idea," I muttered as I rested my hand on his shoulder and tried to let him lead.

Ryder pulled me closer and leaned down until his mouth was next to my ear. "I just haven't had the opportunity to show off my skills."

His lips brushed the shell of my ear, and I shivered. So close, with his arms around me, he didn't miss my reaction. I felt his smile against my neck as he kissed me.

"I...uh...I talked to your mom," I said, pulling back so I could see his face. With eyebrows raised, Ryder waited for me to continue. "She knows."

When he didn't react, I clarified. "About us."

I waited, expecting shock, confusion, *something*, but his expression didn't change. I tossed my right hand into the air in exasperation.

"Why are you so calm about this?" I said a little too loudly. A few people glanced at us, and I gave them an apologetic smile.

Ryder placed his hand I'd dropped in exasperation on my other hip while I rested mine on his bicep.

"Theo gave me a heads up this morning."

"And you couldn't have shared this knowledge?"

He glanced around the room. "You were a little busy putting all of this together. Which is phenomenal, by the way."

"Thank you, but what did Theo tell you?" I asked, brushing past his compliment. "You didn't think this was important enough information to interrupt me for?"

"He told me that she knew, but he didn't tell her anything. He was right last night—we're not all that sneaky," he said.

"Ryder, you should have—"

"He also said that she wasn't upset. That she just wanted the truth."

My eyes bounced between his, and I didn't detect a hint of deceit behind the blue. Taking a deep breath, I let my shoulders relax. "I still wish you would've told me," I said.

He nodded and looked appropriately apologetic. "I'll make it up to you later."

I licked my lips and bit the lower one to hide my smile. Ryder noted the attempt and leaned in like he was going to kiss me.

"Not here," I whispered angrily.

"Everyone you were nervous about knowing knows, so what's the harm?"

"I'm still technically working," I argued and attempted to extricate myself from his arms. Only he tightened his hold, and my attempt wasn't that valiant.

"Okay, you're right. I won't do it again." I nodded, and he waved to one of the other groomsmen who was looking at us with shock and awe.

Freaking hell.

"What did my mom say?"

My eyes scanned his perfect jawline, stubbled with the beginnings of a five o'clock shadow, and the line of his neck where I could see his tanned skin behind his collar.

"She's known since that day in my bedroom," I said, and then dropped my voice lower as I continued, "after I tied you up."

At that, I finally got a reaction. His eyebrows shot up, and he reared back in surprise. "She's known for that long?"

I nodded as we passed an older couple—Miles's grandparents, I think—who were standing in the middle of the dance floor swaying back and forth.

"Something about having repaired that T-shirt of yours I threw on to go out and see her."

His eyes narrowed, and I saw when realization and understanding dawned on him. "Shit, I—I didn't even think about that. I would have stopped you if I had thought—"

His own panic was rising, not for the fact that his mother knew, but I realized because he thought I might assume he had done it on purpose. Ryder was smart and slick, but he wasn't nefarious.

"No, I know you didn't do it on purpose," I said, resting my hand against his cheek. "And honestly, Natalie was more understanding than I ever could have hoped."

He smiled and leaned into my touch. Suddenly aware of what I'd done, I almost removed my hand entirely, but then I considered his reaction. How his face would drop ever so slightly, and his shoulders would slump in disappointment. That was until he realized a second later that he'd shown me how much it hurt him and right his posture and expression.

And I couldn't stomach that reaction.

So, I left my hand against his cheek.

"I told you she would understand," he said, and I rolled my eyes at his gloating.

"That's fine. You can have your 'I told you so' moment, but it only lasts as long as this song." Which was going on forever, might I add. It was something slow and sultry that I hadn't heard before. It was gorgeous, though.

"What if I want it to last longer?" he asked. "What if I want all of this to last a little longer?" His voice dropped, and he tilted his head down until our foreheads were nearly touching. I didn't say anything, letting my hand fall to his shoulder and holding my breath. I could hear the change in his tone, and I could do very little to prepare myself for what he said next.

"Caroline, there is no way you can't feel this. You can claim all you want that it's just sex or just fucking or whatever, but that's not true. There's more. There's *something*."

His voice shook as did his hand as he reached up and clasped my cheek. He didn't try to kiss me, but I could feel how much he wanted to. His desire matched mine. And Natalie's words were echoing through my head. *You wouldn't have done it if it were just for fun.*

So, I successfully pulled myself free from his hold and all but ran toward the closest door.

THIRTY-THREE

STANDING ALONE

Ryder

I DIDN'T THINK, I JUST STARTED MOVING THE SECOND I REALIZED what she was doing. She was halfway across the dance floor before I reacted, but I followed her out the antique French doors and onto the patio.

I don't know what changed or made me want to confess my feelings in the middle of the dance floor at my best friend's wedding. I could blame it on the alcohol or the emotions of watching Stephen and Miles exchange their vows. But neither of those reasons felt right. I think I'd finally just given up trying to hide everything I'd been feeling.

It was stupid. I knew it was, yet I did it anyway. Not that I could have stopped it.

A few people were huddled around cocktail tables strategically placed at the edge of the fountain and under the lights strung from tree to tree. I lost sight of Caroline for a moment but caught a glimpse of her blonde hair as she turned the corner around a hedge, heading deeper into the garden.

My dress shoes, that I should have broken in before today, clicked across the stone patio. Once I rounded the shrubs and I was out of sight of the other guests, I broke into a jog. The freaking garden was like a goddamn maze. Plants and flowers lined grassy trails that occasionally broke off into alcoves that held more fountains or benches or large, old trees.

It was a guessing game. Somewhere between her turning the corner and me turning the same corner, I'd lost her. But I was determined. Taking left and right turns and feigning confidence, I refused to quit.

Finally, breathing hard and cursing my damn shoes, I found her on one of those benches staring up at a tree that looked like it was twice as old as my grandfather. My initial reaction was to start spewing my feelings. I wanted to get them all out before she had a chance to run away again. But I knew that wouldn't go over well.

Instead, I kept my steps light and crossed to the metal bench. I slipped down beside her, but didn't look at her. My eyes were fixed on the tree in front of us. Its trunk was still strong yet worn from years of battling the elements, and its branches, that rose several feet in the air then dropped lower toward the ground, were thick with leaves and a few small purple flowers.

I considered it a small win when she didn't sprint away.

I made it a point to leave space between us. Almost a foot between her thigh and mine, yet it somehow felt like miles.

I'd never felt silence so heavy. Even with the sounds of the reception raging behind us and the odd wind rustling the leaves, it felt like the weight of the world was sitting on my chest and with every breath, I hoped and prayed she would let me in.

"I'm sorry," I began quietly. "That wasn't the time or place for that."

She didn't answer, so I continued, bracing for her reaction. "But it's the truth, Caroline."

"It's your truth," she said, and I chanced a look her direction. Under the moonlight, her eyes were shiny with what couldn't be unshed tears. Caroline didn't cry. Ever.

But the thought made my heart leap into a rhythm I didn't

know if my body could sustain. Especially when I spotted the ring she was fidgeting with in her lap.

Still staring at the tree, she blinked and then slowly turned her head toward me.

"If you're saying you don't agree, I'm not surprised," I said.

I felt her scoff like a knife to my gut. When she stood, I also wanted to cry, but she paced to the tree and turned with her arms crossed over her chest.

"What do you want from me, Ryder? I've been clear from the start—I can't give you a relationship. And you said you would take whatever you could get. I knew this was a horrible idea, but I can't think straight around you."

By the time she was done, she was almost yelling, which might have made me second-guess my actions if it had been anyone else. But not with Caroline. I was just happy she was showing emotion, that her mask was slipping.

"If you can't think straight around me, don't you think that's a good sign there's more here than what we've been doing?"

My legs bounced beneath me, and I was dying to get up and cross to her.

"Oh my god, you're infuriating!" she exclaimed with a frustrated groan. "Why can't you just take no for an answer? Why can't you just drop it? You will find someone else, Ryder. Probably someone your own age who wants the white-picket-fence dream you're craving."

With that statement, I was out of my seat, unable to contain the energy and my frustration with the beautiful woman before me. "Who the fuck said I want that? Now you're putting words in my mouth, and that's not fair."

"Then tell me, Ryder. Enlighten me. If I'm so wrong, what do you want?"

"You!" I bellowed, but I wasn't worried about who was listening. I wanted to fight for her, for *us*. Everyone else be damned. "I want you. Yes, I said that I would take whatever you offered, and I would play by your rules. But between that night in your pool and right now, things changed. I *crave* you, Caroline. You're all I think about, all I want. Yes, I thought you were just my teenage fantasy, but you became my everything."

"Ryder." My name was barely above a whisper, but it was enough to make me close the space between us. She didn't drop her arms when I stopped in front of her, but I didn't care. I reached up and brushed her hair over her shoulders and grasped her neck, using my hold to position her defiant eyes on mine.

"Let me in, baby. I don't understand why, but I know you're scared. And you don't have to be. Don't you want to be something to someone? Something to me?"

A flicker of emotion stirred behind her eyes. It was a moment. One single second among the billions we get to live, and it would be the one I would hang onto forever. I'd replay it over and over again to justify every sliver of hope she would decidedly shatter in the next.

"No." One second, one word, one shattered heart.

She said it so forcefully, so firmly that I took a step back. My hands fell to my sides, but she stood her ground. A force against any feeling. Arms still crossed over her chest, her breathing was even.

I knew what was coming, but I didn't want to believe it.

"I've been something to someone before," she said, her voice eerily calm. "And I won't do it again."

"So, that's it then?"

She nodded once, and I felt like my world was collapsing.

"I'm not going to give up on you, Caroline. I'll give you space to figure it out, but I can't walk away. You're going to have to be the one to do it."

It took a few seconds, but eventually she took one step then another. I didn't move, but out of the corner of my eye, I saw her stop just behind me. My heart stuttered when I thought she might have changed her mind, but the sinking in my stomach felt never-ending when her steps continued.

And I just stood there and stared at the tree where Caroline had stood.

THIRTY-FOUR
BE PATIENT

Ryder

I COULD HAVE STOOD THERE FOREVER. I DIDN'T PLAN ON MOVING until my phone vibrated just a second after Caroline walked away. I barely felt it the first time, and the second it almost pierced my mental fog. Finally, the third time, I retrieved it from my pocket and numbly looked down at it.

> Miles: Hey, man, where'd you run off to? Need best man help.

Fuck. There was still a wedding reception happening in the distance, and I had to be there. I had to put on a happy face and pretend like the only woman I'd ever loved hadn't just ripped my heart out of my chest and stomped all over it.

Taking a breath, I typed a quick response to Miles letting him know I would be back in a second and shoved my phone back in my pocket. I tried to slip back into that carefree, happy Ryder everyone expected when I walked back in there, but I couldn't find him. There was just...nothing.

Turning, I cursed once again at my sore feet and the stupid

dress shoes and walked back into the garden and toward the house. I took a sharp right and made it halfway down the trail before I stopped in my tracks.

Standing in the middle of the walkway was Caroline. Suddenly, I realized her footsteps hadn't disappeared out of earshot, she'd stopped.

"What—" I began to say, but that was all I could get out. She had her back to me and was staring up at the moon that was high in the sky.

I didn't have a second to think up something else to say before she spun around. My breath caught in my throat, and I couldn't move. She looked so beautiful yet defeated under the moonlight.

With her arms crossed over her chest, she shook her head as her eyes landed on me.

"Fuck, Ryder. I made it this far," she said, and I didn't miss the way her voice shook. "I only made it this far, and I couldn't keep going. I walked away, but I couldn't keep going. What— what have you done to me? I'm not supposed to, I'm not—"

Hearing the pain in her voice, I couldn't stand idly by. In a few steps, I was in front of her, but she raised her hands and pushed against my chest.

"No, don't," she warned, her voice angry. "You did this. I was fine. I was *happy*, then you came along and blew up my life. This is why relationships are bad. They never work. Someone always gets hurt. *You did this*. Are you happy?"

Unshed tears shined in her eyes as they bounced between my own. I didn't know if she expected an answer, but it felt like a rhetorical question. I hadn't meant to blow up her life as she claimed I had. I'd just wanted her.

"Now, I don't know how to live without you, but I also don't know if I can give you what you want either. I don't think I can—"

She fought me for a second, but I won. I pushed her arms aside and wrapped mine around her. A quiet sob broke from her lips, and she dropped her head against my chest. My heart broke all over again hearing the sadness and frustration in her voice.

I smoothed my hand over her hair and the other down her back as she stuttered out a broken breath and clenched her fists against my jacket. I peppered the top of her head with kisses and held her as tightly as I could as if that would keep her from walking away again.

Several minutes passed, and I tried to wrap my head around what was happening. I couldn't tell if our fight was about to pick back up or if it was the second chance I wanted. I was never going to stop fighting for her, but I didn't expect to turn the corner and find her standing there.

I knew there was something more to it. Her words minutes before all but confirmed it—*"I've been something to someone before, and I won't do it again."* But I was still in the dark, and until I knew what was going on inside her pretty little head, we couldn't overcome it.

Several minutes passed, and she picked up her head. The tears slowing, she wiped at her eyes and took a shaky breath.

"Is my mascara running?" she asked, and I couldn't help the startled laugh that jumped from my lips. Clasping her cheeks, I tilted her head higher and appraised her beautiful face.

"Actually, it's not. And you're a very pretty crier."

She wiped under her eyes and the beginnings of a smile tilted her lips for a moment before it vanished. Her chin started to wobble again, and I rubbed my thumbs against her cheeks, quietly, but not dismissively, shushing her.

"All I've wanted for the past few months is for you to show some emotion or tell me how you're feeling, but now that you are, I don't like it one fucking bit."

Another humorless chuckle, another deep breath, and she straightened, squaring her shoulders and seeming more herself.

"I'm also not a fan," she said quietly. "Umm…look, I want to keep talking, and I know we need to. But we both have to go back in there, and I can't do it right this second."

I nodded my agreement and smoothed my hands down her arms. "Yeah, yeah, of course."

"I just need to get through this weekend. With the brunch and everything tomorrow, and the reception still going on, I need to be focused on that. Miles and Stephen deserve a wedding coordinator who isn't distracted."

"I understand," I said, and I couldn't help the dejection in my voice. The last thing I wanted to do was let her walk away again without finding a solution. But she was right—Stephen and Miles deserved their perfect weekend.

Her shaking hands clasped my cheeks, and I brought my eyes back to hers. The anger had ebbed, but there was still so much more emotion behind the gray than I'd ever seen before.

"I'm not...I'm not walking away again. At least not until we can have another conversation," she said like she knew I needed to hear that. "Just please be patient with me."

I nodded and tried to tamp down the urge to do everything I could to fix it all immediately.

"Okay," I agreed. "I'll try my best to be patient."

"Thank you."

"I really want to kiss you right now," I admitted quickly. I needed that connection with her. I needed to feel her lips on mine and remind her how good and right it felt. If she was thinking about giving it all up, I needed to remind her why she shouldn't while she was still in front of me.

She licked her lips and glanced at my own. "I would really like that." Her response surprised me, but I didn't question it. I leaned forward and placed a soft, chaste kiss on her tear-dampened lips.

And I just hoped it wasn't our last.

THIRTY-FIVE
A BOX OF MEMORIES

Caroline

My parents' house was quiet. It was Monday afternoon, so my dad was still at work, and my mom always volunteered at the animal shelter until after five. Which meant I had a few hours to myself.

With a shaking hand, I pushed open the door to my childhood home and slipped the key back into my bag.

I wasn't sure why it felt so strange to walk inside. I'd been there somewhat recently for a family dinner and my aunt's birthday. It shouldn't have felt foreign, but it did. And I had to attribute it to the reason I was there.

The entryway was lined with family photos, mostly of my sister and her family, but there were a few of me sprinkled among them. Likely my dad's doing.

I walked past the gallery walls and into the kitchen and living room at the back of the house. Nothing was askew, just as my mom liked it. Each item had its place, and it would never be found anywhere else. If anything, I got that one thing from my mother.

But I didn't stop to look around. To the right, I took the stairs up to the second floor and headed toward the door at the end of another hallway lined with photographs. It wasn't until I braced my trembling hand on the brass doorknob that I stopped and considered what I was doing.

What waited for me behind the door, I wasn't sure I wanted to face. I knew I needed to, that it was time, but I didn't want to do it more than I'd ever not wanted to do anything else.

The breath I sucked in through my nose shook almost as much as my hand. My pulse was racing, and I felt the uncanny urge to sprint the opposite direction. But standing at the door was like standing at the precipice of my future, and I had to take that step.

I pushed open the door and braced myself for...nothing. Because it was just a room. And I reminded myself of that when I shuffled around the new guest bed that had replaced the one I'd grown up sleeping in and when I approached the closet door that once held my belongings.

Another door, another moment of hesitation.

"*Fuck*," I muttered under my breath and dropped my bag on the floor next to me. My anxiety was frustrating yet unavoidable. When I tugged the door open, a large picture frame tumbled toward me along with at least six different types of holiday wrapping paper.

I lunged for everything and only managed to grab the edge of the frame and one roll of paper before everything else fell out unceremoniously around me. With a huff, I righted the frame and propped the rolls in one of the back corners. The disruption had allowed me to momentarily forget about my anxiety or my purpose.

Until I looked up at the top shelf and spotted the box I was looking for. My hands shook as I grabbed it, and it nearly fell, too. I managed to catch it awkwardly in my arms before I set it on the bed and stared at the worn cardboard.

The edges were scratched, and the corners were torn. There

were words written in black marker across each side, most of them scratched out.

But two words were still intact: Caroline & Daniel.

I ran my fingers over my mom's loopy script and sucked in a sharp breath as I pulled it open. The first thing to greet me made my knees buckle, and I slouched on the edge of the bed for support.

One hand covered my mouth to stifle the sob I could feel rising while the other lifted our prom photo out of the box.

My light purple dress was peak mid-2000s fashion, and Daniel's bow tie matched perfectly. We'd spent an hour at the department store sifting through options with a swatch of my dress. And he'd never complained once.

I set the picture aside, squeezing my eyes shut against the onslaught of memories, and returned to the box. There was my dried corsage from that same night and ticket stubs from movies and concerts we'd seen together. Below even more photographs I couldn't bring myself to look at for too long, I found the football jersey he'd given me at his final high school game.

That was when the first tear fell. Hesitantly, I lifted it to my nose and breathed deeply. Only after the odor of age and cardboard hit my nose did I realize I still expected it to smell like him.

I quickly dropped it and reached for the one thing I was after.

I sat on the bed and crossed my legs, setting the scrapbook on my lap.

It was page after page of our relationship, a timeline that included all our biggest moments—like high school graduation and moving to college—as well as the smaller ones that we weren't likely to remember. The time we went to the pumpkin patch or the aquarium.

My heart thumped against my chest, and I let myself remember it all for a moment.

The car crash. The hospital. The machines. The scrapbook I

made for when he woke up, so I could help him remember our life together.

The funeral and the heartbreak.

The car crash happened on our way back to school after summer break. We were laughing, listening to music, nothing out of the ordinary. Until a truck ran a red light going almost twice the speed limit and slammed into us. We spun and flipped and didn't stop until we collided with a pole on the opposite side of the intersection.

I didn't remember much after that until I woke up in a hospital bed the next morning. I had bruises, scrapes, and a concussion that resulted in a brutal headache. There weren't any lasting injuries.

Daniel wasn't so lucky.

He took most of the impact. He broke more bones than I thought possible and most of his body was bruised. But it was the traumatic brain injury he suffered that turned out to be fatal.

The moment I woke up in the hospital, I'd demanded to see him. There were wires and bandages everywhere. But he looked so peaceful lying there.

I'd spent nearly six years of my life with him, so when the doctors said he may not wake up or, if he did, he would likely have many obstacles to overcome, including memory lapses and loss, I made the scrapbook. Every memory I could think of, I added to it. I wanted him to remember as quickly as he could the little part of life we'd shared together.

I sat beside his bed for weeks, creating the book and talking to him. Just *being* with him.

But he never recovered. Now, all I had left of him was a crumbling cardboard box and a fucking scrapbook.

Daniel's death left me raw and heartbroken. And the relationship that followed it was the catalyst for all my barriers.

Flipping through the book was both cathartic and horribly painful. I got lost between those pages. So lost that I didn't hear my dad walk in until he brushed his hand against my shoulder, and I jumped into the air.

"Dad!" I exclaimed, fumbling to catch the book before it leaped off my lap.

"Sorry, Peanut. I've been calling your name."

He glanced around me, at the memories spread across the bed, and smiled up at me with remorse heavy in his eyes. He didn't say anything, just pushed a few photos out of the way and sat down next to me, putting his hand on my knee. It was the silent support I needed.

Never once in the several long minutes did he try to speak or act like I was a bother. He was just *there.* As he had been twelve years before.

"You're home early," I finally managed to say.

He lifted his opposite hand and glanced down at his watch. "I try to leave a little early when I can."

"Right. Umm…I honestly planned on being gone before you or mom got back. Sorry if I startled you."

He chuckled and patted my leg twice. "I saw your car out front, so I figured you were here somewhere. It was a good surprise." His smile turned sad. "What prompted this?" he asked, motioning to the box.

My sigh was loaded. I didn't know how to respond. Telling my dad that I was freaking out because I was feeling emotions I hadn't felt in almost a decade for someone I shouldn't, didn't seem wise.

It was also a lie. Because what I felt for Ryder went beyond anything I'd experienced before, which was more terrifying than the fact I was feeling anything at all.

"It was time," I said, and he nodded.

"You haven't looked since—?"

"No," I responded quickly with a sad smile.

He peered over my shoulder at the page the book was opened to and tried to stifle his laughter with a hand over his mouth. "Sorry, but that Halloween was great."

We looked ridiculous, but it was one of my favorite memories. I was Britney Spears, of course, and Daniel was the Joker. I'd thrown together my costume at the last minute, and by the end of the night, Daniel had sweated off his makeup, but neither of us cared about how we looked.

My dad flipped the page with a nod of approval from me, and we reminisced about each photo and memory. When I'd made the book, I never would have thought I'd be sitting there with my dad sifting through the pages.

It was supposed to be Daniel.

"I remember when you started this," my dad began. "Your mom cried herself to sleep that night."

My shock must have been written on my face. "I know, it's hard to believe. She acts...well, she acts the way she does, but when you were in so much pain, we were right there with you."

I shook my head and looked away.

"I know that what happened with Daniel, and then what happened after—"

"Yeah," I hurriedly said. More memories I didn't want to be reminded of right then. Reminiscing about one relationship was enough for me.

He squeezed my knee, and I looked down at his hand. "All I'm saying is that whoever it is, they're lucky to have you."

I jerked my head up and closed the scrapbook, setting it down on the bed and sliding off the edge. I surveyed the mess I'd made and began putting everything back the way I found it.

"Why do you think this is about...someone?"

He snorted derisively and handed me a stack of photos I rearranged in an envelope. "Peanut, it's hard not to notice. You've been distracted more than usual, smiling at your phone, and your reactions to your mom's questions about your love life has...changed."

"What do you mean? They haven't changed."

"Sure, I guess. You just don't react at all anymore. You used to get defensive, and rightfully frustrated. Now, you just don't say anything at all." I stopped with the jersey in my hands and considered what my dad was saying. I hadn't seen my mom much since Ryder and I had started sleeping together, but when I did, she'd continued her usual questioning of my life choices and lack of partner.

I didn't think my reactions had changed, though.

"Either way, I'm happy for you as long as you're happy," he said as he stood.

"That's if I haven't fucked it all up beyond repair." Even mumbling under my breath, my dad heard my admission.

He stopped, and I watched as he contemplated whether he wanted to respond or leave it be. Then he made his decision that he couldn't ignore it.

"You never know unless you try," he said with a shrug. "You're the most determined person I know. If you want to fix it, you will."

Simple. He made it sound so simple, yet it was anything but. He kissed me on the forehead, patted my arm, and turned like he was going to leave the room. But he hesitated, glancing back at me with concern.

"I promise I'm okay," I said, knowing exactly what he wanted to know. "At least, I think I will be."

He nodded once, approving of my response enough to leave the room. I examined the contents still strewn across the bed and put everything back besides the scrapbook. That, I took with me.

I returned everything to its rightful place and even fixed the bed, so maybe only my father would know I'd been there. Rounding the bed, I caught sight of my appearance in the mirror above the dresser. I looked as rotten as I felt. I couldn't remember the last time I'd left the house looking like that, but I'd spent the past few days feeling like the worst person in the world, so at least the inside matched the outside.

The moment I'd walked away from Ryder, I knew it was a mistake. Probably the biggest mistake I was going to make if I had kept going. So, I stopped. Whether I wanted to or not, my body physically wasn't going to allow me to move forward. And for once, my heart, my brain, my body, were all in agreement—walking away was not an option.

I'd been resigned when I'd left him then felt this sudden anger that he'd disrupted my entire life. He was too good, and it fucked everything up. Without his interference, I would have gone on living my life without the emotions filling up the bottomless pit in my stomach.

He'd entered my life and irrevocably changed it. I just had to get my mind right enough to accept it. Which was why I was standing in my childhood bedroom, clutching the scrapbook I made for my dead ex-boyfriend.

I had things to work through before I could move forward. Mental barriers that seemed impenetrable until Ryder started knocking them down. Quietly at first and without my knowing, until he had crumbled each and every one. Until he made me realize what lay on the other side might be worth it.

That not everyone left, and I could trust him.

Going the rest of the wedding weekend without speaking to him or trying to ignore his watchful gaze was nearly impossible. It felt like walking around with my heart on the outside of my body. But I needed that time to think. And he'd been as patient as I'd asked which I knew had to be killing him.

Clutching the scrapbook in my hands, I walked down the stairs and waved goodbye to my dad who was standing at the kitchen island eating cold leftovers out of a plastic container.

When I got in my car, I set the book in the passenger seat next to me and backed out of the driveway. Without thinking, I knew exactly where I was going.

I just hoped he would open the door.

THIRTY-SIX
SOMETHING TO YOU

Ryder

I parked in the first spot I found and turned off the engine. But I didn't get out. I just stared out the windshield at the exterior of the apartment building.

I didn't want to move or think or do anything really. As Theo put it, I was moping. But he would be too if he were in my position. Hell, he was in a very similar position not all that long ago.

I told her I would be patient, and I was doing my best to keep that promise. But every second that passed felt like we were further away from where I wanted to be. Like the longer we went without speaking and the more space I gave her, the more likely it was that she'd never come back.

The rest of the weekend was miserable, but I'd put on my best happy face for Miles and Stephen. The reception and the brunch the next morning were great. It was watching Caroline work and be so close but not being able to talk to her that was torture. She did a much better job at pretending like I didn't exist.

It was safe to say I was spiraling.

I went from numb to heartbroken every other minute. Staring out my windshield was one of those numb moments.

Finally, I mustered the ability to push open the door and step out into the summer evening. It was uncomfortably warm, and I began sweating almost immediately, my dress shirt and slacks sticking to me awkwardly as I retrieved my jacket and my backpack with my laptop from the back seat.

I wasn't paying attention as I walked up the stairs. I was more focused on thinking about taking a shower, changing clothes, and sitting in the dark, binging reality TV on the couch. It was what I would have preferred to do all day rather than go to work and pretend like I cared to be there.

With my mind elsewhere, I didn't see Caroline standing in front of my door until I was only a few feet away. Immediately, I stopped. She spotted me at the same time and froze.

"What—?" I started, shaking off the surprise and blinking to test if she was just a figment of my imagination.

"I—uh...I thought you just weren't answering the door because it was me."

"I would've answered, but I just got home," I said.

Caroline was wearing athletic shorts and a lightweight jacket that was unzipped, displaying my T-shirt I'd lent her beneath it. A kernel of hope bloomed in my gut as I stepped forward. She didn't have on an ounce of makeup which I only noted because it was unusual for her. Similarly, her hair didn't look like it'd been brushed, tied behind her head in a haphazard ponytail.

"Do you want to come in?" I asked as I stepped forward.

She nodded and let me walk past. "That would be great."

I fumbled with my keys for a second, but finally managed to open the door. I flipped on the kitchen light and dropped my backpack on one of the barstools. I slung my jacket over the back and turned to find Caroline standing just inside the closed door.

"Do you want—"

"I know we both probably have a lot to say," she said quickly, urgently. She dropped her bag next to the door and stuffed her hands into her jacket pockets. "But if I don't get this out now, I don't think I ever will."

Startled by her sudden explosion of words, I nodded.

She took a deep breath and closed her eyes for a moment, like she was trying to ground herself or prepare. I rubbed my sweaty palms against my pants and waited with bated breath. She tilted her head down and stared at her shoes as she spoke.

"When I was twenty-one, my boyfriend died."

Of all the things I expected her to say, that was not one of them. The hurt in her voice made me want to wrap her in my arms and never let go. My heart ached for her.

Then she told me about Daniel. She told me from beginning to end about their relationship—how long they'd been together and how she thought it would be forever. Then she explained the accident and the outcome.

The entire time I gripped the counter for dear life and watched this woman I cared so deeply for pour her heart out to me while she stared at the floor then her hands. She was still my confident, unshakable woman, but that mask she wore so proudly had finally fallen.

I would've never been prepared for what it hid.

"I made him this scrapbook," she said, her voice shook, and the longer she spoke, the harder it was to keep from crossing to her. "It was for when he woke up, all the memories we'd shared, but he never got to see it. And today, for the first time since he died, I looked at the damn book."

Finally, the sob she'd been holding broke free, and she looked up at me.

"I'm so sorry, Ryder."

In the next second, I wrapped her in my arms and muffled her tears and apologies against my chest. I tangled my fingers in the back of her hair and tugged her closer with the other until there was no space left between us.

I could feel her heartbreak, and whatever I had to do to make it better, I would do it without hesitation. I wished I could fix it.

And as much as I hated witnessing and feeling her sadness, something settled within me having her back in my arms. Her tears calmed quickly, and I wiped away my own as she pulled back. "I didn't mean to make you cry. *I* didn't mean to cry," she said sweetly, lifting her hands to dry off my damp cheeks. "And I didn't tell you this so that you'd feel sorry for me. It's not an excuse for how shitty I treated you, it's just an explanation. One of the reasons I'm...closed off."

I nodded and brushed my thumb over her mouth. "I understand, and I'm so fucking sorry." Her smile was sad, but she took a deep breath and stood a little taller. "Do you want to come sit down?"

"Yeah, let's sit."

I led us over to the couch, and when she tried to take a seat on the cushion farthest from me, I tugged her closer with a hand around her hip and another at her knee.

"I've missed you," I admitted, not letting her go. "I didn't know if...I just want you close."

She set her hand on top of mine and nodded. "There's more I should probably tell you." She licked her lips and stared down at where our hands met, running her thumb back and forth over my hand.

"The first relationship I had after Daniel died was with an older guy. He was in his late thirties, and I was only twenty-three. Not that I have an issue with an age difference," she said with a small smile. "But I desperately wanted some sort of connection again, and when I met Jaxon, I *thought* I'd found that."

I already didn't like where the story was going, but I stayed quiet and let her continue.

"It was a whirlwind—flowers, chocolate, trips, the works. I was fresh out of college and barely making enough to afford an apartment with a roommate, so his lifestyle was a very nice bonus. Until it all fell apart in an extravagantly horrible way."

She rubbed a hand over her mouth and sighed. "He had

some important job—I honestly can't even remember what it was—so he was always traveling. Or so I thought. He told me one weekend that he'd be out of town, and I didn't think anything of it. I was working at an event planning company as an assistant event coordinator, and we had the entire weekend booked up for a VIP client anyway. We were supposed to show them a ton of venues, nail down all the details. It was a wedding planning marathon, and my first huge event. I was overly prepared, so I knew it would be perfect. Until Jaxon walked into the first tour and kissed the bride."

God, I was running through emotions today. My numbness had turned to rage, and now, the anger coming off me felt like it would singe my skin.

"You're kidding."

"Nope," she said, popping the 'p.' "Unfortunately, I'm not. The man who had renewed my belief in love had shit all over it in less than a second when he walked into the wedding venue and into the arms of his perfect fiancée."

I shook my head and ground my teeth together. Looking up the address and phone number for every man named Jaxon in his late forties wouldn't be going too far, right? It would take some time, but it would be worth it to find the right one.

"What did you do?"

She shrugged. "I did my job. The look on his face was enough for me in that moment. He'd tried to pull me aside a few times, but I wouldn't talk to him. I didn't care what he had to say. He was dead to me the second I saw him."

Fuck, my tough girl.

"So, I waited until the weekend was over, and I called his fiancée and told her everything. She said she knew he had slept around, and it was unfortunate it had been with me. But that she wasn't really worried. She knew who she was marrying."

Enthralled by her story, I leaned forward and placed my elbow on the back cushion, resting my head on my hand.

"She didn't tell him, and he finally took the hint and stopped talking to me altogether. She knew, so I'd done my part. But she ended up marrying him and filed for divorce less than a year later. They hadn't signed a prenup, so she got more than half of everything. I guess she felt bad for me, and mentioned that she was glad I hadn't told anyone else, so she gave me a tidy sum. And that's how I started my business—with my fuckface cheating ex's money."

A startled laugh escaped me, and I couldn't contain my grin. "Holy shit, you're a badass."

She brushed her shoulder off and smiled her first genuine smile since I'd found her outside my door.

"I guess so, but as sweet as that revenge was, and helpful to the rest of my life, that relationship fucked me up more than I wanted to admit. I couldn't trust anyone for a really long time. Losing Daniel then realizing Jaxon was a despicable human, it made me retreat. And letting anyone in again meant they had the ability to hurt me in so many different ways."

"I would never—"

"I know," she said, squeezing my hand. "But love can make you the happiest or the saddest person on earth. And I didn't want to try for happy when sad was such a real possibility and all I'd known."

My pulse raced, and I sucked in a sharp breath that pierced through my lungs.

Love.

She'd said it so casually I almost missed it. Like it wasn't the word I'd been silently using for years to describe how I felt about Caroline. A feeling that had only grown stronger over the past few months.

I cleared my throat and carefully considered my next words. Caroline Grant was sitting in front of me, holding my hand, throwing around the word "love," and telling me all her deepest secrets. I didn't want to fuck it up because of my big mouth.

Chewing on my bottom lip, I was struggling to find the right way to ask the question clawing at the back of my mind. Impulsivity was more my style.

"How—" I began but stopped just as quickly. She silently urged me to continue just using her eyes, so I did, eloquence be damned. "How did you get here? I mean, a few days ago, you almost walked away, and I swore you were going to end things. I thought you were going to walk away again, only this time, it would be for good."

One side of her mouth tilted upward, and she glanced back down at our hands. Her jacket sleeve had ridden up her hand, revealing that little purple ring on her right ring finger.

"I thought I might, but I couldn't. You changed...everything," she said, her smile widening and a teasing glint appearing behind her red eyes. "I always said that I was open to a relationship, but it had to be with someone who was exceptional. Someone who made me better and would be a partner. My life was already full—I didn't *need* anyone."

She took a breath and lifted her free hand to cup my cheek. "But that was only partially true. I needed someone I could trust, and I needed to trust myself. And then you came along, and I felt that. I felt things I didn't think I'd ever feel again. And it was terrifying. I never expected it, especially with you. No offense."

"None taken," I said with a grin.

"You made me face these feelings, and I just needed to work through my mental blocks before I could fully embrace it. No one else did that. I don't think anyone else could."

I was going to have a heart attack. I was sure of it the way my heart raced, and my pulse skyrocketed. Her eyes dropped to my lips, and her hand tangled in the back of my hair. She pushed up on her knees and scooted closer to me until her legs brushed the side of mine.

"You asked me the other day if I wanted to be something to someone," she said, and I held my breath. I don't know where that had come from, but it sounded good in the moment. "The answer is no. I don't just want to be something to someone. I want to be something to *you*."

My stomach almost dropped out of my ass for a moment, but fuck, that last sentence was really going to send me into cardiac arrest. My smile was unbidden, and I reached for her.

"But," she said, stopping me before I could touch her. "I understand if it's too much. If you can't forgive me for the way I treated you. And since I'm still figuring it all out, I have to ask you to continue to be patient with me. After years of closing myself off, it's a lot. So, if you want to walk away, you can, and I won't stop you."

With a growl, I propelled myself forward and tackled her onto the couch. She let out a surprised laugh and smiled up at me. I hadn't thought about it before I started moving, so I quickly looked her over to make sure I hadn't inadvertently injured her. Thankfully, her head landed on one of the pillows she'd picked out for me and the couch was soft otherwise.

I just wanted her to stop talking about one of us leaving.

"I told you then I wouldn't walk away, and nothing's changed. You may not need me, baby, but I need you."

Kneeling between her spread thighs, I planted an elbow beside her head and placed my other hand against her cheek, directing her to look up at me. She stuttered out a broken breath and sighed, placing her hands on either side of my neck.

She smiled, and I couldn't wait another second to feel her lips against mine.

Like she couldn't resist either, she pressed up as I leaned down. The kiss was everything I'd ever wanted. Finally, when her lips brushed mine and her tongue swiped at the seam of my mouth, I felt the confidence and surety I'd wanted to feel since our first kiss. No more hesitation or barriers. She was there with me one hundred percent, and I could feel it everywhere.

Caught up in the euphoric feeling, I mumbled against her lips, "Fuck, baby, I love you."

True or not, I didn't mean for those words to come tumbling

out in that moment. Beneath me, Caroline froze and let her head fall back onto the pillow.

I fumbled for something else to say, to backtrack before she could run again. Her eyes bounced between mine, and her wet lips opened and closed a few times.

"I did not mean to say that. I mean, I feel it. I meant it, but that was probably the wrong time to say it. Especially after you asked me to be patient. And you don't have to say it back. I don't expect anything. I know you're just now—"

With one hand over my mouth, she stopped me mid-ramble. Her unsure, surprised expression morphed into a small smile, and my thumping heart settled. My pulse returned to somewhere near normal.

"I don't think I'm ready yet, but I feel it, too. I promise I do. What I feel for you, Ryder, I've never cared about someone like I care about you. It makes my heart hurt how much I do."

My response was muffled by her palm which she slowly removed. "I believe you, baby."

She tangled her hands in the back of my hair and tugged me down, kissing me hard and showing me with her actions how much she cared even if she couldn't find the words yet. Then a realization hit me, and I pulled back, narrowing my eyes.

"You haven't scolded me for calling you 'baby,'" I observed. "Is that allowed now?"

She rolled her eyes and shook her head in mock annoyance. "I'll allow it for now," she said. "But only if you give me something in return." She pushed her hips off the couch and dragged them along my aching erection, making her intentions and desires crystal fucking clear.

With a groan, I rolled my hips and watched her mouth pop open on a silent moan. "Anything, baby," I promised. "I'll give you anything you want."

THIRTY-SEVEN
THIRTY-FOUR CANDLES

Caroline

GLANCING OVER AT THE CLOCK ABOVE THE STOVE, I HURRIEDLY grabbed the last platter of food from the fridge and placed it on the island.

I rearranged a few plates and switched the music booming through the speakers mounted around the house. Although my friends who were joining me to celebrate my birthday would have been fine listening to my carefully curated early 2000s playlist, my parents and other family members would not.

After event planning for the better part of a decade and putting together my own parties for even longer, I had hosting down to a science. But I still couldn't shake the nervous energy buzzing through me. It had nothing to do with the party itself, or even turning another year older and had everything to do with the fact that it was the first time I would introduce Ryder to my family as my boyfriend.

It was the natural next step, but he was the first person who had claimed that title since Jaxon, so it felt monumental.

The weeks since I'd shown up at his apartment had been better than I ever expected. Telling him about Daniel and then

Jaxon was rough, but I felt like a thousand-pound weight had been lifted in the process.

After our fireworks-filled reunion, he'd asked me about Daniel. What he was like and about our relationship. It had been cathartic to talk about and even more so when Ryder asked to see the scrapbook. We'd flipped through it for a while. I explained the photos and shared a few stories.

When I got home, I'd placed it on the shelf at the top of my closet where I expected it to stay. The past was once and for all truly behind me, and apparently, it had taken Ryder fucking Calaway to help make that happen.

I glanced down at the ring on my right ring finger and smiled. When Ryder found an upgraded option, a silver band with simple, light purple stones that didn't come out of a coin-operated vending machine, he jumped on the opportunity.

He'd picked it up a few days ago, before my birthday, but he couldn't wait to give it to me. That night, he'd slid the box across the table at dinner with a clarification that it was absolutely not an engagement ring. Neither of us was ready for that step.

It was the sweetest gift I'd ever been given, and I never wanted to take it off.

The front door opened, and a voice boomed, "Baby, I'm home!"

I shook my head and tried to hide my smile as Ryder came around the corner with the largest bouquet of light purple flowers I'd ever seen. His smile was a mile wide, and his black hair was a mess like he'd been running his fingers through it all day.

It wasn't until he stepped closer that I realized he was also holding a smaller, white bouquet, too. It was partially hidden behind the enormous purple one. I scrunched my eyebrows in confusion but happily kissed him over the armful of flowers.

"Two bouquets?" I asked as he placed both on the counter next to the sink and slid his arms around my waist. He ushered me backward until my back hit the countertop behind me, and I had no choice but to heed his hungry kiss and exploratory hands.

The warmth and fullness in my chest still felt so new to me, but I'd finally stopped fighting it.

Ryder placed one final kiss on my lower lip and pulled back. He smiled down at me and cupped my cheek.

"Happy birthday, pretty girl."

"You've already wished me happy birthday several times today."

He shook his head and brushed his nose against mine. "And I'm bound to tell you at least ten more times before the day is over."

He kissed me once more and stepped back. "I left the drinks in the car. I'll be right back."

I nodded, and he jogged around the corner. Crossing the kitchen, I surveyed the large purple bouquet. It was all my favorite flowers and so large it wouldn't fit anywhere in the kitchen. It was as heavy as I expected as I moved it to the center of the kitchen table.

Ryder reentered the kitchen with soda and beer in both hands as I turned my attention to the smaller, but no less pretty, white arrangement. He set the drinks on the counter and started organizing them in the fridge.

"So, two bouquets?" I asked.

Ryder slid the last can into place and straightened, shutting the fridge and turning to me. He leaned against the counter next to me and placed his hand against my hip. With my hands wrapped around the clear glass vase, I spun the flowers slowly.

"The big purple one is from me," he said, tilting his head toward the kitchen table where it proudly sat. His eyes dropped to the white bouquet, and he took a deep breath. "This one, I bought for...Daniel. Or on his behalf, I guess."

My hands froze and emotion welled in my throat. Immediately, I looked from the flowers up into Ryder's sincere blue eyes.

"What?" was all I could manage to ask.

He sighed, and his grip on my hip tightened, his thumb idly rubbing the small strip of skin where the hem of my top met my jeans. "I kind of feel stupid now, but I don't know. I was picking up the other one and saw the all-white one in one of the display cases. After everything you told me, it felt right for him to be represented, too. I think he would have wanted that."

"Ryder," I said quietly, unsure what else I could say in that moment. I turned to face him, glancing from him back to the flowers. My sweet, kind man. And that was just it, he was mine.

He chuckled wryly and shook his head, dragging his hand over his jaw. "I know, it's stupid, but—"

"It's not stupid, Ryder. Not at all. It's really sweet, and...he would have appreciated it. I appreciate it." The hesitance in his expression slowly faded. "Although the idea of you *also* getting me flowers probably wouldn't have been so popular."

He cracked a crooked smile, and I kissed the corner that was tilted upward. Finally, he laughed and lifted me up, setting me on the counter next to the little white bouquet. I giggled uncharacteristically as he stepped between my legs and planted his hands on either side of my hips.

He kissed me softly once, then again. He lingered against my lips, and I cupped his cheeks in my hands. I liked the rough feel of his stubble against my palms and the heat of his breath against my lips. It was a balm to my heart as it grew with the love and care I could feel in his every touch and word and action.

"I really hate that so many things had to go wrong—really, *really* wrong—to get us here, but I'm so fucking happy we are," he said. "Because all I want to do is love you more than you ever thought a person could love someone else."

"And I'm so lucky to be loved by you, Ryder. It's...amazing."

I sighed, and our kiss resumed. More urgent and hurried than before. A tangle of lips and teeth and tongues, I wrapped my legs around him as he tugged me closer to the edge. I raked my fingers through his hair, and I could feel his need meeting mine as his hands groped at my hips and dragged up my back.

"Oh, holy shit!" A voice—not mine or Ryder's—bellowed from my left. I startled and pulled back from Ryder as he did the same. Both of us swung our attention in the direction of the sound to find Natalie covering her eyes and Theo directly behind her, trying, and failing, to suppress his smile.

I rolled my lips like it was going to hide my own smile and felt bad for how sweet I thought Ryder's blush was. He dropped his head against my shoulder as Natalie peeked out between her fingers.

"Is it safe?" she asked.

Theo kissed the side of her head and walked farther into the kitchen. "Yes, baby girl. It's safe. It was payback for the time he found us together."

Ryder scoffed and straightened, helping me down off the counter. "If you'd given us another five minutes, then *that* would've been payback. Catching us making out doesn't exactly make us even."

"Yes, yes," Natalie agreed, dropping her purse onto a barstool and skipping over to me. "Anyway, Happy birthday!"

She stretched on her tiptoes and wrapped her arms around my neck. "Thank you," I said, squeezing her back. "Thank you both for coming especially since—" The doorbell rang, and I sighed. "Since my family is going to be here soon."

Ryder won over my entire family. My sister, mom, and dad already loved him as Natalie's son, but as my boyfriend, I knew it could be an awkward transition.

But leave it to him to win over everyone. My dad had invited him over to watch football, and my mom was hanging on his every word. Even my niece and nephew thought he hung the damn moon. And of course, Ryder was eating up the attention.

He was always the life of the party, and with my family, it wasn't any different.

I was happy it had gone so well, but I was also relieved when I closed the door behind my mother, who was always the last one to leave. She was going on about how proud she was of me for finally finding a nice man to settle down with and blah blah blah. I'd tuned her out the second she said the word *"finally."*

With a forced smile, I waved to her and shut the door without a second thought. I let out a long sigh of relief and leaned back against the door. A second later, I could feel Ryder in front of me, his hands smoothing down my arms and his lips against my forehead.

"That went really well, right?"

I nodded and opened my eyes. "Better than I could have hoped."

"I think so, too," he said with a smile. "Now, if you want to hear it, I have a plan for the rest of your birthday, because as much as this party was for you, it also wasn't."

I hummed in the back of my throat and rested my hands on his chest, against the blue T-shirt that matched his eyes and was stretched across the muscles beneath.

"What's your plan?"

"To take you back to your bedroom and make you come more than you ever have. Over and over and over again. We can shoot for thirty-four times. What do you think?"

I laughed, and he covered his smile with our intertwined hands, pressing them against his mouth. "I think I'd very much enjoy you trying to get to thirty-four, but that's a lofty, likely unattainable, goal."

"But we'll have so much fun trying. What do you want first then? I think my mouth and fingers would be a good place to start."

I moaned and kissed him soundly although quickly. "Yes, but I have to put away all the food first." I stepped around him, and he groaned as he followed me into the kitchen.

"How about a compromise?" he offered.

"What's your compromise?" I asked as I started picking up plates and cups left scattered around the kitchen and living room. Proof that people were too busy having fun to worry about picking up after themselves. It was a good mess. One I liked seeing.

"I'll pour you a glass of wine, you can watch me clean up, then we go to your bedroom. You shouldn't have to deal with this on your birthday."

Ryder crossed the kitchen and pulled open the refrigerator door, retrieving the bottle of rosé Natalie and I had started earlier. It was on the tip of my tongue to argue, but he leveled me a serious, sincere look.

"Please," he said, and I had to nod. He poured me a healthy glass as I leaned against the counter.

He handed me the glass, and I took a long sip.

"So...speaking of parents, I got a text from my dad earlier today," he said, collecting more plates and consolidating the leftovers behind me. "He said that he and Jessica want to have lunch with us sometime next week. I didn't commit to anything, though, before I could talk to you."

I cringed and took another large gulp. Mark was not a bad person at all—he and Natalie had just grown apart, and it had turned out for the best. But he wasn't necessarily my cup of tea anyway. It was remarkable that he'd contributed to creating his son who I cared about more than almost anyone else. But I guess *officially* meeting the parents was necessary in every relationship.

"I know it's going to be awkward and weird, but like your parents, I think he just wants to feel included and make sure we're...*real.*" He came back around the island and dropped a few plates in the sink, looking at me with raised brows and an apologetic look in his eyes.

"That's fine. Wednesday or Thursday work best for me, and if necessary, I can move my Sunday meeting."

With a wink, he kissed my forehead and walked back around

the counter to gather more dishes. "I promise it won't be too bad, and I'll make sure I have an excuse ready, so he doesn't try to extend the meal. I know spending a ton of time with my dad and his girlfriend isn't high on your list."

"Yeah, but I love you, so—" I didn't think. I didn't contemplate the words before they were out of my mouth. Realizing what I said, I froze and waited for Ryder to say or do something.

But a long-extended silence followed. Still behind me, I was nervous to turn around and look at him, so I stood still and considered maybe I hadn't just said what I think did.

I barely heard his soft steps on the tile floor and waited with bated breath as he rounded the corner and came into my periphery. He stopped directly in front of me with three stacked trays in his hands. His jaw slack, he narrowed his eyes.

"What did you just say?"

I had two choices in that moment—pretend like I hadn't meant it and try to change the subject or cop to it. Several weeks ago, I would have been sprinting the other direction. Running from feelings I refused to name or share. But standing in front of Ryder now, I couldn't imagine waiting to say it a second longer.

"You heard me," I said. Energy buzzed through me as I waited for his next move. With a neutral expression, he stepped forward and set the trays on the counter next to the sink. He was so much closer now, I felt the need to hold my breath for some unknown reason. Likely to cover up how hard I was breathing or how rapid my heartbeat was pounding in anticipation.

"Say it again," he said, looming over me and wrapping his hand around the side of my neck. His thumb slipped over my jaw and paused on the center of my chin, just beneath my lower lip.

I wetted my lips and finally breathed again. His eyes bounced from mine to my mouth which he watched in wonder as I admitted, "I love you, Ryder Calaway."

Shock then elation crossed his face, and I'd never seen a smile so wide or proud. In the next second, he was gripping beneath my ass and lifting me into the air. I fumbled to set my wineglass on the counter right before he strode down the hallway and toward the bedroom.

"Fuck cleaning up," he muttered against my neck. "Say it one more time."

Smiling, I leaned down, positioned my mouth right next to his ear, and whispered in a low voice, "I love you."

He groaned and kicked open the double doors to my room. "Fuck, my dick is so hard right now."

THIRTY-EIGHT
LOVE ME, PEG ME

Caroline

THERE WAS COMMOTION ON THE OTHER SIDE OF THE FRONT DOOR, but I knew it wasn't trick-or-treaters. It swung open a second later, and I twirled the tie of my black, satin robe in one hand as I leaned against the wall at the end of the entryway.

Ryder walked in, shut the door behind him, and took a few steps before he noticed me. A slow smile spread across his face.

"Hey, pretty girl."

"Hiya, Trouble."

I'd received an invitation to the opening of an exclusive club that night, but I was craving alone time with Ryder. And I knew my assistant, Addie, needed a night out, anyway. We could partake in the club's exclusive rooms whenever we wanted. And I felt confident in my decision as I appraised Ryder.

With easy, measured steps that didn't bely his earlier eagerness, he crossed to me. I stayed where I was, watching him closely, until he was within kissing distance, and I had to tilt my head slightly to look in his eyes.

"You ready?" I asked.

He reached up and toyed with a lock of my freshly curled

blonde hair between his fingers. My hair was pristine as was my makeup and the mostly smudge-proof red lipstick I hadn't pulled out in a while.

"More ready than I've ever been for anything in my entire life."

"Good, good," I whispered. Dipping just the tips of my fingers beneath the waistband of his jeans, I slipped them against his skin and toward his hip while I held his hungry stare. He stuttered out a shaky breath, and I couldn't contain my slow, seductive smile. I tiptoed my nails up his shirt, over his stomach and his chest, and he shivered, his eyes falling shut for just a second.

"Are you going to be a good boy for me?"

He groaned, and I could feel the vibration against my palm.

He licked his lips as he nodded, and his eyes met mine. "Yes, I'll be the best boy for you."

"I'm sure you will be," I said as I took his hand. I let my eyes linger on his face until I pivoted and led us down the hallway, my heels clicking on the tiled floor.

He eagerly followed, and once we crossed the threshold into my bedroom, I had to remind myself that there was no rush. That we had all night, and I could take my time.

I'd lowered the lights and lit a few candles, casting the room in a warm, dim glow. And it smelled fantastic, too.

"Sit," I instructed, pointing to the edge of my bed. He dutifully did as I instructed and folded his hands in his lap. I didn't linger long, pushing open the bathroom doors. But before I stepped fully inside, I glanced over my shoulder.

His eyes were glued to me as I'd hoped. "Stay," I added and slipped through the doors.

I heard his muffled, "yes ma'am," through the doors and smiled to myself. Everything I needed was laid out on the bathroom counter in front of me. I'd done my research, investigating different types of dildos, vibrators, and harnesses, trying to find the one that would work best for us both.

And I'd finally found it. The one I'd decided on was a double-sided vibrator with a long, thicker shaft I knew Ryder would enjoy and a smaller portion I could slip inside myself. And to make sure it stayed in place, I bought a dark-red leather harness.

I picked up the vibrator and the lube next to it but realized quickly that I didn't need it. All it took was the brief thought that Ryder was sitting on the edge of my bed, waiting for his cock like a good boy to make me wet enough to slip the shorter side inside me.

I gasped at how well it hit that perfect spot but didn't stop until I had the harness tightened around my hips and the longer shaft slipped through the ring. I appraised my image in the mirror before I walked back out into the bedroom.

My short, silk robe was still thrown over my shoulders. Underneath it I'd chosen a lacy, black bra that cupped my tits and complimented the dildo and harness. I'd tried everything on once a week ago when it came in, but I hadn't paused to consider what I looked like. Now, I stared at myself and the unfamiliar yet enticing view of me with a cock jutting from my hips.

I liked the way I looked and the way it made me feel. *Powerful.* That was the word I settled on when I appraised my reflection and how my body felt wearing this new pleasure-giving tool that I was eager to use.

Leaning forward, I double-checked my lipstick in the mirror and tucked a stray piece of hair behind my ear. I slipped the remote to the vibrator into my robe pocket. Excitement buzzed through me, but when my hand clasped the doorknob, a wave of nerves bombarded me.

Still, I tugged open the doors and found Ryder right where I left him. The moment he looked at me, all nerves washed away in one swift rush.

"*Fuck me,*" he muttered, eyes sweeping over me again and

again like he was so captivated by every part of me, he didn't know where he wanted his attention to land.

With a smile, I took a few slow steps to him. "That's the plan."

His hands were tense, grasping his knees and showing off the impressive veins beneath his skin. He raised them as I got closer, but I shook my head.

"Don't touch yet," I instructed as I stepped between his spread thighs. His jaw tensed, but he dropped his hands back to his thighs. My instructions were only for him, though. I wanted to touch him as much as I could. Everywhere and anywhere.

His black hair was recently trimmed, so neat and perfectly styled after a day at work. But I wanted us both undone. I slipped my fingers through the silky strands and dragged them down the back of his head to the curve of his neck.

He stared at my face in awe and appreciation, but I caught him glancing down at the vibrator standing proudly between us. Beneath it, I could see the hard outline of his cock pressing against his pants. My pussy clenched in response around the toy, and my hands dropped onto his shoulders.

"Do you remember your safe word?"

He blinked twice and slowly nodded his head. "Yes, am I going to need it?"

Fisting his hair in one hand and wrapping the other loosely around his throat, I tsked at him. His eyes widened, and I felt him swallow beneath my palm.

"You said you were going to be good, but questioning me about your safe word isn't the best start, Trouble."

"You're right," he said, licking his lips. "My safe word is lilac." He said the word slowly: *lilac*. Emphasizing both syllables and letting it roll off his perfect tongue.

He almost looked disappointed when I let go of his hair and his throat, but when I reached for the hem of his shirt, that disappointment disappeared. He raised his arms, and I tugged it off over his head, tossing it on the floor at the end of the bed. I didn't hesitate to run my hands over his broad chest and the smattering of dark hair in the center.

He groaned, and I glanced down to finds his hands balled into fists against his knees.

"You want to touch me so bad, don't you?" I taunted. I ran my fingers down his toned arms and scraped my nails against the tops of each of his hands. A low growl rumbled up his chest, and I smirked at his quiet but definitive confirmation. And all at once I wanted that, too. Teasing him was fun, but I wanted to feel his hands on me. I wanted to feel that pent up need, and I wanted him to let it out on me. "Then do it."

The second I uttered the last word, Ryder was up, cupping my face and guiding me in a brutal, hungry kiss. He ran one hand down my back and hauled me closer. The vibrator squeezed between us, he rocked his hips against it, rubbing the underside of his cock, still confined in his pants.

The thinner stretch of material that connected one side of the vibrator to the other was perfectly placed against my slit and rubbed against my clit. Powerful waves of pleasure came with every sweep of his tongue, every swipe of the toy against my sex, and every needy touch of his hands. But it wasn't just pleasure that I felt. It was desire, hunger, *love*.

"You picked a pretty toy," he muttered against my lips, reaching between us to palm the toy in his large palm. "Is it one of those fancy double-sided ones?"

"Yes," I whispered. "A little bit of something for both of us."

He smiled and stepped back only far enough that we could both clearly see what he was doing—pumping that pretty silicone shaft like he was impatient for it to be inside him. "You're so perfect," he said with enough reverence that I had to look back up. His hand didn't stop moving, but his eyes were steadfast on mine.

In them, I saw every second of our future together. And it made me want him so much more.

"The only problem with this is that I can't taste your cunt. Are you dripping around the toy? Making a huge mess?"

I nodded as he kissed me. Reaching forward, I dragged my nails over the fabric covering his thick length and was rewarded with a hearty groan.

"You may not be able to taste me," I said. "But you can suck my cock."

THIRTY-NINE
AND IT VIBRATES?!

Caroline

A GLORIOUS, ELATED SMILE TILTED HIS LIPS, AND HE PREPARED TO kneel. But I stopped him with a firm hand on his dick. "Let's take these off first." I slipped his belt off and popped open the button.

Apparently, I was going to slow for his taste, because he unzipped and kicked his pants—followed by his briefs—to the side in less than a second.

"Such an eager boy," I purred. Closing the space between us, my silicone toy and his warm, erect cock pressed together as I attempted to pump us in unison. My thumb brushed over his tip, and he bucked against my hold.

He was so hard I swore I could feel the blood pounding through the thick veins running up and down his length and the pressure building in his balls. I wasn't the only one who was wet. He was leaking everywhere, and I collected what I could on my thumb, lifting it to my mouth and swiping it against my tongue. I loved the salty, tangy taste of him.

He tracked the motion with his jaw slack and a fire in his eyes.

"I need to see how hard you are and what a big mess you make as you suck your new toy. Now, be a good boy, and get on your knees."

Without fanfare or hesitation, he dropped on one knee then the other. He looked up at me through thick, dark lashes with his hands resting on his knees, waiting for instruction. I carefully let my robe fall down my arms and tossed it on the bed.

"Do your worst," I said. "Show me what you can do."

His smile was devious and full of promise.

He reached up and wrapped his fingers around the base of the shaft, directing the tip toward his mouth and licking up the underside. No, of course, I really couldn't *feel* the heat or wetness of his tongue or hand, but what I *could* feel was every slight tug and pressure throughout the rest of the toy. It massaged against my clit and rubbed my g-spot. And the sight itself, of Ryder enjoying slipping his tongue and his mouth over the toy I'd fuck him with later, was so fucking erotic.

He licked up and down, wetting it to allow his hand to make easy languid passes, and then suctioned his mouth around the tip.

"Yes, just like that," I muttered. Dragging my nails through his hair, I gripped it at the root, but didn't direct his movements. I just wanted to touch him.

What started out slow didn't stay that way long. His hand and mouth worked in tandem as he sucked up and down. He twisted his wrist and bobbed along the length. He looked so good in the low light of the room. All his lean, toned muscles in his arms tensing as he worked, I could watch him all day. Especially as he stared up at me like he wanted me to see what a good job he was doing and how perfect he looked.

"You're doing so good. That's exactly how a good boy sucks cock."

My praise was met by redoubled efforts. He sucked and pulled, and the movement of the toy was so merciless against my clit I swore I was going to come.

He let go with a pop, still pumping his hand. "Fuck my mouth," he said quickly, a string of spit connecting from the tip to his bottom lip. "I'll tap your leg if I need you to stop."

In the back of my mind, I could feel the slight nervousness clouding the moment. I tightened my hold of his hair and gripped the base of the toy. Having never done this before, it was like he knew I needed the encouragement.

"Please," he muttered as I tipped his head back. That one word was enough. He opened his mouth and stuck out his tongue, a willing and dirty offering. He dropped his hands to his thighs and let me guide the cock back into his mouth.

He closed his lips around the toy when I let go, adding my other hand to his hair. My first thrust was awkward and clumsy. As were the few after that. But Ryder held my gaze the entire time, taking whatever I was giving him and doing it so well.

Finally, I found my rhythm, and triumph sparkled in his eyes when he realized I had. My thrusts went from shallow and uneven to deep and confident. When I tapped the back of his throat, I pulled back just a little. But then I did it again and again with no reaction from Ryder.

"No gag reflex?" I asked, and the shake of his head was barely noticeable between my thrusts. "Wow, such a good slut."

His eyes fluttered at the praise, and I looked around us to see his cock bobbing angrily between his legs. The tip was shiny with pre-cum that had dripped down onto the rug beneath him, and it looked like it was begging to be touched.

"Are you ready, Trouble?"

I stepped back, and Ryder nodded, wiping his mouth with the back of his hand. He stood, and I couldn't not kiss him. I reached for him and wrapped my arms around his neck, tugging him closer and fitting my mouth over his.

A tangle of limbs, we unceremoniously tumbled onto the bed. He wrapped a hand in my hair, and I scraped my nails down his back. I nipped his lower lip as I rolled on top of him.

I leaned to the side and grabbed the lube and remote from

the pocket of my robe and kicked it off the bed. Ryder watched me set them down next to us while he reached around and unfastened my bra with practiced ease.

"And it vibrates?" he asked, and I nodded. "Fuck, yes. I knew it." He tapped the outside of my thighs, and we shifted until his legs were spread and I was poised between them.

With his heels pressed into the sheets, he bent his legs and readjusted until he was open for me. I smoothed my palms down the inside of his thighs until I reached his cock which I encircled in my palm. He grunted and shunted his hips. My other hand struck out and pushed his hips back down onto the bed.

"Fuck, Caroline," he groaned. My hand slipped easily over his soft, taut skin as his hands grabbed the blankets at his sides. I squeezed the tip and watched a drop of pre-cum bead at the top. Leaning forward, I was about to lick it up when Ryder stopped me with a hand on my shoulder.

"If you put your mouth on me, I'm going to shoot down your throat in two seconds." I froze and sat back up. "I can't wait any longer. Just get inside me."

My hand drifted lower, and my fingers brushed against his ass. Circling the hole, I reached for the lube with my free hand as Ryder moaned.

"Please," he begged, and it sounded so pretty coming from his swollen lips.

"I don't want to hurt you."

Before I'd finished speaking, he was fervently shaking his head.

"You're not going to hurt me, baby. But even if you did, I wouldn't mind. Pain isn't so bad when it's from your hand."

His words hit me directly in the center of my chest. They were heavy, whether he meant them to be or not. I assumed he hadn't meant anything so serious with the way he still writhed beneath me. But I had caused him pain when I'd almost walked away a few months ago and left him in limbo for days. Even if it was always meant to be temporary.

If I hadn't made the right decision—the *only* decision—and come back to him, I would have been responsible for even more pain.

Inflicting pain with the purpose of eventually creating pleasure was the only way I ever wanted him to experience it again.

I flipped open the cap of the lube bottle and dripped just enough along the top of the toy. I spread it over the tip and around to the underside, making sure every inch was covered.

"God, you're so fucking hot," Ryder muttered as he watched me prep the toy from beneath hooded eyes. I loved the way he looked at me. Like I was all his fantasies come to life like he'd once told me. And I knew my expression mirrored his.

I took the excess lube and spread it over his hole. He pressed into my hand like he was silently asking for more as he gripped the base of his cock.

"Please, baby. Please, *please*." I hummed and moved closer, notching the tip of the toy at his ass and taking a deep breath.

"I love it when you beg. Ever since that very first time. You are so good at it. I can't help but give in to you."

"That's the point," he gasped as I slowly pushed forward. With one hand on his thigh, I watched the tip of the toy disappear. I met resistance, but not as much as I expected. His body eagerly accepted me as the silicone stretched him open.

He moaned, and I glanced up at his face which was contorted in pleasure. Eyes fixed on me, his jaw was slack, and his cheeks were flushed. With one hand still on his cock, he wrapped the other around his thigh and pulled it back.

Another inch, then another until the toy was fully inside him, and I could feel the heat of his skin against mine. He panted and swore under his breath. The muscles in his stomach and chest danced and twitched, but I stayed still, wanting to give him enough time to adjust.

But that wasn't what he wanted. "Move, pretty girl," he said through clenched teeth. "Please, fuck me."

I clenched around the opposite end of the toy and carefully pulled back. He gripped it so tight, it was work to move it in and out. Still not used to the movement, my thrusts were jerky and awkward. But Ryder was there to help guide me. He leaned forward and wrapped his hands around my waist, tilting my hips in the tempo he wanted.

"So good," he said. "Just like that."

He held onto me, and I wrapped my arms around his neck, holding onto him. I pumped into him and finally managed to get the movement right. Right enough that his hands migrated to my ass, and his fingers slipped beneath the straps of the harness.

His face dropped into the crook of my neck, and I took the opportunity to reach for the remote next to me. It took a second to press the right combination of buttons, but the toy finally vibrated to life and both of us cried out.

"Oh, fuck, fuck, *fuck*," Ryder groaned as he tumbled back onto the bed. His legs tried to close, but I slammed my palms down on the inside of his thighs and pressed them into the blankets.

"No, *no*," I struggled to say with my orgasm already bearing down on me. The toy perfectly pressed against my g-spot, and even on the lowest vibration setting, I was too turned on to resist the sharp pleasure sparking through me. "I want to see you taking this cock when I come."

With every thrust, his cock bounced and smacked his stomach, leaving a trail of pre-cum on his skin. He was so hard and so turned-on, and I was the one making that happen. My nails dug into his thighs, and I ground onto the toy as I plunged into him again and again.

"Yes, baby," Ryder growled. "Let me see you come. Come all over that toy as you fuck me."

And that was all it took for my orgasm to shoot through me,

followed by unending ecstasy as I stared at the man I loved more than I ever knew possible.

FORTY

OUT OF THIS WORLD

Ryder

I'D TRAVELED TO ANOTHER PLANE, ANOTHER PLANET.

It wasn't the first time I'd had a toy or a dick in my ass, but there was something about Caroline being on the other side that made it better than any time before.

She made everything better.

She writhed between my spread legs, and her thrusts momentarily stalled as her orgasm peaked. God, she was fucking incredible. My own orgasm was so close to the surface, I needed those few moments, watching her fall apart, to keep myself together.

But the vibration continued, and my ass clenched around the rumbling toy. The sensations rushed up into my shaft and pierced through my balls. I was consumed by it and by her.

Caroline shuddered and planted her hands against my hips on either side of my cock. Her eyes slowly rolled up my torso and finally landed on my face. Her cheeks and chest were flushed. Her lower lip swollen from where her teeth dug into it as she came.

Blonde hair fell over her shoulders in tousled waves, and her tits were fucking bitable. She was the epitome of sex and desire. Especially with the dildo strapped around her hips.

I could tell she was a little nervous and was struggling to get the rhythm right. But she was a quick study.

She leaned to her side and grabbed the lube, dripping more of the cold liquid onto the toy. Then she reached for the small black remote.

"Oh, no. I don't think I can—" My words disappeared on a whimpered groan as she ignored my concern and clicked the button anyway.

My entire body tensed as the vibrations shot through me.

"You can do it. Be a good boy and take it," she said sweetly. Every time she called me that, I wanted to do whatever I had to to make her say it again. I wanted to be good. I wanted to be her good boy if only she kept fucking me and looking at me like she needed me.

She dropped the remote back to the bed and resumed fucking me. First with slow, deep thrusts that were impressive and thorough. If I hadn't had to guide her earlier, I would've guessed she'd done it a thousand times before.

She held me in place and dug her nails into my hips as she thrusted in and back out. Every time she retreated, the tip of the toy brushed against my prostate and stars sparked behind my eyes.

But I knew she wouldn't be able to resist pounding into me like she was before her orgasm hit her. She upped the vibration again, and I sucked in a breath through my clenched teeth. The curses coming out of my mouth were unintelligible, strung together between pleading sounds and cries.

Her grip on my hips tightened, and she increased her speed. "Yes, yes, yes," I cried as I wrapped my hands around my thighs and pulled my legs back to give her better access. She leaned forward and glanced down at my cock which was angrily hard and leaking everywhere. I'd never produced so much pre-cum in my life.

I was so enthralled in every sweep of the toy inside me and the feeling of her hands that I didn't realize what she was doing until I felt her wet palm slide against the underside of my dick. My gasp turned into a moan as she wrapped her lubed hand around my shaft and started pumping me in long strokes.

"Come for me, Ryder. I want to watch you shoot all over your stomach."

"Come with me," I ground out. "Come with me."

She nodded but kept thrusting and jerking. Our moans mingled and echoed through the room, growing louder with each punch of her hips. My hands fisted around my thighs, I was desperate to touch her, but I knew moving would chance fucking everything up. And it felt too good to chance.

"Oh, fuck, Ryder," she moaned and went to throw her head back, but I wanted her eyes on me as we came undone together.

"Look at me," I growled, and she complied, dropping her head and squeezing the tip of my dick with her purple tipped fingers. It was enough—the vibration, the toy pressing against my prostate, her hand, and her eyes on me as she came once again—to send me careening into oblivion.

Ropes and ropes of cum shot up my chest as the most intense, mind-blowing orgasm I'd ever experienced over-whelmed me. It went on forever, euphoric relief flooding my veins as I stared into Caroline's eyes. Her pupils were blown, and her body was tense as we rode it out together.

Together. We were together, and suddenly, I had to feel her, too.

I'd just finished coming, my dick still hard and leaking, when I dropped my legs and lunged for her. I fused our mouths together and devoured every little sound she made.

"I need to be inside you," I said.

That was the only warning she got before I pushed her back onto the bed, effectively slipping the toy out of my ass. She fell against the sheets, and I quickly grabbed the towel she'd already had laying on the edge of the bed before we even stepped foot in the room. I wiped the cum off my chest then grappled with the straps of the harness as she turned off the toy. It took longer than I wanted, this burning need to feel her wrapped around me like it was going to ignite us both and everything around us if I didn't extinguish it quickly.

I ripped the pretty gold clasps and tossed the red leather harness to the side. Then I removed the toy and buried my face in her cunt. She was swollen and sweet. My tongue lapped at her opening then teased her clit. She was sensitive, too, bucking against my face and clambering to get away. But that wasn't going to happen.

I would have spent forever devouring her pussy, but that need made me push up onto my knees, widen her thighs and thrust into her in one quick move.

"Oh, fuck!" I cried as she moaned my name. We both shuddered as I wrapped my arms around her. She did the same and hooked her legs around my waist until I didn't know where either of us began or ended.

My hips snapped again and again, searching for that sweet euphoric relief a second time. She was so wet and warm. I wanted to live inside her for the rest of my life. She clenched around me and mumbled my name over and over again.

"Yes, baby. You know exactly who's fucking you," I said as I buried my face in her neck. It was one of my favorite spots. It always smelled faintly of her perfume and shampoo—like flowers in sunshine—but it was always entirely Caroline. I fisted a hand in the back of her hair and doubled my efforts, changing my angle just enough that my pubic bone rubbed against her clit and the tip of my cock brushed against her g-spot.

I knew I'd hit the perfect combination when her legs fell open, but her nails dug into my back. Each breath was shallower than the last, and her moans turned into sweet little whimpers.

She drenched my cock a second before her inner walls strangled me. The tightness keeping me trapped and making it impossible to thrust any longer. But I didn't need to. I let her pussy hold me hostage and milk anything left from my cock.

I kept still and pumped deep inside her, breathing in that uniquely Caroline smell as we came together.

Both of us breathing hard, I waited several seconds before rolling to my back and taking her with me. Her head against my chest, I smoothed my hands down her back. She sighed and took a deep breath, propping her chin on the back of her hands and looking up at me.

"How'd I do?" she asked, and I reached up to brush away a stray lock of hair.

The pleasure-high was still thick, so words were hard. "So good. So, *so* good," was all I could manage.

She smiled softly and nibbled at her bottom lip. Somehow her red lipstick had stayed mostly in place through everything. "Good not great?"

"So great," I clarified.

"Great not amazing?"

I groaned but leaned up and kissed her somewhat awkwardly at our angle. It still made her smile, and that's all I wanted.

"Every time we have sex, pretty girl, it's the best sex of my life. We keep outdoing ourselves."

Her eyes flared with accomplishment and agreement. "We really do," she said, her voice low and sultry. She reached forward and ran a single finger over my jaw then up to my cheekbone. She trailed that single finger across my forehead and repeated the pattern on the other side of my face.

It was so soothing and calming, my entire body relaxed with her weight on top of me and every sweep of her finger.

"I love you so much," she said quietly. I breathed deeply and rested my hands on her hips. My reaction when she said it for the first time a few months ago and now were exactly the same. My heart rate picked up, and I felt this lightness in my chest. I was the luckiest person in the world hearing those words from her lips. And I wanted to hear them every day for the rest of my life.

I opened my eyes and was greeted by her easy, serene smile and wild sex hair.

"I love you, too. So much."

She sighed and continued drawing patterns across my face. Closing my eyes, I focused back on the feeling.

"I'm glad you were trouble," she said after several minutes of silence, and I smiled.

"Is that so?"

I could feel her nod against my chest. "I'm glad you had the confidence to do what I couldn't. To go after what you wanted and not give up until you had it."

I opened my eyes to see her looking down at my mouth where her fingers traced my lips. She was looking at me, but she was lost in thought.

"I was never going to give up on you, pretty girl. You're it for me. Always have been, always will be. I was just waiting for you to catch up."

I kissed her fingers, and her eyes finally met mine. They were clear and bright.

"You're it for me, too, Trouble." And I had to kiss her after hearing the sincerity in every word, so I'd know what my future tasted like, too.

EPILOGUE
MR. PHANTOM

Addison

"This one might be my favorite." The comment came from a man who had stopped beside me. Far enough away that he wasn't in my personal space, but close enough that I could feel him there.

My throat went dry at the sound of his voice. It was low and husky, and I immediately wanted to hear it again.

I was well and truly out of my comfort zone. The sultry, sexy club around me was not my usual scene, but my boss, Caroline, couldn't make it to the opening and asked me if I wanted to go instead. She knew I had been down recently and thought it would cheer me up. Except it wasn't until I walked through the door and pushed back the velvet green curtain that I realized it wasn't just a club, it was the new sex club, Abditory.

Caroline knew everyone in the city, so I wasn't surprised she'd scored an invite. I, however, wasn't likely the person they expected. Although it seemed fine that she transferred the invite.

The first floor was a bar and lounge—velvet green sofas, leather barstools and dark wood finishes—but the upper two floors were playrooms, as the hostess had called them, and an open play area. Those were supposed to open for use in almost two hours, and I wasn't planning on participating.

Until then, I was sipping my drink and walking the perimeter of the panel-lined room, observing the art hung on the wall in the dim light and trying like hell to forget everything that had happened *before* I walked through that curtain.

Like that my boyfriend, Owen, who said he would come with me, had ditched me for who knows what. I tried to forget that it wasn't the first time. I tried to forget the *"we need to talk"* text I'd sent him while getting in the car to come here. I tried to forget the woman I was half an hour before. I wanted to be someone different for the night. Someone who didn't have to deal with that real life mess.

And the man who appeared next to me looked like he might make it easier to forget.

"All of the women grinding on a...uh...large penis, I wonder why it's your favorite," I muttered sarcastically and looked over at him.

He was wearing a white mask that obscured half his face and a well-cut tuxedo. Not that I knew whether it fit well or not, but it looked damn good on him.

He was dressed as the Phantom from *The Phantom of the Opera*. He fit in with everyone else well. Caroline had transferred the ticket to me so last minute, that I didn't have time to pick through the measly leftover costumes the few stores still had on Halloween. So, I'd thrown something together from things already in my closet—a short blue dress, a black belt, matching Mary Jane heels, and white knee-high socks. I'd even put my blonde hair in pigtails.

Voilà, I was freaking Bubbles from the *Power Puff Girls*.

And I didn't fit in at all.

Still, Mr. Phantom had decided to initiate a conversation with me. The one half of his face I could see bore a sharp jawline covered in stubble, and his dark hair was messily tousled in that purposeful way some men pulled off effortlessly.

And beneath his tuxedo, I could tell he was built.

No matter the costume, I knew he was gorgeous. And fuck me, his laugh matched his voice—deep and soulful.

"You're right, it is a little on the nose, although that wasn't necessarily the reason," he said with a smile. "Which one is your favorite?"

He motioned with his tumbler to the rest of the art I'd just viewed. I glanced around at each and carefully considered his question.

"This one," I said, pointing to the one just to his left. It was of a woman and a man lying together. One of the woman's legs tossed over the man's, it was like we were a part of their intimate moment looking down their bodies at where they touched. "It feels…intimate, natural."

He hummed, and I followed as he walked the few steps to the painting I'd mentioned.

"I like how they've painted her especially," I continued, not sure if the next part was too personal a thought to share with a stranger, but for some reason, I felt compelled to share it anyway. "They didn't try to hide what we've been conditioned to believe are her imperfections."

I motioned to the curve of her stomach and the stretch marks on her inner thigh. One breast was subtly larger than the other, and her skin tone wasn't completely even.

"But even with all those so-called imperfections, she's still desired."

A silence passed between us, and I took a long sip of my nearly empty drink, trying to fill the void. In the span of a second, I questioned everything I'd said, and if I'd shared too much.

Concerned that I'd put my foot in my mouth, I quickly said, "Or maybe it says something more about me that I picked out all those imperfections." My laugh was hollow, but I was relieved when he shook his head and turned his half-smile on me.

His eyes were the color of the light emitted from sconces hanging around us—a warm amber.

"Then maybe it says something about me, too," he admitted. "Because I noted those perceived imperfections. Although, to me, they're anything but imperfect. They are often my favorite thing about a woman's body."

My mouth went dry, and I found it impossible to swallow. Silently, I wished I had more of my drink left or that it was socially acceptable for me to eat the ice left in the glass.

Although he wasn't talking about my body, it reacted as if he had. And my reaction was only exacerbated by his long perusal of my body. His amber-colored eyes tracked down then back up, landing confidently on my face once again.

"They are everything that makes her...*her*."

I was going to combust or erupt into flames. Either way, I had a feeling I would enjoy it if it involved Mr. Phantom.

"Would you like another drink, Bubbles?"

"Yeah, that would be—" I stopped and looked up at him, my confusion written all over my face.

"Bubbles?" I asked as we walked toward the bar.

He nodded. "That's who you're dressed as, right?"

We both set our empty glasses on the bar and ordered another round before I turned back to Mr. Phantom. "Yes, but I guess I'm just surprised you recognized it."

"Why?" he asked with a tilt to his lips like he already knew my answer.

"Doesn't seem like your type of TV show."

He smiled, and I damned that freaking mask. I wanted to see it unobstructed and unbound. I wanted to know if he had a dimple on the right side that matched the left.

"I guess it wasn't really," he admitted as the bartender handed us our new drinks. "It came out when I was a teenager, so I wasn't going to be caught dead watching a TV show about three kindergarten girls with superpowers."

Math was not my forte, and I couldn't remember the exact

year the show had premiered, but based on my limited knowledge and even with my crappy math skills, I could guess that—

"I can see you doing the math in your head," Mr. Phantom said. And I shook my head, taking a long sip of my drink. It tasted even better the second time.

"Sorry," I mumbled, and he immediately shook his head.

"Don't be. I'll save you the trouble—I'm almost forty."

Another sip, and I realized I didn't give a shit how old he was. Whether I was supposed to or not, I liked Mr. Phantom. And he could be the key to turning my terrible night around. "Well, I was born five years too late to see the premiere of *Powerful Girls.*"

He seemed unsurprised by my admission which made sense with my outfit and pigtails and overall youthful look. But especially with the damn pigtails.

"So, how did you score an invite?" I asked as we walked to a small empty couch tucked in the corner where we'd first met. He let me sit first and took a seat directly next to me. The outside of his thigh brushed mine as he sat, and I couldn't ignore the shiver that whipped through me.

He chuckled at my question which I'd forgotten I'd asked "Or is it top secret?" I asked.

"Not top secret. My best friend owns the place, and I've helped him a little along the way."

He told me about Abditory and how his friend, Nathan, randomly decided one day that the city needed an exclusive, invite-only sex club where anyone could be themselves and explore their desires in a safe, inclusive way. That then brought us to the topic of how I was invited, and I told him about Grant Events without specifying the name, keeping a few details for myself. He seemed genuinely interested in event coordination and what went in to planning.

I shared some of my favorite memories from the past several months of working with Caroline, and we talked about his work as an attorney. By the time, they made the announcement that the upper two floors were opening, I hadn't realized so much time had passed.

Somehow, in the midst of our conversation, we'd migrated closer to one another. My legs tilted toward him, his knee was pressed against mine and his fingers brushed the top of my leg.

He still hadn't taken the mask off, but I could at least clearly see his eyes which were fixed on me. His smile slowly faded, and I could feel the shift. He glanced from my face down to where his fingers touched my leg, and I felt like the one touch was going to burn me alive.

With two drinks and almost two hours of easy conversation, my confidence was at an all-time high and somehow the world had shrunk to just us two sitting on that velvet couch wanting something just within reach.

Our world was too tiny for anyone else. Especially Owen who was a far-off memory. A twinge of guilt hit me once when I realized how much I was enjoying Mr. Phantom, but I quickly dismissed it. My soon-to-be ex didn't deserve a second thought.

"How does someone go about getting one of those rooms upstairs?" I asked, pushing away any shame or possible embarrassment. It was just a question. A question I normally would never have asked, but behind that green curtain, I was determined to be someone else. At least for tonight.

Mr. Phantom straightened, and I worried I'd misjudged every subtle signal until he reached inside his tuxedo jacket and retrieved a small gold key from its inside pocket.

"You'd need a key." He held it out to me in his large palm like an offering. When I went to reach for it, his next words stopped me. "I just need to know one thing before we go up there, because fuck, Bubbles, I really want to go up there with you."

The tips of my fingers traced his, circling where he held the key and brushing over his wrist. I enjoyed the way his eyes shuddered, and he had to swallow before answering.

"What's your name?" he finally asked.

My heart collided with the inside of my chest, and my name got stuck at the back of my throat. I couldn't pinpoint why, but it was a detail I didn't think he needed. Another piece of information I wanted to keep to myself.

"This is just for tonight, right?" I asked, resuming the pattern I was drawing over his palm.

He licked his lips and considered my question for a moment, his eyes narrowing like he couldn't decide what to say next. "It can be whatever you want, Bubbles," he finally said.

"Then what good is my name going to do you?"

I was staring down at the key when his dark chuckle hit my ears. Immediately, I perked up and looked up at him. He leaned forward and dropped his hand back to my thigh, only higher. He pushed his fingers up until they were just beneath the hem of my short skirt, and I could feel the heat of them between my thighs.

A moan caught in my throat, but I swore he heard my muffled whimper as he dropped his mouth to my ear.

"If I don't know your real name, what am I supposed to cry out when my cock is buried deep inside your perfectly tight, wet cunt in less than ten minutes."

I swallowed my shock and inadvertently squeezed my thighs together, searching for some sort of relief. But his hand was still there against me, and I ended up pushing it higher up my skirt. He grunted and sat back just enough to look down my body, getting the perfect view of my cleavage.

The way the words rolled off his tongue in his low, gruff whisper, and the confidence in each of them was enough for me to want to mount him right then and there. I had never been so thoroughly turned on and confused.

My pulse maintained an impressive, intense pace while I tried to compose myself enough to reply and continue our banter. I wanted to be someone new, but I couldn't completely do away with my old self. "I'm sure you can come up with an alternative," I said, but my voice was breathy. "I like Bubbles. It's cute."

He smiled and opened his mouth to speak when his attention bounced to someone who had approached from behind the couch. So invested in him, I hadn't even noticed.

"Hey, Beckett. I knew I'd see you here, man. How are you?"

Mr. Phantom's name was Beckett. Good to know.

Beckett clenched his jaw and licked his lips. I noted his annoyance at the interruption, but if the other man did, he didn't let on.

"Fine, Jared. How are you?" They had a quick, casual conversation, and the man didn't seem interested in introducing himself to me which was fine. It was a quick chat, just the pleasantries really, but the entire time, Beckett didn't move his hand from my thigh. Normally, I would have stopped such an outward display of affection or attraction. Maybe it was the fact that we were in a sex club, or maybe it was the fact that Beckett had already made me feel ten times more than any man had before, but I liked that he was claiming me. Like he wanted this man to know his intentions with me and wasn't put off by them in the least. He even ran his fingers back and forth against my skin as he spoke.

I felt as desired as that woman in the painting.

"I'm sure I'll see you around," the man said with a nod and finally left.

Beckett's attention was back on me in full force. "Well, now you know my name."

I knew when the man said it, he was bound to point out how inequitable it was that I now knew his name. But I was prepared and had decided exactly how I was going to argue my point.

"Then I won't use it when you, what did you say? When your"—I cleared my throat—"*cock is buried deep inside my tight, wet...cunt?*"

He stared at my mouth with his jaw slightly slack, like he was shocked to hear such language from my lips. Honestly, if he knew me any better, he would have reason to look so shocked. I don't think I'd said the words "cock" or "cunt" before in my life.

But I didn't mind it. I was committed to being this version of Addison tonight. The atmosphere and Beckett's confidence were making it so much easier.

"Fuck, that sounded so good coming out of your sweet, pouty mouth. You can call me anything you want as long as you keep talking like that," he murmured. "What would you like to call me then? Do you have something in mind?"

I readjusted on the couch so I was facing him fully. The outcome of which was his hand slipping even closer to my... cunt, which was aching for his touch. Drawing on my newfound confidence, I reached forward and touched his hair I'd been fantasizing about slipping my fingers through all night. I toyed with a piece that flipped out near his neck and licked my lips.

I did have something in mind, but I wasn't sure how he would react if I offered it as a possibility. I looked back at him and tried to suppress the quiver in my voice when I asked, "What about *Daddy*?"

ACKNOWLEDGMENTS

When I started writing *Somewhere to Stay* (Theo & Natalie's book), it was meant to be a standalone—one book about their forbidden romance. But then I fell in love with Ryder and Caroline and realized it would be a crime not to write their story.

And I'm so thankful I did, because I love how it turned out. They may seem like an unlikely pair, but they fit together so well. Individually, they are whole people. They don't *need* the other to be "complete," but they want to be together because they make each other better.

I hope you loved their story as much as I do! And I promise, you're not ready for Beckett and Addison.

ALSO BY GRACE TURNER

If you love this book, check out Grace Turner's other books. All available on Amazon and with Kindle Unlimited: https://amazon.com/author/graceturner

And to stay up to date on everything else Grace has to come, sign up for her newsletter at graceturnerauthor.com and make sure to check out:

- instagram.com/graceturnerauthor
- facebook.com/graceturnerauthor
- tiktok.com/@graceturnerauthor
- amazon.com/author/graceturner
- goodreads.com/graceturner

ABOUT THE AUTHOR

Grace Turner lives in Houston, Texas with her husband and two rambunctious pups and has a revolving door full of friends and family always visiting. By day, she works as a paralegal, and by night she reads, writes, and breathes contemporary romance.

www.ingramcontent.com/pod-product-compliance
Lightning Source LLC
Chambersburg PA
CBHW072024020726
47501CB00006B/1936